A METHOD TO HIS MADNESS

The man who had once been Nick Turner stood naked in front of the sliding-glass door. As he opened it, the chill of the January air touched his body, drying the perspiration. It felt good. He often stood in front of this door following his morning workout.

He continued to keep his body in shape. He worked out with calisthenics, isometrics, and then went into his martial arts routine.

It was hard to believe he had left Kansas three years ago. Everything had gone so well. He had kept up with the New York newspapers, and, so far, no one had put any of his killings together. That was his doing, of course. He tried to use a different method each time, and even when he repeated, he made sure that those incidents were well-spaced. His experience as a writer and researcher told him that serial killers were usually classified by the method they used to kill. But then, how many different ways could you kill someone before you *had* to repeat?

Other *Leisure* books by Robert J. Randisi:
Thrillers:
ALONE WITH THE DEAD

Westerns:
TARGETT
LEGEND
THE GHOST WITH BLUE EYES

THE SIXTH PHASE

ROBERT J. RANDISI

LEISURE BOOKS NEW YORK CITY

*To the woman who made me the man who
could write this book,
Christine Matthews.*

A LEISURE BOOK®

December 1999

Published by

Dorchester Publishing Co., Inc.
276 Fifth Avenue
New York, NY 10001

This book was previously published as *The Turner Journals*

ISBN 0-8439-4651-2

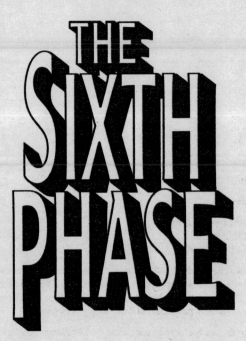

THE SIXTH PHASE

Prologue

Nicholas Turner stared down at Gina's face and swore he'd kill the first person in the funeral home who said "She looks good."

Gina Turner looked like what she was: dead. At the age of thirty-two, Gina had died, just like that. One minute they were sitting there playing couch potato, watching a rerun of *M*A*S*H*, and the next minute she stood up, saying, "I'm gonna get some ice cream," and then she was falling, a blank look on her face. Dead before she hit the floor, the doctors said she hadn't felt any pain. A little bubble in her head had burst, they said, and then she was gone.

Her face, beneath the cosmetics, was pasty, the skin cold and lifeless. Her eyes were closed.

Did they sew them closed? He wasn't sure and wasn't about to ask. Her mouth was closed, though, and that was the giveaway that she was indeed dead. Even in her sleep Gina's mouth had always been open, just a bit. That lovely mouth he had loved to kiss would never open again. His heart felt as if it were in a grip of iron, and he fought back the tears.

"Don't fight it, Nick." Gina's mother stood next to him now, holding onto his arm. A woman who had never liked her son-in-law, Evelyn DeBartolo was nevertheless being supportive. For his part, Nick didn't feel any closer to Evelyn just because her daughter—his wife—was dead. Nick hoped that Evelyn wouldn't be expecting him to come around a lot, now. With Gina gone, he saw little reason to maintain contact with Evelyn, except for his daughter, Lisa. He had no use for Gina's parents, for Evelyn or her husband, Anthony, but they were Lisa's grandparents—the only grandparents she had; his parents had died in a car accident when he was eighteen. He'd make sure Lisa got to see them, but he wasn't going to wear a path to their door.

"Go ahead and cry, Nick," Evelyn said, squeezing her son-in-law's arm.

Nick had no intention of crying—at least, not in front of Evelyn and the others. He had always been a private man. He would grieve in private, in his own way.

"I can't believe she's gone," Evelyn said.

The Sixth Phase

This was the second of the two days that a wake was being held for Gina at Giordano's Funeral Parlor in the Marine Park section of Brooklyn. During those two days Nick had heard every cliché imaginable from Evelyn and Anthony and the rest of Gina's family. Nick had no family of his own, but Gina's parents were both Italian, and that made for a ton of aunts, uncles, and cousins.

"She was such a good girl," Evelyn said.

Sure, Nick thought, that was why they treated her like shit when she said she was going to marry Nicholas Edward Turner.

"He's got no job," Tony DeBartolo had told his daughter.

"He's a writer, Daddy!" Gina had argued.

"That ain't no real job for a man," DeBartolo had replied with a sneer. Man's work was when your hands got dirty.

The more her family tore Nick down, the more supportive Gina became. Nick couldn't believe that someone as good and loving as Gina had come from a union between Evelyn and Anthony DeBartolo.

Nick and Gina Turner had been married for eleven years, and for every one of them Gina's parents never let her forget that she could have married this fella, who had become a doctor, or that fella, who was a lawyer. Instead she was married to Nick, who was eking out a living writing paperbacks.

To Gina, every one of those books was a Nobel Prize-winner. If it wasn't for her, Nick Turner would have given up on himself a long time ago. "You're better than this, Nicky," she had told him time and again. "You're better than most of those best-sellers, and you're gonna prove it."

She almost had him believing it, believing in himself.

What was he going to do now that she was gone?

How could he live without her?

Part I

McQueen

Chapter One

January 1993

Detective first-grade Dennis McQueen knew he was a failure as a husband and a father, but took solace in the fact that he was a good detective. Not unusual for a career cop. Many cop marriages fell prey to the job. At forty-four, with twenty years on the job, McQueen had long ago admitted to himself that he was never meant to be a husband or a parent. He was meant to be a cop. These days, five years after his divorce, he put all his energies into his work.

"Your wife called," Police Administrative Aide Bobby Callan told him as he entered the 61 Precinct squad room. Callan was a civilian aide

13

who'd been hired years ago to handle department paperwork, freeing up the police officers
for the street. He was in his early twenties, a
thin young man with a head of curly brown hair
so unruly that combs and brushes must have
fled in terror at the sight of it.

"*Ex*-wife."

"Yeah, well, she says you forgot your ex-
daughter's birthday yesterday."

McQueen closed his eyes and said, "Shit." To
Callan he said, "Get a haircut."

"Yeah, yeah, bite me." Callan smiled and
shook his head. Of all the detectives in the
squad, McQueen was his favorite. He never
worried about his hair, his shirt, his tie, or his
shoes. If he wasn't the best-dressed man in the
squad, he was the most down-to-earth.

McQueen had forgotten Margaret's birthday.
She was—what, sixteen? No, it was seventeen,
because last year she'd had her Sweet Sixteen
party. He had missed that, too, for the same
reason he had forgotten her birthday yesterday:
He'd been working.

"Damn it," he muttered as he walked to his
desk. He'd have to send Margaret a check—
only, did he have any money in his checking
account?

"Fuck," he said, sitting down.

"Life bitin' you on the ass again, Dennis?"
Ramon Velez asked.

"Chewin' a hole through my pants, Ray,"

McQueen told his partner. "I forgot Margie's birthday."

"Yesterday," Velez said. "And she doesn't like being called Margie anymore, remember?"

McQueen's desk butted up against his partner's, and he stared across the expanse at Ray Velez's handsome face. Velez was everything McQueen wasn't. At thirty-two he was a successful family man, a sharp dresser, and a cop with a future. He was already a detective second-grade, and first-grade was right around the corner. The two men had been partners for three years, and Velez credited much of his success to McQueen. He told anyone who'd listen that he had learned everything he knew about being a detective from the older man. His superiors thought he was just being modest. They praised him for wanting to share the credit for his success with his partner.

McQueen begrudged his partner nothing. He liked Ray, wanted only the best for him.

"You sonofabitch," he said, "how come you remember these things and I don't?"

"You're a self-centered bastard, McQueen," Velez said in his lightly accented English. Ray Velez knew this was far from the truth. Dennis McQueen was the most unself-centered man he knew. Unfortunately, he was also the least ambitious.

"That's what my wife used to say."

"Ex-wife, you mean," Velez said.

15

"Fuck you."

"She wouldn't be an ex if you'd shown more interest in taking the sergeant's exam."

McQueen put one elbow on his desk and pointed a finger at his partner. "If you think a sergeant's stripes would have saved my marriage, you've got a lot to learn about people, Ray—and about marriage."

"My marriage is fine," Ray Velez said. "You need a new woman in your life now, Dennis."

"I repeat," McQueen said, "for anyone in the room who didn't hear me the first time . . . fuck you."

Velez sat back in his chair. "I love you, too, Dennis."

First on the scene was six-one Adam. They had responded to a report of a foul odor coming from the downstairs apartment of a two-family home on Stewart Street, in Marine Park. They both knew what that usually meant, but they had to investigate before calling for help.

The street was lined on both sides with attached two-family brick homes. The only thing differentiating one from the other was the front doors. Some had entry foyers and some didn't, so some of them stood out farther than others. They were like rows of crooked teeth.

As the officers drove down the street they noticed the carcass of a large tree lying in the street near the curb, as if someone had parked it there.

"Now, ain't that just like this city?" Police Officer Wilson Bennett said. "Cut the damned thing down and leave it lying there."

"They send one crew in to cut the fuckin' thing down, and then they send another crew to cut it into sections and take it away," said his partner, Police Officer Ed Simon.

"Of course. Makes perfect sense," Bennett said. "What's this city comin' to?"

"Wonder how long it's been there?"

"Wanna bet it's been a couple of weeks," Simon said. "It's already rotting away."

The address was two doors up from the dead tree. The cops found a parking spot right in front of the tree.

While Simon went upstairs to speak with the apartment's owner, Bennett approached the downstairs door. The smell hit him even before he'd descended the three steps into the entry well.

"Whew!" Bennett said as his partner approached. "You know what we got here, don't ya?"

"A ripe one," Simon said, wrinkling his nose. "Just like we figured. Can we call it in now?"

Bennett made a face and said, "You know we gotta check it out. You got the key?"

"Got it from the landlady."

"Open 'er up."

"I'll open it," Simon said, "and you go in."

"I ain't goin' in first," Bennett said. "You got the key."

"I'm the Operator and you're the Recorder. You go in first. The paperwork's yours."

"Shit. All right, all right. The smell ain't gettin' any better while we're arguin'. Open the damn door."

Simon inserted the key and turned it. The door opened onto a small entry foyer. He allowed Bennett to precede him. When they opened a second unlocked door, the smell hit them full in the face.

"Christ!" Bennett said, rearing back.

"You know," Simon said, "I know guys who can sit on a ripe one waiting for the squad and the M.E. and have a sandwich."

"I ain't one of 'em," Bennett said. He took out his handkerchief, and, for all the good it would do, held it over his mouth and nose.

"Okay," Simon said, "let's go in."

"You get the front windows open. Let's go."

Entering the small downstairs apartment, Simon went immediately to the two front windows, one on either side of the door, to let the stiff breeze in. It would take more than that to combat the smell.

It was a railroad flat, three rooms one right after the other. From where he stood Bennett could see that the third room was the kitchen. He saw a TV in the second room, and he could see the lower portion of a bed, but not the entire bed. He could also see a bare foot—just one bare foot at the bottom of the bed.

"It's in there."

"Let's take a look," Simon said. He was hoping it wasn't a young woman. He hated it when the stiffs were young women.

They moved into the room together until the entire bed was in view. On it was the body of a man. He appeared to have been about twenty-five. He was naked, and there was some blood splattered on his torso, but most of the blood was concentrated on the area between his legs. The blood was so thick there that they could not see his genitals.

They couldn't see his genitals because they were no longer there.

Bennett gagged and then vomited into his handkerchief.

Chapter Two

McQueen and Velez heard the call over the radio for the duty captain, and the M.E. and the squad. They arrived before anyone else.

Driving down Stewart Street, they noticed the

cut-down tree lying in the street, taking up at least one parking spot.

"This city," McQueen said, shaking his head.

"That'll be there forever," Velez said.

They double-parked, blocking in the radio car. A uniformed police officer sat on the front steps, shaken and pale.

"Looks like a bad one," Velez said. "This guy's no rookie, and he tossed his cookies."

Neighbors who had gathered around observed a mismatched pair as they walked up to the uniformed officer. McQueen was a big man carrying, at two hundred and thirty pounds, about thirty pounds too much weight, all of it in gut and love handles. Well over six feet, he could carry the extra weight fairly well, but he knew it was there every time he had to go up a flight of stairs or chase a suspect. His hair, once raven black, was now peppered with gray, and where he had worn it carefully cut as a younger man, it was now shaggy, hanging over his ears and curling up around the back of his collar.

Velez was about five ten, and always impeccably dressed. He worked out three times a week and maintained his weight at a fit one hundred and sixty-five pounds. His hair was always neatly cut, his mustache carefully trimmed. More than once he had been told by women that he looked like Lorenzo Lamas.

"Hey?" The voice came from a man on the

next porch, to their right. White-haired, in his fifties, he looked put out.

"Yes?" McQueen asked.

"You cops?"

"That's right."

"You work for the city, right?"

"That's right, sir."

"Can't you do something about that?" The man pointed to the tree trunk in the street.

"We'll get right on it, sir."

"Been there for two fuckin' weeks," the man said, shaking his head.

McQueen and Velez approached the cop seated on the steps.

"He said the same thing to me," the uniformed cop said.

"Fuck 'im if he can't take a joke," Velez said. "You first on the scene?" The name tag above his badge said BENNETT.

"That's right."

"Where's your partner?"

"He's inside."

"You all right?" Velez asked.

"It's pretty bad," Bennett said. "In fact, it's about as bad as I ever saw, and I've been on the job eight years."

"Okay," McQueen said. "Why don't you just stay out here and keep the people back?"

Velez tapped the man on the knee, and the two detectives went downstairs.

"Shit," McQueen said when he caught the smell.

"Good thing it isn't summer," Velez said.

Inside, they found Bennett's partner sitting on a sofa.

"Simon?" McQueen said, reading the man's name tag. "Where's the stiff?"

He led them into the second room. McQueen and Velez stopped short. Simon, who had already seen it once, was again taken aback.

"Go into the kitchen," McQueen said. "Find some coffee and toss it into a frying pan. Let's see if we can't mask some of this smell, okay?"

"Sure," Simon said, happy to have something to do that would take him away from the body. "Don't touch anything you don't have to," Velez called after him.

McQueen and Velez each took a pair of rubber surgeon's gloves from their pockets and pulled them on.

"Look around," McQueen said. "I'll do the body."

"Right." Velez didn't argue. Officially the case was McQueen's.

McQueen leaned over the body and examined it without touching it. He guessed the man's age at thirty or so. He looked like he had been in good shape when alive, probably worked out a couple of times a week. Middleweight, he guessed, one sixty or so like Velez, except this guy had pumped some iron and had the biceps to prove it.

The man's head leaned to the left. McQueen moved closer to examine the right side of the neck and thought he could see some bruises. The flesh was dead white and it would take special lighting in a lab to tell whether he was right. He couldn't tell for certain whether the man's neck was broken.

Both of the stiff's hands were visible and, while there was dirt beneath the nails, none seemed to be chipped or broken. Careful examination in the lab would tell what was under the nails with the dirt.

The air began to fill with the scent of the frying coffee.

There was a lot of blood on the man's groin. McQueen looked at the man's legs and feet, then came back to the crotch and took a good, close look.

"Ray, this guy's cock is gone."

"What?" Velez looked over his partner's shoulder.

"Looks like his balls are gone, too," McQueen said. "Jesus, somebody sure did a job on him."

Behind his partner's back, Velez made the sign of the cross.

"You crossing yourself, you macho spic?" McQueen asked without turning around.

"Fuck you, Dennis." Velez went back to looking around the apartment.

"Let me know if you find any cocks or balls anyplace," McQueen said.

McQueen had seen all he could without touching the body, so now he started the second stage of his investigation. He lifted the dead man's head just enough to satisfy himself that the neck was indeed broken. There were no ligature marks there, so a wire or a rope hadn't been used on him.

He carefully turned the man's hands over, examining the palms as well as the backs this time. More dirt.

"Got us a working man here," McQueen said. He turned around. "Simon, anybody talk to the landlady?"

"Only to get the key. Want me to question her?"

McQueen looked at the man and figured he was about thirty. "Nah, we'll do it."

Simon looked crestfallen, but didn't say anything.

McQueen continued his examination, touching the body but not changing its position. He'd leave that for the Medical Examiner. In his experience, though, rigor had come and gone. That and the smell indicated that the body had been there at least four or five days—maybe as few as three, depending on how good the heating was.

"Find anything?" McQueen asked Velez.

"Place looks like it's been burglarized, though my guess is it always looks like this," Velez said, coming over to stand next to McQueen. "Whoever did him must have taken the guy's dick with him."

They looked at the body. Velez said, "His books and magazines indicate he was a plumber."

"His hands have dirt in the palms and under the nails, the kind regular soap can't get out."

They stared at the body for a few more moments and then from behind them Simon asked, "Who would want his cock and balls?"

When the duty Captain walked in he looked at McQueen and said, "Did you touch anything?"

"No, Cap."

Captain Leon Rademaker, the executive officer of the 67 Precinct, looked suspiciously at the gloved hands of McQueen and Velez, but said nothing. Rademaker had thirty years on the job, and was bound and determined to make inspector someday. Word in the department was that he didn't have the brains—but then a lot of inspectors didn't have brains.

"Where's the body?"

"In here, Cap," Velez said.

"Let me take a—Mother of God!" The captain held a hand up, palm outward, in front of his face. "Cover that up, can't you?"

"Uh, no, Cap," McQueen said, "we can't just now."

McQueen, Velez, and Simon waited to see if the captain was going to throw up. For a minute it looked as if they were in luck, but the man somehow managed to hold it in. His normally ruddy complexion, however, had paled.

"We got this under control, Cap," McQueen said. "Why don't you, uh, wait outside . . . um, for the press, or something?"

"The press," Rademaker said, backing away from the gruesome sight. "Uh, yes, good idea. I'll, uh, wait outside . . ."

After the captain had left, Velez said, "The press?"

"Magic word with his type."

"Would the press have this already?" Simon asked.

McQueen looked at him. "Not unless you called 'em. Did you?"

"No, sir. Not me."

"Then let him wait out there." McQueen turned to his partner and said, "Ray, you want to talk to the landlady? I'll hold the fort here."

"Sure, Dennis."

"Simon, why don't you stay at the door? When the M.E. and his boys get here, let them in, but nobody else."

"Uh, sure." Simon started for the door, then stopped and asked, "What about the captain, what if he wants to come back in?"

"Don't worry," McQueen said. "He won't. He's seen enough."

McQueen felt that he, too, had seen enough. In all his years on the job he had thought he'd seen it all.

He was wrong.

Dr. Ethan Bannerjee, the M.E., arrived and examined the body, unofficially concurring with McQueen's estimate of the time of death.

"Damnedest thing I ever saw," Bannerjee said, shaking his head.

"When can I get a report, Doc?"

"As soon as I can get to it, Detective McQueen. Check with me in a couple of days."

"Backed up, are you?"

"No room at the inn?" Velez added.

"Let's just say you won't be seeing a vacancy sign out anytime soon. Good day, Detectives."

After Bannerjee left and the corpse was removed to the morgue, McQueen, Velez, and four uniformed policemen canvased the area, asking questions of the neighbors.

The man's wallet had been discovered in the pocket of a pair of jeans hanging on a closet doorknob, and identification in the name of Paul Medco. His driver's license photo confirmed that the wallet belonged to the dead man. He was also a member of the plumbers' union. Canvasing confirmed that a lot of people on the block knew Medco, but he had only done work for a handful of them.

About half a block down, while McQueen was questioning a man called Clayton, he saw a pretty teenaged girl inside the house, listening. She looked about sixteen.

Clayton told McQueen that Medco had worked on their toilet a few times, but that was it. "You'd think he'd give a neighbor a break on the price, but he ripped me like any other plumber."

"I know what you mean," McQueen sympathized. "Did you know him at all?"

"My wife dealt with him, not me. I paid the bill, though."

"I see. Well, thank you for your help, Mr. Clayton." McQueen started down the steps. Before he reached the bottom, the door opened again and the girl came out. She trotted down the steps, but stopped two from the bottom. She leaned on the railing with one hip jutting out, posing. She had long brown hair, a ripe mouth, and the kind of knowing eyes no sixteen-year-old should have, although many do. She did an admirable job of filling out her T-shirt, as well. She was probably a popular girl in school.

"Is it true what I heard?"

"Depends what you heard," said McQueen.

"That Paul Medco was killed."

"Yes, that's true. What's your name?"

"Amanda."

"Amanda, did you know Paul Medco?"

"Oh, yes," she said, her words heavy with meaning.

"How well did you know him?"

"I knew him real well, mister." Amanda Clayton fixed those big brown eyes on him and repeated, "Real well."

"Amanda, are you telling me that you had sex with Paul Medco?"

She bit her lush lower lip, lowered her head a bit, and looked up at him with her big brown eyes from beneath her long eyelashes. "I can't get arrested for that, can I?"

"No."

For a moment he thought about his own daughter, Margaret, and wondered if he'd notice that same knowing look in her eyes the next time he saw her.

"Well," she said, swinging her knee back and forth now, "we did it, ya know, once or twice."

"Would you happen to know anyone else he had sex with on the block?"

"Well, I don't know about on the block, but he did it plenty. He was, ya know, good at it."

"Your father would be real upset if he knew, wouldn't he?"

"Not as upset as he would be about my mother. Paul was doin' her, too."

Across the street and two houses down they found his van. On the side it used to say MEDCO

29

PLUMBING, but much of the lettering was faded.

"Who would want to do this to him?" the landlady, Mrs. Stiller, asked Ray Velez.

Mrs. Stiller was a white-haired woman in her sixties whose skin shone like it was oiled. All she knew was someone had killed her tenant. She didn't know about the mutilation. McQueen and Velez had no reason to inform her of that fact.

"We don't know, ma'am," Velez said. "Did you hear any strange noises downstairs recently?"

"What kind of noises?"

"Well, sounds like someone was having a fight: banging, yelling, screams?"

"Detective," she said, her tone tired, "I wouldn't think nothin' of screams comin' from Paul's place."

"You wouldn't?"

"He wasn't the ideal tenant, you know. I mean, he was a nice enough man, and he worked on my drains and stuff, but he had a taste for women, ya know? And he brought some of them home with him. Believe me, when I *didn't* hear screams comin' from down there, then I would get worried."

"And last night?"

She thought a moment and then said, "I believe he was quiet."

"Thanks, Mrs. Stiller," Velez said. "If you think of anything else, would you give me a call?" He handed her one of his cards.

He started down the steps and she called out, "Detective?"

"Yes, ma'am?"

"Could you do anything about that tree trunk?" She pointed to the big wooden carcass in the street.

"I'll see what I can do, ma'am."

Chapter Three

After his shift the next day, McQueen stopped at the morgue before going home.

He and Velez had worked their usual 8 × 4. The day before, because of the murder, they had worked nearly through the 4 × 12 as well, but today they finished their shift at the regular time. Even after five years, McQueen wasn't used to going home to an empty apartment, so he often found an excuse to go someplace else. Usually, it was some cop bar. Today it was the morgue.

Being in a hospital was bad enough. The morgue was in the basement of the Kings County Hospital on Clarkson Avenue in Brooklyn, over in the confines of the 71 Precinct. The hospital's buildings, most of

which had been built just after the Second
World War, sprawled over a two-block radius.
The morgue was in the basement of the main
building. Office workers did their jobs just one
level above a bunch of people who would never
work again.

As he entered the morgue, an attendant
looked up from his desk and frowned.
"McQueen, right?" the man asked. McQueen
had only been there a handful of times—and
that was too many for him.

"That's right," McQueen said. "Is the G-Man
around?"

The man cringed. "Jeez, don't let him hear
you call him that. He hates that. I have to listen
to him bitch and moan about it all day."

Some of the detectives found Bannerjee's
name too difficult to pronounce, so they short-
ened it to "G-Man." When it was discovered the
M.E. hated it, the nickname became permanent.

"He's inside," the attendant said. "I think he's
working on your cock and balls victim. Boy, he
loved that one."

"What's your name?"

"Jeffers," he said without looking up from his
desk.

"Jeffers," McQueen said, "listen up. If that
cock and ball reference shows up in any newspaper, I'll know where it came from. Do you
understand?"

Jeffers looked up at McQueen, was about to say something, and then thought better of it. "Uh, sure, Detective . . ."

"You won't only lose your job," McQueen said, "but I'll walk out of here with your cock and balls in my pocket. Do I make myself clear?"

The man wasn't sure whether to be annoyed or frightened. He nodded and said, "Crystal."

McQueen was about to go looking for Bannerjee when the doctor stepped out into the reception area.

"Why am I not surprised to see you here?"

"I was on my way home and thought I'd stop in on the off chance that you, uh, had something for me."

Bannerjee put a chart down on Jeffers's desk. "Come with me."

McQueen followed the tall, good-looking East Indian doctor down a hall with cracked and peeling bile-green and tan walls until they reached his office. McQueen closed the door behind him.

"Have a seat, Detective."

McQueen sat in a chair opposite Bannerjee. Out the high basement window behind the M.E. McQueen saw a man's legs from the knees down passing by.

"You are quite right in assuming I have something for you," Bannerjee said. "As it turned out, I could not resist starting work on Mr. Medco."

"Because of the missing genitals?"

Bannerjee waved a hand in a gesture of dismissal. "I've seen that before."

"You have?" McQueen asked, surprised.

"There was a case some years back of a murder where the victim's penis had been cut off and taken away, but that was different."

"The killer left the balls?"

"Well, yes," Bannerjee said. "But beyond that, the amputation of the penis was done in a surgically correct manner. The killer turned out to be a man with some medical training."

"And this case?"

Bannerjee spread his hands. "Once I cleaned up the body and took a closer look, it became obvious that this killer had no surgical knowledge. The genitals of this poor young gentleman were hacked away, or dug out with . . . with I'm not sure what."

"A knife?"

"Possibly," Bannerjee said, "but I wouldn't be surprised if something less sharp had been used. The genitals were ripped away, not cut off."

"I see."

"It's entirely possible that the victim was still alive when it was done. In the beginning, at least."

"Jesus." McQueen paused to catch his breath and then said, "But, I thought the neck was broken."

"It was," Bannerjee said, "and it may have been the cause of death, but the amount of blood indicates that the heart may have still been pumping when the amateur surgeon started."

· The men sat in silence, considering the enormity of what they had inherited.

"And under the nails?" asked McQueen.

"Not yet done," Bannerjee said. "You'll get a report. I simply wanted to satisfy my own curiosity as to what was done to this young man."

"And the neck?"

"Broken, as you say, probably by a powerful man's hands. There were no indications that the victim was struck with any kind of object." McQueen couldn't recall the last time he had seen the usually stoic M.E. so shaken.

"All right, Doc," McQueen said, standing up. "Thanks for the quick work."

Bannerjee waved a hand, and McQueen left the office, relieved that he hadn't had to see Paul Medco's corpse again. He had seen enough of him to last a lifetime.

The case made the papers, without any "cock and balls" references, which pleased McQueen. However, the fact that the genitals had been removed was prominently played up, specifically by the *New York Post*. Articles and interviews appeared, usually containing what

McQueen considered to be psychobabble about what the missing genitals represented. Every doctor and would-be crime columnist had an opinion. McQueen thought he knew what they represented, and he guessed it had more to do with sex than plumbing.

This kind of mutilation often carried homosexual overtones, and the newspapers tried to play up that angle. However, in McQueen and Velez's investigation, Paul Medco appeared to have been a raging heterosexual. In fact, they had already discovered and talked with no less than half a dozen women who had recently been involved with him sexually.

Velez wondered how a man could keep that many women happy at one time. McQueen suggested that Medco's current condition might indicate that he couldn't. However, it did seem that he had his pipes cleaned out more than regularly.

There were no indications that Medco was homosexual, or any proof that he swung both ways.

McQueen and Velez checked out the boyfriends, fathers, and husbands of the women—and girls—connected with the case. They all checked out with alibis. Most did not seem to possess the strength it would have taken to break bodybuilder Medco's neck and then remove his genitals with a dull instrument. Of course, a case might be made for rage and adrenaline, but for the moment the detectives discounted these men as viable suspects.

Which left them with nothing.

It's an accepted fact that murders not resolved within the first seventy-two hours— and that's being generous—usually go unsolved. Within a week, McQueen and Velez were working on other cases, as well. Paul Medco was on the back burner.

Chapter Four

March 1993

After a year of living on a sofa bed in a one-room basement apartment, McQueen had finally gotten himself a decent place to live. Since his divorce five years ago McQueen had lived in a variety of one-and two-room apartments, none of which he had ever stayed in long enough to turn into a home. He had found his most recent—on Nostrand Avenue between Avenues S and T—while investigating the Paul Medco murder two months earlier. Medco had been killed a couple of blocks away from this apartment, and it was while widening the canvass of the area that McQueen spotted the sign taped in the window of a cleaner's, advertising a four-room apartment on the second floor, above the Italian restaurant next to the cleaner's. McQueen wrote the phone number down on his pad, and discovered it a week later. Calling, he found that the apartment was still available, at a reasonable price for the area. It was manageable for him, even though he was still paying off the mortgage on the house his wife and daughter lived in.

Even before McQueen looked at the apartment, he knew he would take it. The location was good. It was above a good Italian restaurant, with the cleaner's on one side and a luncheonette on the other.

Across the street from the cleaner's, on the corner of Nostrand and T, was a 7-Eleven. The old Brooklyn had never had these, but now they were here and there, and McQueen appreciated their convenience—especially since they were open twenty-four hours a day. Often awake in the early hours, either from insomnia or because he was coming home from work late, it was handy to live across the street from some place that always had coffee available. If he wanted to eat something more substantial, there was a diner about two blocks away, on the other side of Avenue U.

Five years since the divorce and he still couldn't

afford a decent car. When he wasn't using a department car, he took the bus. It was no hardship, really. You could get almost anywhere in Brooklyn by using a bus or the subway, and if you were in a hurry, there were plenty of car services available.

He had moved into his new apartment a month earlier, long enough to become known to the Koreans running the 7-Eleven. As he crossed Avenue T for some morning coffee, McQueen ran into another familiar face.

Joey Dante was a security guard for the apartment houses on the block, one on McQueen's side of the street and the other across the street. He was swarthy, with a heavy mustache and sleepy eyes. Dante patrolled both buildings and the street outside all night long. He was a fixture on the block.

They had first met when McQueen moved in, and their paths had since crossed often enough that they had taken to exchanging a few words.

"Mornin', Joe."

"Hey, McQueen," Dante said. "How goes the fight against the bad guys?"

"Going slow, Joe," McQueen said. "Real slow."

"Headin' for Seven-Eleven?"

"Yup," McQueen said. "Regular, no sugar?"

"You got it. Thanks."

McQueen didn't mind buying Dante coffee

now and then. Hell, while he was on the sidewalk watching his building, he kept an eye on McQueen's place, as well. For his part, Dante liked being friends with a cop. It made him feel like he was "on the job."

The two Koreans behind the counter both nodded to McQueen as he walked in. He went to the back where the coffee machines were and poured himself and Dante twelve-ounce cups. He put milk in Dante's, his stayed black. He idly wondered if Paul Medco had picked up coffee here, or a six-pack of beer, or a newspaper. Odd to think they might have been neighbors if someone hadn't killed him.

He took the coffee to the register and paid for it and a *New York Post*. He read the *Post* for its sports section and little else. But today, the front page caught his eye. The headline read "Woman Slain and Sexually Mutilated in Brooklyn." Underneath, in smaller print, it said "Body found by motorist on Belt Parkway."

"Excuse me," one of the Koreans said.

McQueen looked up and saw the man holding out his change.

"Oh, thanks."

Velez was picking him up today because they both had to go to Manhattan to testify in court. He crossed back to his side of the street, gave Dante his coffee, then waited for Ray in front of the Italian restaurant. He opened the paper and read the gruesome story.

* * *

"Why do you have to pick him up all the time?" Cookie Velez complained. Complaining was something she did well and often.

"He's my partner." Velez took his wallet, change, and keys off the dresser in the bedroom and transferred them to the pockets of his pants.

"Why can't he buy his own car?"

Cookie was a beauty, no one could deny that. She was model-thin, with a face highlighted by prominent cheekbones and a wide mouth that declared her Spanish heritage. This month, her hair was red. Velez preferred her natural black.

Behind Velez's back his colleagues called her a royal bitch. What they didn't see, though, was the Cookie Velez he saw now, as he turned. She lay naked in bed, where they had made love upon awakening. Something always stirred inside Ray Velez when he saw his wife like this. She had small, firm breasts, and he loved the chocolate brown color of her nipples. The hair between her legs was bushy and black—the natural black that the hair on her head should have been. He felt his body again responding as he stared at her. Her legs were spread carelessly, unconsciously.

He briefly entertained the thought of crawling back into bed with her, but she opened her mouth again and talked him out of it without realizing it.

41

"And why do you have to take my Caddy?"

"Cookie, you know my car's in the shop."

"So what am I supposed to do?"

"Ask Susan to give you a ride wherever you have to go."

"I don't have to go anywhere."

"Then why are you worried about the car?"

"Because it's my car, Ray," she said. "And because your partner is a slob. Plus, he doesn't even like me. Why should he ride in my car?"

She pouted, folded her arms across her breasts, and then crossed one ankle over the other.

"Cookie," he said, walking to the bed to kiss her good-bye. "Don't . . ."

She turned her face away so that he had to kiss her cheek.

"I'll call you from work to let you know the car's all right," he said with a sigh.

As he was going out the door she shouted, "Don't let McQueen eat in it!"

Velez went outside and pulled the Fleetwood Cadillac out of the garage. He paused and looked at the house while the garage door automatically closed. It was a two-story Tudor with a two-door garage in an expensive, upper-mid-class neighborhood in Bay Ridge. Most of his neighbors' homes were even bigger and more expensive, but then most of his neighbors were stockbrokers and lawyers, and doctors and CPAs. He was the only cop who lived in the area, and it made him uncomfortable. But Cookie had wanted the car, Cookie had wanted the house, and he had wanted Cookie.

The dead woman was Bonnie Green, a hairdresser at a beauty parlor in the Mill Basin section of Brooklyn. That, McQueen realized, was the 63 Precinct. Sure enough, further on the article quoted a spokesman for the 63 Precinct, a lieutenant who said, "We have no information as to motive. Everyone who knew her said Miss Green was a nice woman."

McQueen read further, but there was no description given of the kind of sexual mutilation the woman had suffered. As for the cause of death, her throat had been cut and she had bled to death. She had been alone in the beauty shop, having just finished working late on a customer. She either accepted a ride from someone she knew or had been dragged into a car. Her body was later found by a motorist having trouble with his car on Belt Parkway.

McQueen was roused from the *Post* article by Velez's car horn.

"You fall asleep?" Velez asked as McQueen got in.

"I was reading." McQueen showed him the front page of the *Post*.

"What's so interesting?" Velez asked.

"You don't know?"

"Humor me," Velez said. "I'm just a dumb Mexican."

"The sexual mutilation, Ray," McQueen said. He briefed his partner on the case, how he thought Bonnie Green's murder might be connected to Paul Medco's.

Velez shrugged. "Was she raped? Paul Medco wasn't sexually assaulted."

"The story says 'mutilated,' not 'raped' or 'abused'."

"So what does that mean?"

"I don't know," McQueen said. He removed the cover from his coffee and sipped it.

"Don't spill that on the seats," Velez said. "Cookie would kill me."

He said the same thing every time he picked McQueen up in the Caddy.

"Why do you have Cookie's car today?"

"Mine's in the shop."

"Again? Why don't you junk it?"

"I can't," Velez said. "We need two cars."

"Well, if you hadn't bought your wife this Cadillac, you probably could have bought two new cars."

Velez frowned and looked at McQueen for a second before looking back at the road. "She wanted it."

Velez turned right on Avenue T and drove to Ocean Parkway. He was thinking about the *Post* article. "Listen, Dennis, just because the paper used the phrase 'sexual mutilation' doesn't make it the same as the Medco case. Jesus, he was butchered. Don't you think if something that drastic happened to this woman, the *Post* would play it up?"

"If they knew."

"Dennis, don't go making a sandwich when you ain't got any cold cuts."

"What?"

Velez grinned and said, "I heard that on *Law and Order* last night. I didn't think I'd get to use it this quick, though."

"Jesus . . ." McQueen said, shaking his head.

"You can't connect these two cases from a newspaper article."

They drove along in silence until they were on the highway heading toward the Brooklyn Bridge.

"You know," Velez said, "if you found your-self a woman, you wouldn't be trying to look into other people's cases."

"Ray."

"Cookie's got this friend—"

"Ray."

"She's just about your age and—"

"Ray!"

"What?"

"Shut up or I'll spill my coffee."

Chapter Five

They didn't have to return to the squad room because they were testifying and had been taken off the chart for the day. However, McQueen wanted to make some calls and Velez agreed to drive back to the precinct after they got out of court.

"I can catch up on some work," he reasoned.

"What about Cookie? Won't she want her car back?"

Velez made a face. He knew McQueen felt he catered to Cookie too much.

"She'll just have to wait until I get home."

"Ray, I don't want to cause any problems between you two."

"There's not going to be a problem just because I didn't bring the car back early," Velez said. "We're not that immature that we argue about things like that."

"If you say so."

"I know what you're thinking," Velez said.

"Reading my mind?"

"It's not hard, Dennis."

When they walked into the squad room,

Callan looked up from his desk. "You two are not supposed to be in today."

"Tell me something I don't know," McQueen said.

"Okay," Callan said. "Your ex-wife called."

"What's she want now?"

"I don't know," Callan said. "I told her you weren't here, she said a word it's against my religion to say, and hung up."

"What religion is that?" Velez asked.

"I belong to the Holy Order of Good Language," Callan said.

The detective's squad room had rows of desks leading to a holding cell in the back. There was one partitioned office, which belonged to the lieutenant running the squad.

At that moment, about half the desks were occupied by detectives working the shift. At his desk, McQueen phoned the Six-three and got Sam Lacy, the detective investigating Bonnie Green's murder.

"Yeah," Lacy said, "it went around and around for a while, but I got stuck with it. I argued that the perp probably killed her on the BQE, but the powers that be still decided to dump the case in my lap, thank you very much. What's your interest?"

"I had a case in January, had to do with sexual mutilation."

"A woman?"

"No, a man."

47

"Killed with a knife?"

"A broken neck."

"So what's the connection?"

"I don't know that there is one," McQueen said. "Did you get word from the M.E. yet?"

"Not yet," Lacy said. "Still waitin' for the report."

"Why don't you call him?"

" 'Cause Dr. Bannerjee don't give reports out over the phone, Detective," Lacy said.

"You could go talk to him."

"Did you call to tell me how to do my job?" Lacy said, an edge to his voice now.

"No, I didn't," McQueen said. "I just—"

"I tell you what. I find out anything I think you should know, I'll call you. How's that?"

"Hey, listen—" McQueen started, but he was talking to a dead line.

"Sonofabitch!" he shouted, slamming the phone down.

This attracted the attention of a number of the other squad members. Velez walked over to McQueen's desk.

"What happened?"

"The asshole at the Six-Three doesn't want to talk to me," McQueen said. "He got insulted, thought I was trying to tell him how to do his job." He got up and put on his jacket.

"Now where are you going?" Velez asked.

"To the morgue."

"How are you going to get there, Dennis?"

"I'll sign out a car."

"You're not officially on duty."

"I'll take a cab," McQueen said, and went through the doorway.

"Wait!" Velez shouted. "I'll—" He was going tell McQueen he would drive him, but he was already gone. Besides, he had to get her car back to Cookie.

Chapter Six

"Jeffers, right?" McQueen said.

The attendant looked up and frowned. "You got a good memory, Detective. I remember you, too. You had the case with the guy who lost his balls."

"Among other things," McQueen said. "Medco."

"Right," Jeffers said, "Detective Medco."

"No," McQueen said. "The victim was Medco. I'm Detective McQueen."

"Oh . . . yeah," Jeffers said. "You threatened me."

"I don't remember it that way," McQueen said. "Where's the doc?"

"In his office."

McQueen went down the hall to Bannerjee's office and knocked on the door. When he entered, he saw Bannerjee seated behind his desk. The blinds behind him were closed.

"Why doesn't your presence surprise me, Detective McQueen?" Bannerjee asked. "Have a seat."

McQueen sat in the same chair he'd occupied two months earlier.

"Are you here about the woman who was found yesterday?"

"As a matter of fact, I am."

"It's not your case."

"I know that, Doc," McQueen said. "I talked to the detective assigned, but he's . . . well, he just didn't seem interested in what I had to say."

"And he's content to wait for my report," Bannerjee said, "so he really didn't have all that much to tell you anyway, did he?"

"No, he didn't. I don't even think he figured you'd get to it for a while. Did you, uh, get to it?"

"As a matter of fact, I did," Bannerjee said. "You know I'm not really supposed to discuss a case with anyone but the detective assigned."

"I'm aware that—"

"Detective," Bannerjee said, rising from his desk, "would you mind waiting here for me for a few minutes? I've got to take a wicked leak."

"Uh . . . okay."

"I'll finish reading this later," Bannerjee said,

very deliberately closing the file folder that had been open in front of him. "Be back in a few minutes."

McQueen leaned forward to look at the file folder. It was marked "Bonnie Green".

"Hot damn," McQueen said, turning the folder around so he could open and read it. "Another mind reader."

He scanned the file quickly. All of the dead woman's particulars were there. Scars, deformities, height, weight, general condition—she *had* been in good health—and the cause of death was loss of blood and oxygen due to a particularly severe wound to the throat, which severed her carotid artery as well as her windpipe. In fact, from the doctor's notes, McQueen determined that the woman's *head* had almost been severed. It would have taken a tremendous amount of strength to do that—the kind of strength it had taken to snap Paul Medco's neck.

McQueen slowed when he got to the part about the sexual mutilation. The woman's external organs had been removed in much the same fashion as Medco's—that is, with no apparent surgical expertise. In Medco's case, Dr. Bannerjee's report had actually used the word "hacked." Here he stated that it was as if they had been "scooped" out.

Like with a trowel, McQueen thought as he closed the report. Back in January Bannerjee

51

had mentioned that a trowel could have been used.

The file was back in place, right side up, when the doctor returned.

"Now," he said, taking his seat once again, "where were we?"

"I was about to leave, Doc," McQueen said. "I just remembered something."

"An appointment?"

"No," McQueen said, heading for the door. "I'm off-duty."

Emerging onto the street from the morgue, McQueen was surprised to see a police radio car waiting there. One cop was behind the wheel, and another stood outside, leaning against the side of the car.

"Detective McQueen," said the officer outside the car.

McQueen thought he recognized him. His insignia indicated that he was from the same precinct, the Six-One. His name tag read HARDY.

"Yeah?"

Hardy pushed off the car. "The CO sent us to get you."

"Your CO?" McQueen asked.

"Our CO," Hardy said. "Captain Austin?"

Captain Austin was the CO of the precinct, but McQueen worked directly under his squad commander, Lieutenant Guiliano.

"We do have the same CO, don't we?" Hardy asked.

"I suppose so," McQueen said. "How'd he know where I was?"

"We don't know that," the cop said. "We were just sent to get you." He was clearly unhappy about the assignment, the look on his face saying that he had better things to do than chauffeur around the "squad."

"All right, I appreciate the ride, anyway." As they pulled away from the curb, McQueen asked, "What's on the old man's mind?"

"He didn't confide in us, Detective," Hardy said. He looked about thirty-five, probably had at least ten years in. The back of his partner's head was gray, indicating that he was somewhat older.

"What kind of mood was he in?"

"Don't know," Hardy said. "The desk officer called us and told us to pick you up, orders of the CO. That's all we know."

McQueen and Captain Austin didn't get along. They had come on the job at about the same time. Obviously, they had not risen through the ranks with the same speed, but McQueen did not hold Austin's captaincy against him. It puzzled him, however, as to why the man seemed to have it in for him. If he were the captain and Austin the detective, he could understand some animosity—Austin was the kind of man who would hold it against

McQueen if McQueen had risen through the ranks faster than he had.

McQueen settled into the backseat and tried to figure out what he had done to piss the man off this time. Then he gave up. He'd be finding out for himself soon enough.

Chapter Seven

When McQueen entered the clerical area outside the captain's office, he saw Lieutenant Guiliano there, leaning over and talking to the exec, Captain Mulligan. Mulligan was an old hair bag serving out his time behind a desk, shuffling papers. Guiliano, in his late forties, had an outside chance of making captain by the time he was fifty. He was competent, but unimaginative.

"McQueen," Guiliano said, straightening.

"Lieutenant," McQueen said. "What's this all about?"

"I'll let the captain fill you in," Guiliano said. "I'll tell him you're here."

"How are you, Captain?" McQueen asked Mulligan.

"Just fine," Mulligan said. He was about sixty-three, with snow-white hair and a belly that kept him from sitting too close to his desk.

"Do you know what this is about, sir?"

"No, I don't. Nobody around here tells me anything."

"I don't think that's true, sir."

"Oh, it's true," Mulligan said. "I'd be doing more good here if they'd hand me a broom."

McQueen felt badly for the older man. There had come a time in Mulligan's career when he realized he wasn't going to make inspector, and from that point on he had started coasting— and boozing. McQueen knew that he always kept a six-pack of beer in the left-hand bottom drawer of his desk.

Guiliano appeared and beckoned to McQueen.

Captain Edward Austin did not stand up as his two subordinates entered the office. He remained behind his desk, glowering at the wall. He did not even look at McQueen as he presented himself.

"You wanted to see me, Captain?"

Austin looked up at McQueen, then flicked his eyes at Lieutenant Guiliano. A cadaverous man, tall and extremely thin, Austin had a pale complexion, a long jaw, and huge hands. He would have looked more at home on a farm in coveralls than in an NYPD uniform. Though about McQueen's age, he looked a good five years older.

"McQueen, I got a call about you from the CO of the Six-Three, Lieutenant Daniels. Why were you asking Detective"—he stopped a moment to look at a name he had written on a piece of paper—"Lacy about one of his cases?"

"I was curious, sir."

"And were you telling him how to handle his case?"

McQueen took a deep breath. His butt was probably in a sling anyway. "I thought he needed to be told."

"Is that a fact?" Austin looked at Guiliano and asked, "Do you encourage your detectives to meddle in the cases of detectives from other squads?"

"No, sir, I don't," Guiliano said, "but perhaps Detective McQueen was simply offering his advice or his assistance to Detective Lacy. After all, McQueen is an experienced man—"

"That's enough," Austin said. "You can go, Lieutenant."

Guiliano hesitated, then said, "Sir, I'd prefer to stay while you continue to talk to a detective under my command—"

"I'll call you if I need you further, Lieutenant," Austin said. His tone was firm.

Guiliano hesitated, considering whether or not to argue further. In the end, he simply said "Yes, sir" and left the office.

"Close the door behind you!" Austin shouted. He waited until the door was closed before speaking again. When he did, McQueen was surprised at his tone. It was gentle, almost pleasant.

"Sit down, McQueen."

"Yes, sir." McQueen pulled over a metal folding chair and sat down.

"We went through the academy together, didn't we, McQueen?"

He knew very well that they had, but Austin was playing some sort of game.

"Yes, sir, we did."

"You're a detective . . . first-grade, is that right?"

"That's right."

"And you have been for some time," Austin observed. "Why aren't you a sergeant at this point?"

"I don't want to be a sergeant, sir."

Austin stared at him, not sure he'd heard right.

"That's nonsense," he finally said. "Everyone wants to advance."

"No, sir," McQueen said.

Austin looked annoyed. "That's ridiculous. Why would you *not* want to advance?"

"I'm not cut out for it. I like being a detective."

Austin frowned. "That's . . . a funny attitude to take, Detective, isn't it?"

"That's what my ex-wife thought, too, Captain."

"And you have no ambition, Detective?"

"No, sir," McQueen said. "I mean, I did at one time. My ambition was to be a detective—and now that's what I am."

"And you're satisfied with that?"

"Very much, sir."

Austin remembered Dennis McQueen from the academy. Even then he had been a strange one, keeping to himself, acting like he was better than everyone else. Now here he was, just a detective, while Austin was not only a captain but McQueen's CO to boot.

"Do you want to remain a detective, McQueen?"

"Yes, sir."

"Then keep your nose out of other detectives' cases," Austin said. "Especially detectives from other commands. You should be grateful that I was called by the squad commander, and not the CO of the Six-Three. If I'd heard from their captain, I'd have to take stronger measures."

"I understand, sir."

"Do you?"

"I understand you fully, sir."

"Well, I can't say I understand you," Austin said. "You can go, Detective."

"Thank you, sir."

McQueen left the office, leaving the door open behind him.

McQueen found Lieutenant Guiliano in his office. In fact, it wasn't a real office, since the walls—two of them, anyway—were partitions. Still, it afforded him some degree of privacy, for moments like these.

McQueen told him everything, starting with the Medco case. When he got to the case of the murdered woman, Guiliano rolled his eyes.

"Dennis," he said, interrupting, "you're not trying to build a serial-killer case, are you? Come on—"

"Lieutenant," McQueen said, "it was not my intention to build anything. All I wanted was some information on Bonnie Green's murder. This Detective Lacy got all huffy and hung up on me."

"What were you doing at the morgue?"

"I was—hey, wait. How did the CO know to send a car for me there?"

"I wanted to know where you were, and your partner told me," Guiliano said. "Now, you want to tell me why you were there?"

"To talk to Dr. Bannerjee."

"About Medco?" Guiliano asked. "That's an old case, Dennis—"

"No, not about Medco. About Bonnie Green."

"Who?"

"The woman who was killed."

"The Six-Three's case?"

"Right."

"And Bannerjee talked to you about another detective's case?"

"No, but I did get a look at the file when his back was turned."

"Oh, great," Guiliano said. "You're looking to get both our butts in a sling, Dennis, and I'm not willing to swing with you."

"I really don't know what all the fuss is about. I just wanted some information so I could compare the cases."

Guiliano, despite himself, was interested. "And?"

"Well, they weren't killed the same way, but both were killed by someone with tremendous strength."

"People in a murderous rage often exhibit tremendous physical strength, Dennis."

"But both victims had their genitals removed."

Guiliano made a face. "What about the MO? Isn't that different?"

"It is. Medco had his neck snapped, and Green's throat was cut."

"You're reaching, Dennis. There's not enough to connect the cases."

"Lieutenant—"

"Work on your own caseload. You've got enough to do without looking after someone else's case—from another precinct!"

"Is that all, sir?" McQueen stood up.

"Stay away from this Detective Lacy. He sounds like the type to go running to his boss every chance he gets."

"Don't worry. I won't go anywhere near him."

"Good. Just take it easy, Dennis. If you build a serial killer, the department will have to foot the bill for a task force. They won't like that. Now go home, you're off the chart today."

Chapter Eight

July 1993

Ruth Nash couldn't believe her luck. Last month she had gone to The Shamrock Inn with her girlfriends just for something to do. When the gorgeous blond-haired bodybuilder had come over and sat with them, she had been sure he'd be interested in her friend Diane. Diane worked out, after all, and had one of those tight little jogger bods. Granted, she didn't have much in the tits department, but she had a to-die-for tight butt and hardly any belly at all.

But it hadn't been Diane the guy had been interested in, or Esther or Kate. From the beginning it had been obvious he was interested in Ruth.

She'd been married to Harry for eighteen years, and for ten of those their sex life had been—well, boring. She put up with it like a good little wife. It was only last year that she had started having these little nights out with the girls. After all, both her kids—Harry Jr. and Linda—were in high school now. They didn't need her at home every night, looking over their shoulders while they did their homework.

The bodybuilder had said his name was Ned Tyler, and that he was new in the neighborhood. He was looking for an interesting place to drink and wondered if Ruth would show him around. That night she had said maybe, but after she and the girls left they told her she would be crazy not to go for it. The guy obviously had the hots for her.

Ruth Nash was thirty-eight years old, and the idea that anyone would have the hots for her had never entered her mind. She knew she had nice breasts for a woman her age, but she also had stretch marks and love handles. Even Harry thought it was too much trouble to make love to her. Of course, there was that history teacher of Harry Jr.'s last year. He had actually asked her out after a PTA meeting. She had turned him down, and she never told Harry about it. Not that he would have done anything.

For a while after that she thought that maybe she *should* have gone out with the history teacher, but he was skinny, balding, and had bad breath. Maybe, if he'd been better-looking . . .

And now there was Ned the Bodybuilder. That's what the girls were calling him.

The next time she went to the Inn, Ned was there. She came without the girls, and was so nervous her knees were shaking.

They sat and drank for a while and then he leaned over, put his hand on her knee, and kissed her cheek.

"I'm sorry," he said. "I had to do that." He didn't remove his hand.

"That's all right. I—I think I wanted you to."

"Really?" He slid his hand further up, to her thigh, and she felt something right between her legs—something she hadn't felt in a long time.

He leaned over, obviously intending to kiss her on the mouth.

"Not here," she said, turning away.

"You're right," he said. "It's a neighborhood bar. Come on."

"Where?"

"Someplace where nobody will see us." He took her by the hand, stood up, and said, "Come on," tugging at her gently.

She liked the fact that he was obviously so strong, and yet he was gentle with her. He could have yanked her from the chair with ease, but instead he just tugged until she came willingly.

Outside, they started down the block. Suddenly he pulled her into a darkened doorway and kissed her. She moaned as his tongue entered her mouth. She hadn't been kissed like that in—well, ever. And his *hands*, they cupped her ass, kneaded her.

The kiss left her breathless and dizzy. "Oh God, Ned . . ."

He put his mouth next to her ear and said, "I want you, Ruth. I want to make love to you. I want to fuck you."

When he said "fuck" she felt a thrill run through her. She had never heard Harry say that word. Even when they had sex, he refused to talk dirty.

"Oh, Ned, I can't . . . can I?"

"Yes, you can. Come on." He held her hand as they walked down the block to his car. He helped her in, then ran around to the driver's side and got in.

"But where are we going?"

"I told you I'm new in the neighborhood," he said. "I don't have an apartment, but I do have a hotel room." He reached over and put his hand on her leg. "Will you come there with me?"

"Oh, God," she said, and he took that as a yes.

"Good," he said, patting her thigh. "Very good, Ruth." He touched her face and said, "I'm going to make you feel very special."

They entered the hotel near the Belt Parkway through a side door.

"I don't want anyone to see you," he told her. She thought it was sweet that he cared about her reputation.

He put his arm around her waist and ushered her into his room. Once inside, he kissed her and immediately started to unbutton her blouse.

"Please," she said, grabbing his hand, "I'm nervous."

"Do you want me to undress first?"

"Yes," she said, licking her lips.

"Sit here." He led her to the bed.

He slowly removed his clothes. It had been a hot day, and he wore just a T-shirt and a pair of slacks, and sandals. Her eyes widened at the sight of his bare chest. He kicked off his sandals, then removed his pants and underwear. She almost gasped when his penis came into view. It was only semi-hard, but large. He took it in his right hand and moved closer to her.

"Is this what you want, Ruth?" he asked, stroking himself. She watched in fascination as it filled with blood and swelled. With his other hand he reached down and fondled his testicles. "Does this turn you on, or would you rather have a woman? I can bring a woman in for you, Ruth."

She wasn't sure she had heard him right. "W-what?"

"A woman," he said. "Do you want some pussy, Ruth? I heard that you like to eat pussy."

She was confused. He was beautiful, there was no doubt, and she *had* been getting aroused by his strip, but now she was confused—and was beginning to get frightened. "W-what are you talking about?"

"Down on your knees, Ruth," he ordered.

"What?"

It was clear she had made a mistake coming here, and if she didn't leave now, she was afraid it would too late. "Ned . . . I—I have to go—" She got no farther. He reached for her, grabbed the front of her blouse roughly, and tore it away from her.

She cried out and brought up her hands, but he knocked them away and slapped her. She tasted blood in her mouth as her teeth punctured her lower lip. Panic set in. She had the thought that she might not get out of the room alive.

He slid his hand into her bra and yanked. It didn't break right away. He pulled harder and it did, allowing her breasts to bob free. She wanted to scream, but was so frightened now that no sound came out. Her shoulder hurt as if it had been dislocated. He yanked her to her feet and tore the blouse and bra completely off her. Then he put his hands on her shoulders. He pressed down until she had no choice but to drop to her knees.

His penis was fully rigid and right in front of her face.

"You want to suck it, Ruth?" he asked. "Or should I get you some nice pussy?"

"Ned . . . please . . ." Her swollen lip distorted

her voice so that she barely recognized it as her own. "D-don't hurt me . . . I—I'll do whatever you want . . . Just d-don't hurt me—" She broke off with a sob.

"Bitch!" he said, and slapped her again.

Her head rocked to the side, but before she could say anything, he closed both hands around her neck and lifted her up. She thought he was bringing her to her feet, but then her feet were off the ground. She couldn't breathe.

Blackness was closing in on her. She could barely hear him as, over and over again, he said, "Bitch . . . bitch . . ."

Chapter Nine

When the call came in, McQueen was at his desk in the squad room, taking care of some paperwork.

"Who's catching?" Bobby Callan called out.

"I am," Detective Jack Dent said. He looked around sourly. "Where's my partner?"

"They're callin' for the squad at the Gateway Inn," Callan said. "Sounds like they got a DOA."

"Great." Dent stood up and removed his jacket from the back of his chair. He was a humorless man in his thirties, tall and slender except for a twenty-pound beer belly. A detective third grade, he was a workmanlike cop who hated to do any more than he absolutely had to.

"Ralph went for donuts, Jack," McQueen said.

"Jesus," Dent said. Detective Third-Grade Ralph Samuels, a fat man in his forties, had been known to take forever selecting his half dozen or—God forbid—dozen donuts, most of which he would consume during a single tour of duty.

Dent looked at his watch. McQueen looked at his. They were an hour into their 4 × 12 tour. "Ralph'll be picking a dozen," said Dent. "He'll take forever. I'll have to go and yank him out of there."

"That's in the other direction," McQueen said. "I'll go with you. Who's catching, you or Ralph?"

"I am."

"Then there's no harm," McQueen said. "I'll go in his place."

"Where's Velez?"

"Called in sick," McQueen said, "so I'm free."

"Okay, then, let's go."

There were already two radio cars there when they pulled up in front of the hotel. One would have brought the responding unit, and the second would be the sergeant's car. The next radio car would bring the duty captain. With any luck, McQueen thought, it wouldn't be Captain Austin.

It had been raining for a while, and although it wasn't yet dark it was a gray enough day that the hotel lights had been turned on, reflecting off the wet blacktop of the parking lot. McQueen could hear the angry hiss of cars going by on the parkway.

Inside they were met by a uniformed cop in his twenties. His name tag read CHAPMAN.

"Who's got the duty?" McQueen asked.

"Far as we know," Chapman said, "Captain Keepsake, from the Six-Seven."

McQueen had heard his name, but had never met the man.

The young cop led them down a hall off the lobby. For many years this had been a hot-sheet hotel, a place where couples came to spend an hour or two in the throes of something resembling passion. Lately, though, the management had made renovations, even opening a restaurant bar in the hope of attracting a more stable clientele.

"We get a name from the register?" Dent asked.

The cop said, "Yes, sir. Smith."

"Surprise, surprise. And the body?"

"A woman."

Just outside the room were the sergeant and his driver. McQueen recognized the sergeant as a man named Phillips. The room's door was open. Chapman stepped aside to let Dent and McQueen past.

"What's the matter?" Dent asked.

"I, uh, been in there before, sir," Chapman said.

"And?"

"She's, uh, chopped up pretty bad."

"I don't blame him," Sergeant Phillips said. His driver nodded, looking solemn. Apparently, they all had taken a look and one was enough.

McQueen felt a knot forming in his stomach.

"How—" he said, and then stopped short.

"Sir?" Chapman said.

"Never mind," McQueen said. "We'll take a look for ourselves."

"I hate this," Dent said, and they went into the room.

The air was filled with the coppery odor of blood. McQueen imagined he could taste it.

Inside was Chapman's partner, an older cop named Bert Brine. On the bed was the woman.

"Can't even make out for sure what killed her," Brine said.

"You can go outside," Dent said. "We'll take a look."

As Brine exited, McQueen ran his hand over his face. "Jesus, not again."

Dent looked at him. "You got somethin' to tell me, Dennis?"

"I had a man like this in January, Jack," McQueen said.

"What makes it the same?"

"You're going to find that her privates are gone."

"Gone?" Dent asked. "You mean . . . cut up?"

"I mean hacked out and removed," McQueen said.

"Jesus . . . she does look a mess . . ." Dent peered down at her as McQueen took a pair of rubber gloves from his pocket.

Dent looked at him and asked, "You carry those wherever you go?"

"I've been known to," McQueen said, putting the gloves on. As Dent searched the room, McQueen moved closer to the bed. The woman lay sprawled on her back, her eyes open and swollen. Her tongue, protruding slightly, was purple. He used one finger to move her head back and forth, then returned it to its original position. Her neck was not broken. She'd been strangled. There were some blood splatters on her torso. Below the waist she was all blood.

"Nothin' here," Dent said, coming up behind him. "This look like your doer?"

"I'm going to keep my opinions to myself for a while. All right?"

Dent made a disgusted noise. "Sure, big help. You might as well go for donuts, too."

71

There was some commotion outside the room as the duty captain arrived.

"Look, Jack," McQueen said, "don't mention what I said about my other case, all right? I have to talk to Guiliano about this. Let's not get anyone else involved just yet."

"Involved in what?" Dent asked.

"Right," McQueen said. He pulled off his gloves.

Captain Keepsake was a few years younger than McQueen, but seemed at case with himself. Some young officers feel awkward around subordinates of comparable age, but Keepsake obviously felt he had earned his bars. McQueen immediately liked him. If he needed to talk to a captain sometime in the future, it would be this one rather than Austin.

Bannerjee arrived soon after Keepsake, giving McQueen an odd look as he passed him in the hall. McQueen stayed outside while Dent went in with the M.E.

"Ever seen anything like this before?" Keepsake said to McQueen.

McQueen didn't know quite what to say, then decided on something neutral. "Messy."

"You can say that again."

Bannerjee came out and told his men they could bag the body. Both he and Dent gave McQueen meaningful looks.

"We got an ID on her from her purse," Dent said to McQueen. "I'm going to take a ride over to her house. You want to come along?"

At that moment a large figure came down the hall, eating a powdered donut.

"Looks like your regular date has arrived," McQueen said. "I think I'll go back to the house."

"Okay. Thanks for filling in, Dennis." He gave McQueen the keys to the car. "I'll ride with Ralph."

As the group dispersed, Dr. Bannerjee approached McQueen. "Is this case yours?"

"No, it belongs to Detective Dent."

"Are you haunting me?"

McQueen leaned against the wall. "It's the same, isn't it, Doc?"

Bannerjee looked away. "I won't know until I take a closer look."

"Bullshit."

"Cause of death is different," Bannerjee said.

"The cause of death is not the only thing that marks a serial, Doc."

"I'm not calling this the work of a serial killer, Detective," Bannerjee said. "That's not my job."

"I know, I know."

Bannerjee pointed a finger at McQueen. "Don't come to my office on this one, Detective."

"I won't, Doctor."

He wouldn't have to. This case was being carried by one of his own squad. He'd be able to get all the information he wanted from Jack Dent's paperwork.

Chapter Ten

McQueen made a decision. Lieutenant Guiliano would be seeing Dent's report soon enough. He decided to wait and see if the lieutenant brought up the subject of the Medco and Bonnie Green murders. As far as McQueen was concerned, there was a serial killer running around Brooklyn with three kills to his credit—so far.

"Three that we know of," he said to Ray Velez. It was the day after the Gateway murder and he was expounding his theory to the one person he thought might listen.

They were in Sheepshead Bay an hour before they had to report to work. McQueen had asked Velez to meet him at a Roy Rogers. They bought some chicken and coffee and took it outside, in the back of the building where there were tables overlooking the water and the docks. They could look at the boats while they ate.

"There are three that I know of," McQueen said. "All within a seven-month period. Who's to say he didn't hit somewhere else during that time and I just haven't heard about it? It's time to do some research. If there have been other cases like this, I'm going to find them."

"Then what?"

"Then I'm going to line them up one after the other and show—"

"Show who? Captain Austin?"

McQueen made a face. "First I'll find the cases. Then I'll worry about who to show them to."

"You expect to get a promotion out of this, Dennis?" Velez asked.

"You know me better than that, Ray."

"That's why I don't understand why you're doing this."

"It's simple. There's a guy out there killing people."

"There are a lot of guys out there killing a lot of people," Velez said. "We can't catch them all."

"Maybe not. But this sick fucker is killing people, cutting them up and taking the parts with him. I want to find out what he's doing with them."

"Well, shit," Velez said.

"What?"

75

"That at least I can understand."

"What?"

Velez spread his arms and said as if he'd just discovered the word, "Curiosity!"

McQueen planned to start his research the next day, his first RDO—regular day off. Now he sought out Dent.

"What'd you get on the girl yesterday, Jack?"

"Her name was Ruth Nash. She lived in Marine Park. Married eighteen years. Two kids, a girl fourteen and a boy sixteen. The husband fell apart when I told him."

"What else?"

"What else what?"

"How was she killed?"

"Don't have the M.E.'s report yet."

"Did you call him?"

"Yeah, I called him."

"What'd he say?"

"He said I'd get the report later today."

McQueen knew that he would have gotten something from Bannerjee over the phone, but he let it go. With any luck, he'd be around when the report came in.

"Dennis, what was that you said yesterday about a case in January?"

"I had one something like this," McQueen said. "A man. His neck was broken."

"Well, on the scene the M.E. said Mrs. Nash

was strangled. No broken neck. Different MO."

Jesus, McQueen thought, nobody's got any imagination anymore.

"Who's catchin'?" Bobby Callan shouted.

McQueen and Velez caught a burglary with special circumstances. Seemed that the owner of the house was a gun collector, and some operational weapons had been stolen. That meant that instead of closing the case out and leaving it to the owner and the insurance company, they had to start checking pawnshops and other gun collectors. Some legwork, lots of telephone work. The case was officially Velez's, but McQueen got on the horn as well.

Dent and Samuels were up next and caught a robbery in which the victim could ID the perp. That meant they had to go to the hospital to talk to her. The report arrived while they were away.

"I got an M.E.'s report for Detective Dent," a uniformed cop said as he entered the squad room. He held a folder in a raised hand.

McQueen hastily tried to hang up his phone and missed. The receiver clattered to the floor.

"I'll take it," he said, pulling the receiver up by the cord and replacing it.

He signed for the folder, and the uniform left. Velez hung up his phone and stared across the expanse of their two desks at his partner.

"That's not yours."

"Tell me something I don't know." He opened the folder and read the report.

"So?" Velez asked.

" 'The victim's genitals were removed in such a manner as to suggest no surgical knowledge was involved,' " McQueen quoted.

"Which means?"

"Her privates were hacked out, Ray." McQueen closed the folder. "Just like Medco, just like Bonnie Green."

He swiveled around in his chair, walked to Dent's desk, dropped the report on it, and went back to his own.

"So what do you think?" McQueen asked his partner. "Are there three different killers stealing cocks, balls, and vaginas?"

"It would be a bit of a coincidence, wouldn't it?" For the first time, Velez seemed to give some credence to McQueen's speculation. "Now what?"

"I'm going to do my research," McQueen said, "and I'm going to see what Guiliano does when he reads Dent's five," referring to the DD 5, a detective's follow-up report.

"Don't you think the papers might put this together without you?"

"Seven months apart?" McQueen asked. "Only if the same reporter wrote up all three stories."

"What about Bannerjee?"

"He's an M.E., not a detective. He writes his

reports and sends them in. Those kinds of conclusions are not his to draw."

"You know," Velez said, "if you hadn't read about the second one and started asking questions, and if you didn't just happen to be available yesterday to respond with Dent . . ."

"But I did and I was, and I can't just forget about it."

"Jesus, Dennis, you know how the brass feel about serial killers."

"Yeah," McQueen said, "they hate them." McQueen also knew how the new breed of cop went by the credo "Don't rock the boat." He wasn't the new breed of cop and he wasn't going to just rock the boat. He was going to sink it. "The brass hate serial killers because when they're not caught right away, the newspapers bring heat down on them. I hate 'em because they're sick motherfuckers who ought to be put away and fried."

"So you're making this your personal business, huh?"

"It's falling in my lap, partner," McQueen said, spreading his hands in a helpless gesture. "It's not going to go away just because I ignore it."

Chapter Eleven

August 1993

McQueen sat at the small secondhand desk in front of his apartment's one window. It looked out over Nostrand Avenue, virtually right above the entrance to the Italian restaurant. He had set the desk up so that he had a view. On nice days, when his window was open, he'd smell the food from the restaurant.

This was August, though, and he had an air conditioner in the window. It was humming, and he couldn't smell the food cooking. He stared down at his notes.

Paperwork had never been his strong point. That was why he was amazed at how well he had done with his research.

Going back through newspapers for 1992 he had found four stories about murders where the phrase "sexual mutilation" had been used. There were plenty of stories about rape/murders, and sexual abuse, but only these four used the words "sexual mutilation."

Two had been in Brooklyn, one in Queens,

and one on Long Island. It was then when he decided that instead of using the main Brooklyn library, he'd go to the main library in Manhattan. A year's worth of *The New York Times* revealed two more cases in Manhattan, eleven months apart.

Now he had six cases of murder and sexual mutilation. Nowhere in any of the stories did it reveal that the victims' genitals had been *removed*. In order to learn that, he was going to have to either get a look at the police files, or the M.E.'s files.

The first thing he did was contact Dr. Ethan Bannerjee at the Kings County morgue.

"You want me to do *what*?"

"I've found six other cases of murder and mutilation, from 1992, Doctor. I want to know if the mutilations were the same as the Paul Medco, Bonnie Green, and Ruth Nash cases."

"I have been given no indication, Detective, that these three cases have been linked."

"Officially, they haven't, Doctor."

"You mean they haven't by anyone but you."

"That's what I mean, Doctor."

"The three victims we've talked about were killed by different methods. Why are you so determined to build a serial-killer case?"

"Maybe it's just falling to me," McQueen said, and his tone sounded weary even to himself. "It would be a lot easier, though, if I knew about these other two cases."

81

"Just two?" Bannerjee asked.

"The two in Brooklyn," McQueen said. "I've found two more in Manhattan, one in Queens, and one on Long Island."

"What, nothing on Staten Island?" Bannerjee said.

McQueen hesitated, then said, "You agree with me, Doctor. You just don't want to admit it."

"Do me a favor, Detective, and don't include me in your fantasies." Bannerjee hung up.

McQueen wasn't about to be put off that easily. He photocopied the two newspaper articles, and sent them via department mail to Bannerjee's office. He hoped that when the doctor got them he'd at least look up the cases to satisfy himself.

A week passed with no word from Bannerjee.

No progress had been made on the Medco case and he had heard nothing specific about the Bonnie Green case. Of course, McQueen was steering clear of Detective Lacy and the Six-Three generally.

As for the Ruth Nash case, he *had* seen Jack Dent's reports. McQueen found it interesting that two of Ruth Nash's girlfriends had said that the murdered woman had met a man in a bar called The Shamrock Inn. A big man, they had said, "a bodybuilder." A man like that would certainly have the strength to snap someone's neck, or strangle them with ease. Neither girlfriend knew the man's name, though, or where he lived.

The motel clerk told Dent he remembered a big bodybuilder type checking in. He had registered as Ned Smith.

The fact that the man had used the first name Ned led McQueen to believe that the killer's real first name started with the letter *N*. Criminals, in choosing their aliases, usually used their actual first and last initials, an oddity that was a plain and simple fact in police work. Most criminals had very little imagination.

Dent had put out an alarm on a man named Ned Smith with the description given him by the two women. McQueen wondered if Dent had asked either of Ruth Nash's girlfriends if the name Ned rang a bell.

In any case, Dennis McQueen needed some concrete findings to convince the brass that a serial killer was at work. Then a task force could be formed to catch him.

McQueen knew that there could be any number of motives for murder—jealousy, envy, hatred, money, and the age-old one, love. The mutilations were another matter. Why would the killer take his victims' genitals with him? What did he do with them?

He collected his findings in a folder and put it in one of his desk drawers. He'd give Bannerjee another few days, maybe a week, to get back to him. Right now the M.E. was the only one who could corroborate his theory. Without him, McQueen would have to find a someone high enough in rank to believe him and support him on his findings alone. Right now he didn't have a helluva lot.

Chapter Twelve

It wasn't until January second that Dr. Ethan Bannerjee surprised McQueen with a call at home.

He returned home from work that evening to find the message light on his answering machine flashing. Retrieving his messages, he found three hang-ups, each more annoying than the one before. Later that night when the phone rang, he was ready.

"This is McQueen's machine, and if you hang up this time, your ass is mine!"

There was a pause, and then Dr. Ethan Bannerjee's voice said, "Detective McQueen?"

"That's right. Bannerjee?"

"That's right, Detective."

"Have you been hanging up on my machine all day, Doctor?"

"Uh, yes, I have."

"Why?"

"Because I don't want my voice on your machine, Detective. In fact, I don't even want to talk to you on the phone. Now do you want to meet me or not?"

They arranged to meet a few hours later at an Atlantic Avenue bar that claimed to carry three hundred different kinds of beer. McQueen got there a little early and discovered that they also had eleven kinds of beer on draft.

"You've got such a great selection, I don't know what to have," McQueen said. It was almost a complaint.

"Do you like Killian's?" the bartender asked.

"Very much," McQueen said. "Not many bars carry it on tap."

"Well, we do," the bartender said, "but I like the Michael Shea's better." He gave McQueen a small taste. It turned out to be so smooth that McQueen had two before Bannerjee's arrival. He had just decided to put this bar on his list of regular places to go when he couldn't face going to an empty apartment when Ethan Bannerjee walked in.

It was the first time McQueen had ever seen the doctor not wearing either a suit or a white lab coat. He was dressed in a leather bomber jacket, matching leather gloves, and a pair of dark blue jeans. When he opened the jacket,

McQueen saw that he was wearing a cotton flannel shirt in blue and green stripes.

A couple of women at the bar noticed Bannerjee as he entered. Only then did McQueen realize that the young doctor *would* be attractive to women. He wondered if the man was married.

Bannerjee spotted McQueen at the bar and walked over. On McQueen's recommendation, he ordered Michael Shea's.

Bannerjee looked at McQueen. "Can we take these to a table?"

"Sure."

The M.E. led the way to an empty table in a corner, and McQueen felt like an old west gunfighter, sitting with his back to the wall.

"What's this all about?"

"I think you know."

"Humor me, Doctor."

"Okay," Bannerjee said, "so I made you wait a few months."

McQueen just stared at the man.

"It's about that material you sent me in the mail in August. I didn't do anything with it right away, but I kept it—God knows why. About a month later I took it out again, and it got my curiosity up."

He reached into the leather jacket and came out with a sheaf of paper folded lengthwise. He put it on the table between them.

"What's this?"

"Photocopies of the files on those two old Brooklyn cases you asked me about."

McQueen stared at the papers, picked up his beer, and took a sip. "Why don't you tell me about them?"

"One was suffocated, apparently with something like a plastic bag, and the other was stabbed in the back, down low. And in each of the cases, they were sexually mutilated."

"In the same manner?"

"The same, yes," Bannerjee said. "And their genitals were removed from the scene." He looked embarrassed. "I don't know why I didn't remember them or make a connection, except that they happened so long ago, so far apart from each other . . . I get so many cases—"

"You don't need to make any excuses. You're not a detective. You're not supposed to be."

"So I'm not Quincy, either," Bannerjee said. "Are you still interested in following this up?"

"There's still a serial killer out there, Doc."

"I can help—but unofficially."

"How do you mean?"

"You said there were other cases? Manhattan? Long Island?"

"And Queens."

"I can talk to the medical examiners' offices in those boroughs and possibly get some paperwork."

"You'd do that?"

"Unofficially," Bannerjee said again. "Don't forget that."

"Tell me something, Doctor," McQueen said, "when would you come forward officially?"

"When I get some official word that there's a serial killer at work in the city."

"That means when a task force has been formed."

"Yes. But in the meantime, I'll let you know if and when I get something from the other offices. If they corroborate the information on these old cases, and on the three current cases, I don't think you'll have any trouble convincing the powers that be that there's a serial killer at work here in New York."

"That remains to be seen," McQueen said. "Nobody likes to admit to that, not since Son of Sam and the panic he caused. Look at that nut we had running around jabbing women with a pin or a needle a couple of years ago. People were afraid to ride the subways and walk the streets."

"With enough evidence, they'll have to act on it," Bannerjee said.

"I don't have much faith in the brass, Doctor," McQueen said. "Still, I don't expect them to shout it to the newspapers. If they begin an investigation, linking all the cases, I'll be satisfied."

Bannerjee leaned forward and said, "You're not after a spot on that task force—like heading it up?"

"I don't have much faith in the brass, Doctor, and I sure as hell don't want to become one of them."

Chapter Thirteen

March 1994

"So what's happening with your serial killer?" Ray Velez asked.

"Jesus Christ, Ray," McQueen said, "he's not *my* serial killer."

They were alone in the squad room. It was early, the start of an 8 × 4.

"Well, when you think about it," said Velez, "he's yours until you can convince someone else he exists." Velez hesitated. "Can you do that yet?"

McQueen looked across their desks. "I think I can."

Dr. Ethan Bannerjee had come through for McQueen in grand style. Over the course of the

past two months McQueen had received unoffi-
cial copies of reports from the M.E.'s in
Manhattan, Queens, and Long Island.

Just the night before, McQueen had gone
over all the material again. There were some
discrepancies in the earlier cases. For one
thing, in the first three murders the genitals had
not been removed. They'd been hacked at, but
apparently the killer had not yet gotten to the
point where he actually removed them. That
development came later. Counting those three
recent cases, though, he'd taken the genitals in
the past six murders.

"Nine cases over the past two years, Ray."

"You have proof?"

"I have the M.E.'s report for each case,"
McQueen said, explaining the similarities and
differences. "Come on, Ray," he said when his
partner did not reply, "it's not such a hard sell,
is it?"

"Not to me, Dennis, but the brass?"

"I know, they're anal retentive to the max,
right?"

"The max?" Velez said, looking amused.
"That sounds like something Cookie would
say."

McQueen waved that away. "How is Cookie,
anyway?"

"Just fine, Dennis. She sends her best."

I'll bet, McQueen thought.

"We're having a little trouble with her brother, now, but that's nothing serious."

"What kind of trouble?"

"He needs money."

"For what?"

"For whatever it is he spends money on," Velez said. "Probably a new lens for a camera or something. I don't want to talk about it."

"What I need to do," McQueen said, getting back to the point, "is find a boss who'll listen. Someone who's not part of the good ol' boy network. Somebody who's *not* worried about when his next promotion is going to be."

Velez laughed. "Now where are you going to find a boss like that?"

McQueen said, "I think I might have just thought of the right guy."

It was funny about the position of executive officer in a precinct. It was usually a captain, and although he was on equal terms with the captain of the precinct rankwise, he was subordinate to him within the command.

The position was usually filled by one of two different types. One was like Captain Mulligan of the Six-One, a veteran looking to finish out his time.

The other was like Captain William Keepsake, a young captain waiting for his turn at the helm of a precinct somewhere.

Keepsake was forty years old. He'd been married for seventeen years and had two children, both teenaged girls. His wife, Eve, was, he thought, the perfect cop's wife: patient, independent, supportive. It didn't hurt that she was beautiful.

He had made captain at thirty-eight, in his fifteenth year. He had served as exec in the Six-Seven Precinct for the past nine months. He was anxious to have his own command, and wouldn't have minded this one. Keepsake liked the men of the Six-Seven, and they seemed to like him. Giving him command appeared a perfectly logical move—which meant that the department would probably never do it. Instead, he'd probably get a precinct in the Bronx, or maybe even Staten Island.

When Keepsake got the phone call from Detective McQueen, he remembered the man from the mutilation murder he'd covered as duty captain eight months before. Now McQueen said he wanted to talk to him about something important.

"Come to the Six-Seven then," Keepsake suggested, but McQueen did not want to talk in the precinct.

"Do you drink beer, Cap?" McQueen asked.

"I do."

In the end, Captain Bill Keepsake agreed to meet McQueen on Atlantic Avenue.

* * *

Dennis McQueen was sitting at the bar talking to the bartender, Julian, when Keepsake entered. The captain wore a tan trench coat, open to reveal an emerald-green cotton shirt and a pair of black, pleated gabardine pants. On his feet he wore a pair of black boots that zippered up the inside.

McQueen waved. Keepsake saw him and walked over.

"Nice place."

Because the walls were mostly brick and stone, the bar gave the impression of being deep in a cellar somewhere. McQueen liked the effect, and, apparently, so did Keepsake.

"A beer, Cap?"

"Something on draft. What are you drinking?"

"Something I discovered here called Michael Shea's."

"I'll try it," Keepsake said.

It was raining lightly out, and the droplets glistened in the captain's tightly curled black hair. Julian drew him a Michael Shea's and pushed it across the bar.

"Very good," Keepsake said, examining the mug with raised eyebrows.

"Let's move to a table, Cap."

Keepsake laid his trench coat on an empty chair. McQueen's worn raincoat hung on a hook. They sat opposite each other.

"Your call made me curious," Keepsake said. "What's this about, Detective?"

"It's about murder and sexual mutilation."

"That woman in the motel, right?"

"That's right. That woman and many others."

"Why don't you tell me all about it, Detective McQueen?" Keepsake said, sitting back in his chair.

"I'll get us both another beer first, Cap," McQueen suggested. "This might take a while."

Chapter Fourteen

McQueen talked nonstop through a second beer, then a third. Bill Keepsake listened intently, asking a question only when he deemed it absolutely necessary. When McQueen stopped talking, the young captain took a few moments to formulate his thoughts.

Without looking up, he asked, "Why did you come to me with this?"

"I thought you were a boss who would listen."

"And what were you hoping I'd do with this information?"

"I was hoping to get it to the C of D."

Keepsake looked up now. "What makes you

think I have an in at the chief of detective's office?"

"You're what, forty?" McQueen asked. "And you're a captain."

"Are you saying that you don't think I came up through the ranks the normal way?"

McQueen shrugged. "No offense, Captain, but at one time or another we all have a rabbi of sorts."

"And what if I told you I didn't?"

"Then I guess I've wasted my time and yours."

They sat in silence for a few moments.

"As it happens," Keepsake said, "I do know someone who might be able to help, though I'm not saying I'm totally convinced yet."

"Do you want to see the paperwork on the cases before you make up your mind?"

Keepsake used a thumb and forefinger to wipe the corners of his mouth thoughtfully. "I think that might be a good idea."

"They're in my coat."

McQueen walked to the hooks on the wall and pulled a brown envelope from his coat pocket. It had been folded lengthwise, but was too thick to have creased. When he removed it, it sprang flat again. He carried it back to the table and put it down.

"I stated most of the pertinent information," he said, sitting back down again. "Of course, if I hadn't left some stuff out, the file would be twice as thick."

"File?"

"My file," McQueen said. He tapped the envelope and said, "I consider this my file on the case."

"How did you get all the papers from the other cases, from the other commands?"

"I talked to the right person," McQueen said, "which is what I hope I'm doing now, Bill."

"Okay, let's say I get us to the C of D with this. Then what do you hope to have happen?"

"Well, I'd hope that the department would assign a task force to look into these murders. This nut has to be stopped."

Keepsake hesitated a moment, then said, "If there's a task force, I'd want to command it. Do you have a problem with that?"

"Hell, no. Look, I realize you're ambitious, Bill. You can command, and when the guy is caught, you'll probably make DI. I'm not looking for a promotion. I just want this crazy caught."

"If there's a task force, and I command it, I'd want you on it. I mean, it's your case."

"That's fine, too," McQueen said. "Right now it's a lot of cases to a lot of people. I'm the only one who thinks of it as one case. I'd want my partner with me, though."

"No problem. If this happens, I think I'd be able to handpick my men. I'll, uh, want your help with that."

"You got it."

"All right," Keepsake said, "let me take this stuff home and look at it, and I'll get back to you."

"You'll excuse me for saying this," McQueen said, "but don't take too long, Captain. Too many people have already died."

"I understand." Keepsake picked up the file, then stood and took his coat off the empty chair.

"Do you need a ride somewhere?"

"I'll think I'll hang out here a while," McQueen said.

Keepsake looked around. "Not your usual cop bar."

"That's why I like it."

Keepsake extended his hand. McQueen shook it.

97

Chapter Fifteen

Four days later Dennis McQueen sat at his squad-room desk, a half-finished coffee at his elbow, reading *New York Newsday*. The story on page five made him jerk his arm, and his elbow knocked over the container of coffee. "Oh, shit!"

Ray Velez looked up and saw the coffee spreading over his partner's desk.

"It's just coffee," he said. "I've got some napkins here in my drawer."

"It's not the damned coffee," McQueen said. He walked to his partner and opened the newspaper on his desk.

Velez saw the screaming headline that had upset his partner: "College Student Murdered and Mutilated."

"Here," Velez said, handing McQueen a few napkins. "Clean your desk while I read this."

"What's to read?" McQueen demanded. "It's the same old shit, and nobody's going to put it together."

"It happened out in Stony Brook," Velez said. "You know that *Newsday* covers a lot more

98

Long Island stories than any of the other newspapers."

"The killer probably knows it, too. Look at how he's spacing out his kills, Ray, moving all over the place. This bastard is smart!"

"And you're going to catch him?"

"Somebody better," McQueen said. "Or he'll just keep on doing it."

"Unless he runs out of victims."

"How could he run out?" McQueen asked. "There are millions to choose from."

"Maybe not."

McQueen stopped fiddling with the coffee spill and stared at his partner. "What do you mean?"

"Maybe he's not just taking people at random."

"That would mean that all of the victims have some connection with each other."

"Or a common connection to something else, if not each other," Velez said, sitting back in his chair.

"That's good, Ray," McQueen said, thoughtfully, "but it still doesn't do us any good unless we can convince the brass that these killings are connected, and get some kind of task force together."

"Where are you going?" Velez asked as his partner headed for the door.

"I've got a phone call to make."

"Why can't you make it from here?" Velez called, but McQueen was already gone.

McQueen went to the pay phones in the entry foyer of the precinct, where nobody could hear his side of the conversation. He dialed the number for the Six-Seven Precinct.

"Captain, this is Detective McQueen."

"What can I do for you, Detective?" Keepsake asked.

"Well, for one thing you could look at a story on page five of today's *Newsday*."

There was a moment's hesitation on the other end. Keepsake said, "Another one?"

"It sure looks like it."

"Damn."

"What's going on, Captain?"

"I can't talk now," Keepsake said, lowering his voice. "Are you working days?"

"Yes."

"Meet me at the bar at one?"

"I'll be there, Cap."

McQueen was nursing a cup of coffee when Keepsake showed up at 1:20. He wore a black windbreaker zippered up over his uniform shirt. Lots of cops kept windbreakers in their lockers for just that purpose. When it was zipped, and they were wearing an off-duty gun that didn't show, the uniformed pants simply looked like dark slacks. In effect, he was incognito, though he wasn't out of uniform.

Keepsake nodded to McQueen and pointed to a table. "I can't stay long. Sit down, Detective McQueen."

McQueen sat and asked, "So what's happening?"

Keepsake looked around, as if someone might be listening. "My guy was on vacation. He just got back today. I'm meeting with him later."

"And then what?"

"Then I'll call you," Keepsake said. "I haven't forgotten about this, believe me. We're going over a lot of heads here. If we do get a meeting with the C of D, we'll both have to be there. My neck's going to be on the block right along with yours."

"I appreciate that, Cap."

"Never mind appreciating it," Keepsake said. "Just tell me you'll be there."

"This is me, remember? I did all the research on this thing. If it goes the distance, I'll be there. I just want a chance to do what I'm trained to do."

"And what's that?"

"Catch a bad guy."

It was two days later, a Friday, when McQueen came home and found a message on his machine.

"Dennis, it's me. It's a go. Meet me in the C of D's office Monday morning, nine o'clock

101

sharp—and bring all of your material. Don't be late!"

McQueen stood still for a few moments, listening to the message tape rewind, and then suddenly twirled around, punched the air, and yelled, "Oh, yeah!"

Chapter Sixteen

Monday, Dennis McQueen took the subway from Brooklyn to the police headquarters building at Manhattan's One Police Plaza, a huge, boxlike brick structure near the Brooklyn Bridge.

He walked into the downstairs lobby at 8:50 and showed his badge, which gave him free passage into the building. He took the elevator up and looked for the chief of detectives' office. Although he had been a detective for many years and had been in this building on many occasions over those years, he had never before been to the chief of detectives' office.

Walking down the halls he was struck by the difference between this building and the precincts out in the field. It was like day and night, the offices he and other working cops worked in, and this, the big brass's offices. This building even smelled different, with none of the sharp and sour smells found in the real world. Up here in the clouds, the air was unsullied by the rank odor of druggies or whores or pimps. In this upper stratosphere, the only impure odors were those of expensive cigars and pipe tobacco.

When he entered the C of D's office, he saw a woman sitting at a desk, dark-haired and pretty. He had known bosses before who'd transfer pretty civilian aides simply because of their looks.

"Can I help you?"

"Yes," he said, "Detective Dennis McQueen. I'm, uh . . ." He wasn't sure whether he should say he had an appointment, or what. He settled on, "I believe I'm expected."

"Detective McQueen," she said. Her tone indicated that she wanted to make sure that *he* had it right.

"Yes, that's right."

She raised an unamused eyebrow and pushed her chair back. "Wait here, please." She went through a door to the right of her desk and reappeared seconds later.

"You may go in," she said, leaving the door open. She stood aside.

He found himself in another office, though

not yet the C of D's. Behind a desk sat a civilian wearing a very expensive suit.

"Detective McQueen?" the man said.

"That's right."

The man stood up, revealing his impressive height, probably six two or three. He was somewhere in his forties, but it could just as well have been early as late. His hair was slate gray, and his complexion, even in early March, tan. As he came around the desk, hand extended, McQueen saw that his eyes were also gray. He looked to be in excellent physical condition, and would have looked at home on the deck of a yacht with a white polo shirt, white shorts, white deck shoes, and maybe a kerchief—or ascot—around his neck.

"I'm Inspector Pyatt," the man said. "Glad you're prompt."

"Actually," McQueen said before he could bite his tongue, "I'm early."

"Perhaps," the inspector said with a small smile, "but the others are already here. Come this way."

This time McQueen did bite his tongue as he followed the inspector through another door. He was surprised to find that he was nervous. He recognized the chief seated behind his desk. Robert Sands had come up through the ranks. He was a heavyset, bald black man in his fifties who smoked cigars incessantly, though he never allowed himself to be photographed with one. His office reeked of them, and the ashtray on his desk, even this early, held the remnants of a couple of dead soldiers.

Also in the room were Captain William Keepsake, in full uniform, and a man McQueen did not know. He was about five nine, barrel-chested, in his early fifties, and he looked calm and well-rested. If this was Keepsake's rabbi, he did not look concerned that he might be sticking his neck out. Maybe McQueen and Keepsake were the only ones in a position to have their heads roll.

"Chief, this is Detective McQueen," Inspector Pyatt said. "Detective, Chief Sands."

"Detective," Sands said. He stood just long enough to shake hands. "Please, have a seat. Do you know these gentlemen?"

McQueen sat in a chair directly across from the chief. In his lap he held a brown envelope.

"I know Captain Keepsake, sir," McQueen said. "Captain."

"Detective," Keepsake said with a nod.

"This is Inspector O'Brien," Sands said. "He's here to observe."

McQueen still didn't know whether Inspector O'Brien was Keepsake's rabbi or not, but he chose to believe that he was. A lot of the department's old guard were still Irish.

McQueen turned slightly in his chair to see

Inspector Pyatt seated in a chair against the far wall. So there would be five of them.

"Detective McQueen." Chief Sands folded his hands on his desk. "Inspector O'Brien and Captain Keepsake seem to feel you have something I would be interested to hear."

So O'Brien's ass was on the line right along with his and Keepsake's.

"I believe that I do," McQueen said.

The chief sat back in his chair. "Enlighten us."

McQueen nervously wondered if this wasn't a waste of time. Maybe he should have just forgotten the whole thing, adopting the same uninvolved attitude most of the detectives today had.

The chief was staring at him intently. McQueen opened his mouth and started to talk.

After he presented his facts and suppositions, he theorized about what might happen if this killer was not stopped. "He will either go on killing, or he will disappear . . . never caught, unpunished for the murders he's committed. I don't know about you, sir, but I don't think I could sleep well if that happened."

The moment that last statement was out of his mouth he wished he could have taken it back—and then decided, What the hell, let the chief deal with it.

Chief Sands sat quietly for a few moments.

McQueen sat still, aware of the movement of the other men in the room. Peripherally, he saw that Captain Keepsake crossed his legs one way, and then back the other way, betraying his nerves. Inspector Pyatt cleared his throat.

McQueen was determined not to fidget or appear nervous in any way. As soon as he'd made that determination, he got an itch right in the center of his back that began to drive him crazy. He pressed back into the chair harder to see if that would relieve it, but it didn't work.

"Interesting, Detective McQueen," Sands said finally. "Well-thought-out and well-presented."

"Thank you, sir."

"Is that your documentation?" Sands asked, indicating the envelope in McQueen's lap. "I'd like to look it over."

"Certainly, sir."

McQueen rose just as much as he had to in order to pass the envelope over. The itch in his back seemed to be trying to dig a hole.

"I'll get back to you," Sands said, setting the envelope aside.

"Sir?"

"I'll need some time, Detective."

McQueen wasn't sure how to react. He stood up and reached for the itch, finding it with his thumbnail and scratching it. He started to turn to leave, exchanging glances with Keepsake as he did. Inspector Pyatt rose and reached to open the door for him. Inspector O'Brien, on the other hand, had not seemed to move at all during the entire presentation.

McQueen started to leave, then turned back again.

"May I speak freely, Chief?"

"Of course, Detective McQueen," the chief of detectives said. "That's why we're here."

"I don't think we have a lot of time, sir. This nut's been killing people for two years . . . that we know of. His most recent one was just a few days ago. That may or may not have been his last. I don't see that we *have* a lot of time to waste, sir."

Sands sat back in his chair and looked pained.

"Wait outside, Detective," he said finally.

"Yes, sir." McQueen went through the door that Inspector Pyatt held open for him.

Chapter Seventeen

Chief of Detectives Robert Sands stood up, turned, and looked out the window at the plaza below for a moment. Keepsake exchanged a glance with Inspector Pyatt, who was worrying his lower lip.

When Sands turned, he exploded.

"I want to know what the fuck—" he snapped, and then just as quickly as he'd blown, he stopped. He was aware that, if he shouted, McQueen would be able to hear him through the closed door, that his booming voice could be heard all the way out in the halls.

Also, his doctor had warned him about losing his temper, about the things it could do to his blood pressure.

He sat back down, taking a long moment to compose himself. He very deliberately wet the tip of a fat cigar and lit it while the other men in the room watched and waited. When he spoke again, it was through a blue cloud of smoke.

"Why the fuck do I need a first-grade detective telling me what my own people should be telling me?"

"Sir—" Pyatt started, but Sands wasn't finished yet.

"That we've got some nut going around killing people and taking off with sex organs!" He looked directly at Pyatt now and said, "Don't we have people who are supposed to catch this sort of thing? Aren't I supposed to know about serial-killer situations before anyone?"

"Chief," Pyatt said, "we don't really know that Detective McQueen knows what he's talking about. After all, even he admitted that the victims he's discussed were killed in different ways."

"Excuse me, sir," Keepsake said, "but I believe that Detective McQueen does know what he's talking about. He's got documentation."

"Yes," Sands said, putting his hand on the envelope McQueen had given him. "Captain, have you seen this file?"

"I've seen stats of enough pages to warrant my bringing it to your attention, sir."

"Yes," Sands said, "that much is obvious." He looked at Inspector O'Brien and said, "Andy?"

"No, Bob," O'Brien said, "I haven't seen the papers myself, but I trust Captain Keepsake's judgment."

"I see," Sands said. He turned his attention to Keepsake now. "Are you an ambitious man, Captain?"

Keepsake shifted uncomfortably in his chair.

"I suppose I am, sir, yes."

"What would you have me to do with this information, Captain?"

"Well, sir, I think the facts warrant the formation of a task force to look into it further."

"With you as the whip, I suppose?"

"Yes, sir," Keepsake said, "that was my thinking."

"I see," Sands said. He looked at Pyatt and said, "George?"

"Well, sir," Pyatt said, "I think forming a task force is a little hasty."

"What would you do?"

"Well . . . I might assign a task force to determine if a, uh, task force should be, uh . . ."

"Never mind," Sands said, waving the inspector into silence.

The chief looked down at the envelope in his hands for several moments, and then very carefully placed it on the outer edge of his desk. "I'm not going to read all of this now, gentlemen. I'm sure Detective McQueen has been very thorough in his research."

He looked up from his desk, directly at Captain William Keepsake.

"You've got your task force, Captain, and

you're the whip. Get yourself together six detectives. We'll find a place to put you."

"Yes, sir," Keepsake said, trying to hide his satisfaction.

"Your job is to determine if we actually do have a serial killer in our city. If your determination is that we do, then your job will be to catch the sonofabitch. Do I make myself clear?"

"Yes, sir."

"I don't want any press releases, Captain," Sands said, "and no little informal chats with the press. Understood?"

"Yes, sir."

"When you've made your determination, you'll report directly to me, not to Inspector Pyatt, and not to your friend Inspector O'Brien. Is that quite clear?"

"Yes, sir."

"I will then have you cease and desist, or proceed with your investigation," Sands said. "By that time I will have read all of this material that Detective McQueen has collected."

"Yes, sir."

"If this turns out to be a witch hunt," Sands said, "heads will roll."

O'Brien nodded, and Keepsake said, "Yes, sir."

Pyatt hoped that the chief was not also talking to him.

"That's all, gentlemen."

Keepsake, having been the only man seated,

rose and started for the door behind the other two men.

"Oh, Captain . . ." Sands said.

"Yes, sir?"

Sands was looking down at his desk top. "Don't bother assigning yourself a second whip."

"Sir?"

Now the chief looked up and directly at the young captain.

"McQueen will be your second whip."

"Sir," Keepsake said, "McQueen is a detective."

Sands smiled a decidedly humorless smile and said, "I just promoted him to detective sergeant. You'll inform him of that fact, won't you?"

"Yes, sir."

"Good," Sands said, lowering his eyes again. "Then that's all."

The Two Inspectors and the captain exited the chief's office. Pyatt, looking pale and ill, went through another door.

McQueen watched while Keepsake and O'Brien shook hands.

"I appreciate the support, sir," Keepsake said.

"Don't let me down, Bill."

"I won't, sir."

O'Brien turned to McQueen and said with a slight smile, "Good luck, Sergeant."

As O'Brien went out the door, McQueen stood up and asked Keepsake, "What did he call me?"

"Sergeant," Keepsake said. "The chief himself just made you a detective sergeant."

"What about the task force?"

"We've got it," Keepsake said. "I'm the whip, and you're the second. Congratulations."

McQueen looked stricken.

"I'm a boss?"

Part II

Turner

Chapter Eighteen

It had been two months before Nick Turner had been able to rouse himself from a drunken stupor long enough to begin packing away his dead wife's belongings. For those months their six-year-old Lisa stayed with Gina's parents. Nick couldn't take care of himself let alone his young daughter.

So, on a night approximately seven weeks following Gina's funeral, while he was alone in their Brooklyn home, Nick Turner started packing his wife's belongings into suitcases and cardboard boxes.

And found her journals.

He stared at the eight leather-bound books in surprise. He had always been the writer in the family. He hadn't even suspected Gina of keeping a diary, let alone a journal of the past six years.

He immediately sat down and began reading.

Dear Journal,
I'm not really sure how to do this. I mean, I never even kept a diary as a girl. It was Dr. Forslund who suggested it. He said it would be a way for me to get my thoughts out where I could deal with them. After all, I can't talk to Nick about these things. He's busy with his writing. He says if he doesn't write, we won't eat—and even though he hasn't sold anything yet, I guess he's right. I just wish he had stayed in school and gotten some sort of education to fall back on.

This surprised Nick. He didn't recall Gina ever suggesting he go back to school, that he might not make it as a writer. Why would she write that here? Was it a symptom of her depression?

Nick could never understand Gina's bouts with depression, but as expensive as her psychiatric visits were, he had been determined to see that she kept them up until *she* felt she could do without them. Unfortunately, now that day would never come.

He read on, and certain entries stood out to him:

Dear Journal,
Today Nick sold his first short story. He was so excited, and I was as happy for him as if I had written the story myself.

Nick remembered that day well.
There was an entry in the second book, for 1983, for the day he sold his second book. But another entry for that year surprised him.

Dear Journal,
Today I agreed with Nick that we would not have children yet. It broke my heart, but Nick was so insistent that he needed the time to devote to his career and not to fatherhood that I didn't want to argue, but God, how I want children!

He remembered that day, and it seemed to him that she had felt as strongly about not having children as he had. Now, reading her thoughts, he felt like a bastard. She should have told him how she really felt. He was sure that they could have come to some compromise.

Still later, toward the end of the year, was the entry when she found out she was pregnant. He remembered how frightened she had been about telling him. Then another shock.

Dear Journal,
Today I told Nick I was pregnant. I
explained that it was an accident, but he
got very angry, and stormed out of the
house, saying I had betrayed him. While he
was gone I remembered seeing a movie
about a woman who aborted her own baby
with a coat hanger. I thought about it,
Journal, I really did. I even got as far as the
closet, but I couldn't do it. No matter how
unhappy the baby made Nick, I couldn't
kill it.

Nick put the journal down in his lap and put
his hand to his forehead, rubbing gently, then
more vigorously. He remembered being very
understanding, not angry. It shocked and hurt
him that Gina had even considered an abor-
tion—let alone *that* kind.

Puzzled, he read on.

In the third book, for the year 1984, there was
an entry for the day Lisa was born. At least Gina
remembered them both being happy about
that.

He was actually smiling—something he hadn't
done for two months—as he opened the fourth
book.

Dear Journal,
Today I had sex with the plumber . . .

The words burned their way into Nick's mind, seared to the insides of his eyelids. Closing his eyes, he was able to see them.

He stared, aghast. Could it be a joke? Someone else's diary? The handwriting, however, was unmistakably hers.

It was like reading one of those letters they printed in the men's magazines, where people wrote about their sexual experiences.

He steeled himself and, heart pounding, proceeded to read the entry through:

The toilet backed up, and I had to call a plumber.

When he arrived, I *knew* it was a miracle. He was GORGEOUS! He was tall and muscular, but not muscle*bound* like some of those ugly bodybuilders. He was only about twenty-two—five years younger than me—with curly black hair. When he spoke, my legs went weak.

I showed him to the bathroom, and before he started working he took off his shirt. He *knew* I was staring. My heart pounded so hard I swore he could hear it. I had to leave the bathroom or I would have thrown myself at him.

Fifteen minutes later I went back upstairs. I had been sitting in the kitchen, trying not to think about him, but I couldn't stop myself. I made a pitcher of iced tea, and brought a glass up to him. He said he was finished and washed his hands in the sink. I watched the muscles in his arms flex as he rubbed his hands together. I was looking at his butt when I saw him watching me in the mirror. Our eyes met, dear Journal, and I *knew* he was going to fuck me. I wanted him to fuck me.

He dried his hands with a towel, then reached for me. He touched my face, then ran his hands up and down my arms. I could smell his sweat. I wore a sundress and he reached under it and pulled down my panties. He got on his knees and worked them down to my ankles. I lifted my feet and he removed them and tossed them away. Then he raised my dress all the way up so he could kiss my stomach.

I came like I had never come before, just from the feel of his lips on my belly.

My back was flat against the wall. His tongue went into my navel, then lower and lower! I spread my legs wider. He stood up, unbuckled his belt and dropped his pants and shorts. He reached behind me, cupped my butt, and lifted me up. I never saw his erection because I couldn't take my eyes from his beautiful face, but I *felt* it. He lifted me higher, my back still against the wall, and then he was inside me. I wrapped my arms and legs around him, and he fucked me like that, riding me up and down his cock, his mouth on my neck, on my mouth.

I heard the baby in the crib down the hall. It was strange. I was moaning and crying, and the baby was just cooing. Nick was at work, but the backdoor was unlocked, and I imagined that any minute someone might walk in on us—and, oh, Journal, that made it so exciting!

Nick cried out, throwing the journal across the room. A huge sob exploded from deep inside his chest. He stood up, ran to the bathroom, and vomited in the bowl. After he had washed his face and hands and stood drying himself, he realized with a jolt that this was where Gina had been with the plumber.

He dropped the towel, violently recoiling, almost tripping and falling into the tub. When he regained his balance, he went back into the bedroom, where the remnants of Gina's life were strewn about.

Nick couldn't remember the plumber she'd written of. Had he come back again? How long had this gone on?

He glared at the journal as it lay on the floor, spine up. There was only one way to find out. He sat down and continued to read.

* * *

By the time he'd finished, he no longer recognized the woman who kept these journals. He didn't recognize her at all.

She'd seduced the teenaged boy who lived next door:

... oh, Journal, his body is so young and hard. He smelled so clean, and his penis is so cute! Not like Nick's at all ...

She'd had the mechanic in the backseat of their car one time when she took it in to be serviced:

... he smelled dirty and oily, and it was so exciting to be naked in the backseat with him, knowing that other workers and customers were right outside the car ...

She'd had sex with a man on her bowling team right in the locker room, where anyone could have discovered them.

Dear Lord, she'd had sex with the girl who did her hair one night when they were the last to leave the beauty shop.

And she had seduced several of her friends' husbands.

The list went on and on, and Nick forced himself to read it all, all through the night and into the next morning.

She'd had several lesbian experiences, the one in the beauty shop being the first:

Debbie is the redhead who's been doing my hair for the past three years, and I never *suspected* that she was *that* way. She often talked about her boyfriends with her customers.

Today I had a late appointment, and we were the last ones in the shop. While she worked on my hair, she told me what a pig her boyfriend was.

Just once, she said, she'd like to have sex with someone who knew what she wanted, what she liked. She said that it would probably have to be another woman, and was I bi?

Our eyes met. It was like that time with Paul, the plumber. Suddenly, Debbie's lips were on my neck, and I was leaning my head over to one side, my eyes closed, reveling in the sensations. She slid both hands down the front of my dress, into my bra, squeezing my breasts. Then she was in front of me, undoing my dress. Removing my bra, she started to suck my nipples. Oh, God, it was amazing—

He stopped reading to swallow and wipe the sweat from his brow. Angry and ashamed, he realized he had an erection.

He continued reading about Gina and

Debbie, of how they touched each other with their mouths and hands. Gina had learned to make love to another woman that day, and although she had thoroughly enjoyed it, she wasn't sure it would ever happen again.

But it had. From that point on her encounters were with men *and* women.

She had slept with Lisa's second-grade teacher—a young woman Nick remembered as pretty and demure. Gina wrote:

> . . . I knew Miss Perry flirted with the fathers, but that she never did anything with them. She was so pretty, and such a challenge that I decided to push her past the flirting stage . . .

And she did. One night, after they were cleaning up together following a parent/teacher's meeting, she had seduced the young teacher and made love to her in the school kitchen, on the table.

He put the book down and hung his head. He had a raging, throbbing hard-on and was afraid if he moved he'd come in his pants. He held his breath until the erection subsided. It was approaching evening of the second day, and he still had one more journal to read. One more record of Gina's betrayals of their vows, of their *love*. How he had mourned her and cried for her when she'd died!

What more could he read in that last book that would shock him? A lot.

On the very day of her death, just hours before she had sat down with Nick to watch *M*A*S*H*, she had given a blow job to the kid next door, right in their living room. In fact, she'd pointed out in that very entry that the boy was the only repeat lover she'd had. She'd been fucking him and blowing him for two years, since he was seventeen.

> . . . he was so sweet and eager to please that I kept seeing him. He says he loves me, Journal, and I get a big kick out of thinking of myself as his Mrs. Robinson. And he's sweet in more ways. He always makes sure he's clean when we have sex, and his penis is so delicious . . .

Nick put the book down and wept, remembering how the boy—nineteen now—had looked at the funeral. You never would have known that the big, handsome kid had been fucking his wife for two years.

In a panic Nick suddenly wondered how many of his neighbors, how many friends, how many people who attended the funeral *knew* what was going on? Were they laughing at him behind his back?

By the time he closed the last of the journals,

he had made his decision. He was going to sell the house and move away. He couldn't possibly stay, not when he had no idea how many people knew what had been going on for all those years! Everyone on the street, everyone on the subway or bus probably knew what a fool he had been.

He wondered now if her friends had known what was going on. Would she have been able to keep from telling them about her adventures?

And how about the times *he* had taken the car in to be serviced. Had everyone there known about Gina and the mechanic? How could some mechanic resist telling his friends and coworkers about that?

He was the only one who didn't know what was going on. The more he thought back over the years, the more incidents he recalled where Gina had made a fool of him. How about that time she'd disappeared at a writer friend's publication party? From the journal he now knew she had been in a closet giving an editor a blow job. It hadn't even been Nick's editor!

There was no way in hell he could stay in Brooklyn—or New York, for that matter. He'd sell the house, the car, and everything else that he and Gina had ever owned. He'd move. Gina's parents would love to keep Lisa for a while longer, at least until he figured out what he was going to do.

Maybe he'd finally write the book he'd always wanted to write. Didn't writers have to suffer for their art? He'd been suffering for the last two months—or he thought he had. He now knew that the suffering had only begun.

Chapter Nineteen

July 1990

It wasn't working for Nick Turner. Not the way he had planned.

He had thought coming to Kansas City would help him deal with the trauma he had suffered: of Gina's death, and then the discovery of her betrayal.

In April 1990, he had gotten an apartment in a beautiful section of the city called Country Club Plaza, a relatively small area near downtown Kansas City. It was like a midwestern Greenwich Village, but cleaner. It was filled with small specialty shops alongside Gucci and Tiffany, funky bars and clubs that afforded some of the finest dining in the city. He rented, not wanting to own anything. The money he had gotten from the sale of the house enabled him to live in this upscale neighborhood. He also managed to get an apartment in a building that resembled a Brooklyn brownstone, making him feel at home.

He thought he would be able to write once he was settled, but he was unable to concentrate. One minute he missed Gina, the next he hated her. Sometimes he wished she was alive so that he could kill her for what she had done to him.

He had brought the journals with him, and he read them again and again. He didn't want to miss Gina, he wanted to keep hating her, and so he refueled his hate by rereading her journals. Sometimes he even took them to one of the Plaza fountains. People would walk by him, having no idea that he was reading about lies and deceit within those beautiful surroundings.

In occurred to him in May. What Gina had done wasn't actually her fault. These other people, her lovers, had taken advantage of her. She had been seeing a psychiatrist for many years. Maybe she had been more unstable than he had ever thought.

These people were the reason Nick couldn't mourn Gina the way he should. They were also the reason he couldn't write.

They had taken advantage of her condition, her weakness. It was their fault that whenever he closed his eyes he saw dirty pictures of Gina with other men—and women.

He remembered a book written by a friend, the kind of book he wanted to write. It had been about a man who decided to become a killer. First, he changed his physical appearance. He worked out, pumping himself up. He changed his hair color and style and, in the end, he got away with it. His friend's editor had wanted him to change the ending, but he had refused. He wanted his killer to get away with all of the murders because he felt that they were justified. Every person his character killed deserved to die.

Nick grew excited by the memory. If they were all gone, all dead, the slate would be wiped clean. Then he could mourn Gina. Then he could write.

Could he kill?

He joined a health spa that month, working out under the tutelage of one of their trainers.

"Everybody needs a reason to work out, Nick," the trainer told him. "Focus on that reason while you're exercising."

He focused on his rage, on the hate he felt, and his body began to change, even after the first month. His trainer told him he was developing much more quickly than most students. Nick gained weight, and it was muscle that he was gaining. Meanwhile, he worked on the rage and the hate. As he grew stronger, it grew stronger.

One June night he stood in front of his bathroom mirror posing, flexing. His biceps were hardening, his chest was expanding, even his neck was getting thicker. Within three or four months, his trainer said, he could probably compete as a bodybuilder if he chose to. Nick didn't tell him that wasn't his goal.

Staring at himself in the mirror, he wondered what else he could do to change his appearance. He would shave his head. After that, he'd either be able to grow the hair back and do it differently—change the color—or he could wear wigs.

He'd be able to return to the old neighborhood unrecognized. When he was ready, that was where he would start: with the people who had corrupted his Gina. None of them would know him at first, but he'd tell them who he was just before he killed them. After all, they'd have to know why they were dying.

Of course, there was a lot more to do. Just changing his appearance and his attitude wasn't enough. He had to learn how to kill.

He started reading bodybuilding and martial arts books and magazines, then graduated to soldier of fortune publications. You could hire personal trainers to teach you almost anything. All you had to do was be willing to pay. The money he'd be spending was an investment in his future. Once he was finished with his mission, he'd be able to sit down and write again. His mind would be clear, and he'd be able to sleep, think straight.

What he wouldn't give for a good night's sleep. He'd kill just for that.

Through all of this, however, he just couldn't stop reading:

Dear Journal,
Today for the first time I had sex with a man and a woman at the same time. I didn't know which way to turn, but when they started working on *me* with their hands and their mouths . . . oh God, it was wonderful!

Dear Journal,
Today a salesgirl paid a lot of attention to me while I was trying on sweaters in the mall. She kept bringing more sweaters to me in the fitting room, and finally came into the room with me to show me one. I didn't have on a bra, and there I stood, naked to the waist. She closed the fitting-room door and, with a very sexy grin, took my breasts in her hands, leaned over, and started to suck my nipples . . .

Dear Journal,
My goal was to have sex with two women. I picked the salesgirl from the mall and that

cute girl I met in my exercise class, the one I seduced in the shower. Well, I achieved my goal, and had so many orgasms I lost count . . .

On some nights he read them with a sense of horror, on other nights, fascination. On still other nights, they aroused him.

Each and every night, they fueled his hate.

At the end of June, Nick Turner was a different man.

He had found himself a personal trainer in the classified section of one of the soldier of fortune magazines. The man was not only teaching him martial arts, but was also training him with weapons. Not guns, but knives and bladed weapons. Within months, the man told him, he'd be as competent as any soldier, able to kill quickly, efficiently, and silently.

The man accepted the money Nick paid him, meeting him four times a week for training and instructions. It didn't matter why Nick was doing all of this training. It was none of the trainer's business.

In July, Nick decided there was another kind of training necessary for what he wanted to do.

At first he had thought it would be a betrayal of Gina. Just because she had betrayed him didn't mean he should do the same. Not being with a woman showed that he was better than she was.

Now, however, he felt the need, the urge to be with a woman, and since he no longer felt betrayed by Gina—having become convinced that none of what had happened in the journals was her fault—he felt it was time.

He began to go to bars and clubs, pleasantly surprised when women hit on him. Having been married for a long time, he didn't know how to approach women. He needn't have worried. With his new looks, they came on to him.

Still, he was unsure about sex. He had never strayed in his years with Gina, and these days you had to be careful about disease. He decided that at first he would just talk to women and buy them drinks. Eventually, the talk would get around to the subject of sex—and safe sex. It turned out to be remarkably easy, because they were concerned about it, too.

"It's so refreshing to find a man who's not afraid to talk about safe sex," one little hard body called Stacy told him. She was ten years younger than he was, but that didn't seem to bother her.

He had seen her for two weeks now at a bar named after a famous sports figure. But tonight was different: She sat closer, with her hand on his thigh. He could feel the heat from her palm right through his pants. His penis swelled.

"My God, you are built, aren't you?" Stacy asked. "I mean, I work out, but you're built." She left her hand on his thigh and with the other hand felt one of his biceps.

"You're shy, too, aren't you?" she asked. Stacy removed her hand from his arm and touched his face. "That's cute."

"I don't want to be cute," he said.

"Oh, honey," she said, leaning closer. She wore cut-off jeans and a low-cut top. As she leaned over, he found himself looking down at her impressive breasts. "You're not just cute."

"Oh?" he asked. "What am I then?"

She slid her hand over his thigh until she could feel him through his pants. "Ooh, you're sexy, that's what you are."

"So are you."

Stacy leaned closer and kissed him, an enticingly fleeting touching of lips. He could smell her perfume, and the scent of her sweat, and his heart started to race.

"We were talking about safe sex." She flicked her tongue out and licked his ear. "I want to fuck you, honey, but I have to know that you're clean."

"Oh, I am," he said.

She sat back on her stool and studied him, biting her lush lower lip. She had long dark hair and tanned skin, and Nick was aware that other men in the bar were looking at her, envying him.

"I have to take your word for that, you know," she said. "Can I trust you?"

"Stacy," he said, "up until January, I was married."

"Really? Did you get divorced?"

"She died. I haven't been with a woman since."

Her eyes widened. "All that time?"

"Yes."

"Did you . . . did you ever cheat on her, Nick?"

He felt a flash of annoyance, as if she'd insulted him, but now he wanted to go to bed with her and he didn't want to drive her away by reacting badly to her questions. After all, she had said she had to be sure about him.

"No," he said, shaking his head, "I never did."

"How long were you married?"

"Eleven years."

"Well," she said, squeezing his erect penis through his pants, "I guess you're about as safe as a man could be, honey, aren't you?" With her hand on him he thought he was going to come in his shorts, but Stacy removed it just in time. "Just let me fix my face, honey, and we can go."

He watched as she got off the bar stool and walked to the ladies' room. Her cut-off jeans rode high on her butt, showing off the cheeks of her ass. Every man in the place was watching her. She was leaving with him, though, and that made him proud—and terrified.

Compared with what was written in Gina's

journals, their sex life together had been mundane. What made him think he'd be able to perform to this young woman's satisfaction?

He started to sweat, and he had almost convinced himself to leave when Stacy came out of the ladies' room and walked across the room to him. Her breasts were big and firm, and in her halter and cutoffs she was a breathtaking sight.

He told himself he had to do this. This was part of his training.

Chapter Twenty

August 1990

A month with Stacy changed Nick Turner.

That first night he had been nervous. Remarkably, she had been patient, gentle, and understanding with him, not only that night, but for several nights after. And each night he grew in confidence. A week later he was matching her sexual intensity, amazing himself with his stamina and passion.

Sex had never been like this with Gina. It had always seemed a chore to satisfy his wife. After a while it seemed to him that Gina was grateful he wasn't all over her all the time. That was one of the reasons her journals had amazed him so. There had been no hint that Gina had ever thought of any of those things while they were making love.

And yet he wasn't thinking about the journals so much, anymore. Since the second week with Stacy he hadn't even read them.

Stacy worked as a bartender in Overland Park. She usually worked nights, so Nick had taken to waiting for her at the bar where they'd first met. Some nights she showed up, some nights she didn't. When she did, they'd go back to his place and make love all night. She said he was a monster that she had created. Other women approached him at the bar, and he turned them away. He'd discovered he was a one-woman man. He hadn't known that before, but then he'd never looked the way he did now. Stacy said that since he had started up with her he walked differently, stood differently, and even talked differently.

He was sexy.

A month after their meeting, he sat at the bar, wondering why he couldn't just go and meet her after work. Why did they always make love at his place? And where did she go when she didn't meet him after work? She had told him that sometimes she was tired and just wanted to go home.

139

However, sitting at the bar on this night, drinking his third beer, he started to wonder if she was seeing someone else.

And with that thought the old rage rose to the surface. He'd been betrayed by one woman, why not by another?

He slammed his half-finished beer down on the bar and stalked out of the club. He would not let another woman do to him what Gina had done.

He parked within sight of the bar's entrance. Nick had found a spot in a corner, underneath a tree, which this late at night shrouded his car in total blackness.

The place was starting to empty out. He had no idea how soon after it closed Stacy would emerge. He was willing to wait.

At 2:40 she came out the front door, hanging onto a guy's arm. They were laughing. The guy was a yuppie, wearing a powder-blue shirt, white pants, and loafers. He looked to be her age, about twenty-five or so.

Nick's first instinct was to confront her. Maybe he'd even use everything he'd recently learned to teach the guy a lesson. Instead, Nick watched as they walked to her little Toyota.

Before getting into her car, they embraced, kissing deeply. He watched as Stacy ran her hands down his back until she was cupping his yuppie buttocks. Nick knew how that felt: She had done it to him that first night in the parking lot, before they went to his place. He guessed that right now the guy had a hard-on the size of a missile, and it was threatening to blast off.

They broke the kiss, and the guy touched her tits. She laughed and slapped his hands away playfully, but not before giving him a good, long feel. He got in on the passenger side, and she walked around her car and got in on the other side. The guy grabbed her right away and they kissed again in the front seat, long and deep. Nick had a hard time staying in his car. He gripped the steering wheel tightly. He could see their silhouettes melded together. Then they parted, and she started the car.

He didn't know where Stacy lived, so he didn't know if they were going to her place, the guy's place, or to a hotel. He followed.

They drove to an Overland Park apartment complex. Before turning in the driveway behind them, Nick shut off his headlights.

As they got out of the car, he could hear their laughter. Their hands roamed all over each other. The guy even got inside her top, squeezing one firm, round breast. Nick closed his eyes for a moment, then opened them to watch them go inside the building.

He parked in a spot away from Stacy's car, walked to the doorway, and saw the mailboxes. On one of them was the name S. Cates and the apartment number, 2E.

He took the stairs to the second floor. In the back, 2E had a front door on an open balcony, like a motel. The rear of the building looked onto dense woods. There was no danger of anyone seeing him lurking.

At 2E, he pressed his ear to the door. He could hear them laughing inside. Was she telling him how her boyfriend now waited for her in a bar? Were they laughing at him the way all of those people who used Gina had laughed?

The rage boiled to the top. He growled like an animal and struck the door once with his shoulder. It popped open as if it were plywood.

He found himself in a living room. There was a lamp lit, and Stacy and the guy were standing in the center of the room. Stacy was naked, and the guy had his mouth on her breasts. His pants were down around his ankles.

Stacy saw Nick and her eyes went wide.

"Nick!" she said. "What—"

"What's goin' on?" the guy demanded. When he saw Nick, *his* eyes went wide. Nick was a frightful apparition because of his size and especially because of the look in his eyes. His bulging eyes seemed more white than anything else, and they were glazed, as if he were drugged.

"Jesus," the guy said, and then Nick was on him.

He pushed Stacy away. She stumbled over the sofa and fell to the floor. The guy was shorter than Nick, about five nine, and when Nick grabbed him by the throat he was able to lift him off his feet.

The guy tried to say something, or yell, but Nick's hands on his throat held too tightly. His hands clawed at Nick's, but his strength couldn't match that of the larger man's.

"Nick, stop it!" Stacy shouted. "What are you doing? Stop it, you'll kill him!"

He was vaguely aware of her fists bouncing off his broad back. Abruptly, he released the man and tossed him aside, like a rag doll. The guy struck the wall, slumping to the floor, semi-conscious.

Nick turned on Stacy.

"Is this what you've been doing, Gina?" he demanded. "When I'm waiting for you at the bar, and you don't come, you're with him?"

"With him?" she shouted. "You big ape! I never saw him before tonight."

"He's not your lover?" Nick shouted. He grabbed a handful of her hair. "Don't lie to me."

"Let go!" she said. She pulled away. "You fucking asshole! What did you think, that I was only putting out for you? He's just some-body I picked up at the bar, like any other night. Did you think I was faithful to you, you dumb sonofabitch? You're just somebody I picked up for laughs, Nick. A big idiot who doesn't know anything about women, or about sex. I was having fun with you, baby, but when I wanted a real man, I reached out and grabbed one."

She was beautiful, standing there naked, her breasts heaving, her hair wild, her nostrils flaring and her eyes wide. She looked the way she did when they were fucking. Through the rage and hatred, he felt his excitement building, as well.

"A real man?" he asked. He walked over to where the guy sat on the floor, trying to regain his senses. His breath came in hard, raspy inhalations. "This is a real man? *This* is your idea of a real man? Watch closely, Gina."

Nick knelt next to the seated man. He grabbed his head the way his instructor had taught him.

"Hey, wha—" the man said. With a swift, twisting motion Nick cut the man off in mid-sentence. With an audible crack, Nick ended his life. His lifeless form fell over, his head at an odd angle on the now broken neck. The man's eyes were wide open, staring.

Stacy screamed in horror. "What did you do? You killed him?"

"Yes," Nick said. "I killed him, Gina." It hadn't been hard at all. In fact, it had been extremely satisfying.

"Nick . . ." she said as he advanced on her. "Nick, baby, what are you gonna do?"

"You'll see, Gina."

"Why do you keep calling me Gina?"

He didn't hear. "Come here, Gina. Let me show you what a real man is like."

"Nick . . . stop!"

He grabbed for her. She almost slipped away, but his right hand closed over one of her breasts and he held fast. She screamed, but he didn't care. He threw her on the sofa, knelt on her with one knee and began removing his clothes, pinning her down while he removed his sandals and pants, then his underwear.

His erection was huge, pounding. He was more excited than he had ever been before. It was not only Stacy's nakedness and her scent, but the smell of her fear, and the fact that he had killed.

"Come on, baby," she was saying. "Come on, honey, I want you to fuck me." She began to croon to him, but she stopped when he roughly spread her legs and thrust himself brutally inside her.

She screamed. He put a hand over her mouth, the other around her throat while he continued to fuck her. He didn't even notice when her eyes glazed over and she stopped moving. He just kept pounding into her, grunting with the effort, then bellowing as he came, exploding, experiencing the most intense, dizzying orgasm he'd ever had.

When he got off her, he realized she was dead. He'd done it twice now.

He kicked his clothes away and stood there naked, looking down at her, then over at the dead yuppie. She had betrayed him. The man had taken something that was his. Neither had suffered enough for it.

In a flash of insight he suddenly realized how he could make his point. He went to the kitchen to look for a knife.

An hour later in Nick Turner's apartment, he ran the water in the shower, then stepped beneath the spray. Dried blood, liquefied once again, ran along the base of the shower and down the drain. Satisfied he was clean, he stepped from the shower and dried himself. Still naked, he took his clothing to the kitchen. He opened a cabinet and took out a box of plastic garbage bags. He put his blood-splattered clothes inside one. He upended the kitchen trash basket into the bag, dumping the garbage on top of his bloodied clothes. In the morning, he'd dump the bag.

Still naked, he walked into the living room, to the corner desk where his computer was. He opened the bottom right-hand drawer and took out all of Gina's journals. He had not even looked at them since the night he'd first met Stacy Cates. Now he turned on his desk lamp, sat back, spread one of the journals open in his naked lap, and began to read.

Chapter Twenty-one

December 1990

Christmas Eve, 1990

Nick Turner sat in his living room, dog-earing pages of Gina's journals, marking passages with different-colored highlighters.

With yellow he marked off the names and locations of the men his wife, Gina, had sex with. With pink, he marked off the names and locations of the women.

Over the past three months he had intensified his training, until, at the beginning of December, he paid off his instructor. The man had taken the money, no questions asked.

He had prepared to leave Kansas behind without a trace. He stopped going to his health club and began selling his furniture and other belongings. He was only taking what he could fit into a single suitcase—along with all of the journals.

He was still unsure as to where his base of operations would be, but once he found it, he'd be able to begin his mission: to wipe out every man and woman who had corrupted his Gina and turned her into the perverted, hateful bitch she was when she died.

He fondly remembered killing Stacy Cates and her lover. Those were the moments of his rebirth, when the old Nick Turner had died. He wasn't even sure what name he would use in the future, but he knew Nick Turner was no more.

Now he was a single entity with many names and one mission in life. Thanks to Stacy Cates and her lover, he knew that he was eminently qualified to successfully execute his mission.

The big man who used to be Nick Turner giggled—an odd, high-pitched sound—at his own unintentional pun.

How appropriate.

The first of Nick Turner's executions took place in January 1991.

He was lucky: This one was easy. All he had to do was go back to his old neighborhood in Marine Park to the garage where he'd taken his car for work. The mechanic Gina had written about was still working there.

His name was Ed Ruiz. Nick could still remember the entry about Ed, the mechanic:

> . . . Journal, Ed had always liked me. This time, when I took the car in, he looked so attractive. His real name was Eduardo, and he looked a lot like Julio Iglesias.

I drove the car over at lunchtime. He told me to pull it into the last bay. He wore his garage shirt with his name on the breast pocket. It was warm, and he had it open. I could see the dark hairs of his chest, and the sheen of perspiration beneath them.

I knew he wanted me, but I made the first move. It was more exciting that way. We both had to lean under the hood so I could show him what was wrong. I could smell him, and couldn't resist putting my hand inside his shirt and rubbing his chest. His hair felt wiry. His nipple got hard. He called me something then—I think he said *chica*—and put his hand under my dress. The next thing I knew we were in the backseat and he was on top of me. His shirt was off and his pants were down. My skirt was hiked up. I don't know where my panties were. Jesus, Journal, he was inside me and he was hitting just the right spot with every movement of his hips. He had his hands underneath me, holding my behind, and his mouth was all over my neck and shoulders. He *grunted* with every thrust. I *love* it when men grunt . . .

Nick took his time setting up Ed Ruiz. He followed him home from work for a few days and found out that he frequented a neighborhood bar in Canarsie. He always stopped in on his way home from work.

That established, Nick discovered that Ed Ruiz was married, with two kids. By watching the house Nick discovered that his wife was a pretty, dark-haired woman in her early thirties.

Nick started drinking in the Canarsie bar, making sure he was there whenever Ed came in. The guy always had two draft beers, then went home. After a week he got used to Nick being there and they started to talk. Little by little the conversations grew in length and substance, until finally they were drinking buddies, talking about women and sex. Ed even bitched some about his wife, giving Nick his approach.

"You must get a lot of women in that garage of yours. You know, good-looking women needing their cars worked on?"

"Oh, yeah." Ed had a slight Spanish accent. "Lots of women, *amigo*."

Nick nudged Ed's elbow with his own and said, "Come on, Ed, you can tell me."

"Tell you what?" Ed looked at Nick sideways, a half-finished draft in his hand.

"You nailed some of those broads, didn't you? Huh? Come on!"

"Yeah," the bartender said, getting in on the conversation. "Come on, Ed, you can tell us."

"Nah." Ed shook his head. "Hey, fellas, I'm a married man. I got two kids."

"How about in the summer?" Nick asked.

"When they come in wearing shorts and little dresses, huh? Their sweet little tits hanging out in your face? Don't some of them come on to you, Ed? Huh?"

Ed looked a little sheepish.

"Well, yeah, sometimes they do. And they don't all have *little* tits, either." Ed held his hands out in front of his chest to illustrate his point.

"And you sucked on a few of them melons, huh, Ed?"

Ed looked at Nick, then at the bartender. "Well, yeah, okay, a few. But only when they really wanted it, man." He puffed up his chest. "Some of them really want it, ya know?"

Nick drew back from Ed a bit, studying him. "Anybody ever tell you you look like that singer? What's his name—Julio . . . something?"

"Hey, you know? A woman told me that once."

"Oh, yeah?" Nick said. "While you were banging her in the backseat, huh?"

"Well . . . yeah . . ." Ed was sheepish again. He was as good as dead.

Monday, Nick showed up at the bar. He decided that this was to be Ed Ruiz's last day on earth.

After his second beer, Ed readied to leave, but Nick cajoled him into staying for one more, saying he'd buy.

"Hey, man, my wife, she's gonna worry . . ."

"Let her worry, Ed. It'll be good for her. She'll appreciate you more. You *could* be appreciated more, couldn't you?"

They were on their fourth beer when Nick said, "Ed, you gotta help me out."

"Whatsamatta?"

Nick moved closer.

"I know these two blond girls, they're sisters, see? With the biggest, roundest, most luscious tits you ever saw."

Ed lowered his voice and asked, "Are they twins?"

"You guessed right, *amigo*. They're waiting for me in a motel right now," Nick said. "Here's the deal." Nick lowered his voice and put his arm around Ed's shoulders. "I only want one of them, but she's gonna have her sister with her. I need your help."

"Me? What for?"

"I told them about you," Nick said, "and they want to meet you. I told them you look like that Julio guy. Man, the sister—her name's Wendy—she said she *loves* Julio."

"Hey, man." Ed held up his hand. "I gotta go home."

"Ed, *Ed*," Nick said urgently. "You gotta help me here, man. This cunt is hot, man, and she's ready. She'll lie down and spread 'em for you—you ever had a real blond, man?"

Nick talked and talked, and halfway through their fifth beer Ed Ruiz agreed.

They walked to Nick's car, both of them weaving a bit, Ed more than Nick because he usually only had two beers. They drove to a motel on North Conduit out near Kennedy Airport.

Nick had rented a room on the side, allowing them to enter without going through the lobby. He had checked out the place at different hours, and it was never really busy. He'd checked in a few hours earlier, asking for two rooms with empties on either side. Nick told the desk clerk he had a friend coming in on a plane, and they were going to have a meeting here.

"This is it, man," Nick said, stopping in front of room 214.

"They're in here?" Ed asked.

"They're waiting next door. Go inside and shower, man. Get naked, ya know? When you hear a knock on the connecting door, open up."

"Naked?"

Nick smiled. "This chick is gonna be all over you. Make sure you got a hard-on when you open the door, ya know?"

"I'm gettin' one now." Ed grabbed his crotch.

Nick slapped the man on the back, then unlocked the door and let him in.

Then he went to room 216. A gym bag was on the bed. From it he took a black-handled butcher's knife.

He opened the connecting door on his side. He could hear the shower running. He was

153

starting to sweat despite the air-conditioning.

He waited with his ear against the door, the sweat dripping down his face and off his chin to form a damp spot on the rug at his feet. His heart raced, and he had a raging erection. He hadn't killed anyone since Stacy and her boyfriend. This was the one that was going to put him on his path.

The shower cut off, and he caught his breath. He stood back from the door a step, counted to ten, then knocked. When it didn't open right away, he panicked. What if Ed had changed his mind?

Nick knocked again. This time the lock turned. The door opened.

Ed Ruiz, naked, his hair wet, sported an erection that wasn't much to speak of. He had a broad grin on his face and a glazed, unfocused look in his eyes.

"*Chica*—" he said, but he got no farther.

"This is for Gina," Nick said, and drove the butcher knife into the man's belly right to the hilt.

Chapter Twenty-two

January 1994

The man who had once been Nick Turner stood naked in front of the sliding-glass door. As he opened it, the chill of the January air touched his body, drying the perspiration. It felt good. He often stood in front of this door following his morning workout.

He continued to keep his body in shape. He worked out with calisthenics, isometrics, and then went into his martial arts routine.

It was hard to believe he had left Kansas three years ago. Everything had gone so well. He had kept up with the New York newspapers, and, so far, no one had put any of his killings together. That was his doing, of course. He tried to use a different method each time, and even when he repeated, he made sure that those incidents were well-spaced. His experience as a writer and researcher told him that serial killers were usually classified by the method they used to kill. But then, how many different ways could you kill someone before you *had* to repeat? He made sure that he never repeated a method back-to-back, or even close to each other.

He closed the glass door and went to the bathroom. After standing in the doorway, he enjoyed a long, hot shower. He liked this apartment. He had been here the entire time, ever since his first killing. When his mission necessitated a stay somewhere else, he missed this place. Not that he wouldn't be able to leave it if he had to, but it had become home to him. He hadn't *had* a home since his with Gina had been destroyed.

And then there were the jars in the hall closet with his treasures.

He rubbed his face vigorously. He did not want to think about that. He turned the hot-water faucet to the OFF position and stood stiffly beneath the relentless, cold spray. When he stepped from the shower, he was in control once again. He took a towel from the rack and dried himself. As he dried his crotch, he noticed that his penis had become semierect.

He'd had women occasionally since his arrival here. He picked them up in bars and either went to their place or took them to a hotel. And he never saw them more than once. Sometimes they were whores, so they didn't *expect* to see him again, except as a customer.

When they weren't whores, he told them he'd call them, then never did.

He'd already made that mistake with Stacy. Had he fucked her once and then moved on to another woman, then another, he could still have sharpened his sexual skills, and not had to . . .

He shook his head, once again trying to dispel unwanted thoughts. He dropped his towel, stood in front of the toilet, masturbated dispassionately, and spewed his seed into the water.

He was again in control. He cleaned himself off, forced himself to urinate, then lathered his head and face and shaved. He had kept his head bald since leaving Kansas, and had three different wigs that he alternated. When he wasn't in New York, he simply went without. He had come in to like the way his head looked cleanly shaven.

He packed a small cloth bag with a few belongings. He'd be away a few days.

His quarry was a man. Well, he was a man now, but when this *man* had perverted his Gina, he'd only been a boy. By now he must be twenty-one or so. Nick had ascertained that the young man had moved away from his family's house—next door to Nick's old house—and into a college dorm. He would not be difficult to find.

Another thing Nick did to avoid detection

was to never execute his plan in the same place twice. If he killed two people in Brooklyn, there was always at least one in between, in Manhattan or Queens. This kept any pattern from emerging.

It was amazing to him that not only was his physical training put into effective use, but also all of the research he had done over the years writing police and crime novels. Everything he had learned as a writer had helped transform him into an effective killing machine.

Nick sometimes thought of himself as a machine, although he wasn't exactly emotion-less. He *enjoyed* the killing. That fact no longer surprised him. While all of his executions were necessary, he'd come to terms with the fact that he enjoyed them both physically and mentally.

He walked over to a small desk and looked at his laptop computer.

He hadn't started writing fiction again until a year ago. He'd had the urge to write, but it wasn't until after he'd dispatched the first few names in Gina's journal that the urge became *urgent*. At that point, he sat down and began keeping his own journal, a sort of sequel to Gina's. In *his* book, he would be undoing what she had done in hers.

The journals failed to satisfy his urge, how-ever, so he sat down and wrote a crime novel about a cold, heartless, relentless killer. He sent it to his agent with no return address. He included a letter that said he'd follow up with a phone call. When he finally did call, Daniel Foster was very excited to hear from him.

"Nick, this manuscript is great. Jesus, I've been wondering what happened to you. I tried to get in touch with you in Kansas."

"I moved."

"So I gathered," Foster said. "But where to?"

"That's not important," he said. "Do you like the new book?"

"It's inspired. I don't know where you've been or what you've been doing, but your writing has changed. It's more powerful and compelling. I always knew you were capable of this, Nick, if you could only get off that paperback treadmill."

"So you can sell it in hardcover?"

"I'm sure I can," said Foster. "But let's pick a pseudonym. I want to market it as a first novel. I don't want your past reputation influencing the way editors will look at this."

"I can understand that." In fact, he agreed. "Okay, go ahead and sell it."

"How do I get in touch with you?"

"I'll call you."

"Wait," the agent said, "how will you know when I've sold it?"

"I'll call you once a week."

Four phone calls later, Daniel Foster had an

offer on the book. The advance was twenty-five thousand, five times what he usually got for a Nick Turner book.

Nick had arranged to pick up the money at an American Express office in the city. He had the contracts delivered to a P.O. box, also in the city. The publisher rushed the book into production, and it was published six months later.

The reviews were outstanding. According to his agent, the sales were so good that the publisher wanted to sign him to a two-book contract. He was offered fifty thousand apiece. He wanted more.

Writing had solved the money problem. He had been living frugally on his savings, and the money from the sale of the house, but his cache had been dwindling. The sale of the first book had come along just in time. He needed to make sure that he got enough money for the next two so that he could continue his work.

He checked his watch. He had time now to call his agent before he caught his train. If the publisher had agreed to their demands—a hundred thousand a book, half up front—he would be in a very good mood. When he was in a good mood, his "plans" came together so much more effortlessly. In fact, he planned his kills the same way he plotted his books. In the past, the more effortlessly the idea came to him, the easier it was to write. It had been the same with this, what he had come to think of as his second career.

And when it all flowed well, that was good for both him and his victims. When the plan was difficult to formulate *and* carry out, they usually paid for it.

He took it out on them. He knew that made him a bad person.

He put his hand on the closed laptop, then picked up his bag and headed for the door. He hoped Daniel Foster would have good news. He was eager to start the next book.

Before that, though, he was anxious to get the next kill over with. Actually, he was just anxious to get started.

It didn't occur to the man who had once been Nick Turner that maybe he liked this second career too much.

Part III

The Task Force

Chapter Twenty-three

April 1994

The Task Force was given a room in the back of the second floor of the 61 Precinct building. This suited McQueen; it meant he didn't have to leave "home" to do the job. As second whip he reported to Keepsake, which meant he owed nothing to Captain Austin or Lieutenant Guiliano beyond the normal respect for their rank.

It was Monday when McQueen came into the squad room and found Keepsake at his desk, looking lost. He felt sorry for the younger man, for anyone who let ambition push him into situations he wasn't prepared for. Whether or not that was the case with Keepsake remained to be seen.

"I think I've got our task force, Cap."
McQueen put five personnel folders down on
the desk. He picked one up. "Detective Second-
Grade Jason Van Shelton. Fourteen years on
the job, the last eight as a detective. He's thirty-
eight. Good record of closed cases. Right now
he's assigned to the Four-One in the Bronx. I
don't know him personally, but his reputation's
good. Word is, he's reliable, a hard worker. He
gets the job done."

McQueen pulled out the second folder.
"Detective Third-Grade Neil Chapman. Eight
years on the job, three as a detective. He's
twenty-seven, will make second grade any day
now. We can get him from the Two-Four
squad."

"Personal opinion, or word of mouth?"

"Word of mouth."

Keepsake nodded, picking up the third folder.

McQueen could almost recite these creden-
tials without looking at the file. "Marie Scalesi,
detective third grade, forty-three. Eighteen
years on the job, she's been a gold shield for
only five. She got it by being stubborn and
working hard against the bias."

Being a cop was damn hard work, but it was
even harder for a woman. Any woman who
made detective deserved it.

"Know her personally, Dennis?"

"Yes, sir, I worked with her when she was in

uniform, and a couple of times since she made gold shield."

"Where is she now?"

McQueen made a face and said, "At the academy, going to waste as some kind of instructor."

Keepsake studied McQueen for a few moments. "You're not fucking her, are you, Dennis?"

"No, sir, we're not fucking." McQueen was fine as long as he made this statement in the present tense. The past was an entirely different matter. "She's just a good cop."

"Okay. Who's next?"

McQueen handed the fourth folder to Keepsake without reading from it. "My partner, Ray Velez, a good man with eight years in, and he's already made—"

"Save it, Dennis." Keepsake cut him off with a wave of his hand. "If he's your partner and you want him, he's in. Who's next?"

McQueen picked up the last folder. "Detective First-Grade Sam Lacy, Six-Three squad. He's got his twenty in and he's sticking around. We had a little run-in a while back about one of his cases, which is now one of our cases, but he's a good man."

"Can you work with him?"

"I think the question will be, can he work with me, sir."

"Well, maybe you should ask him. In fact, you should ask all of them. I want the squad assembled by Friday. I'll leave it to you. Call the chief of detectives' office, and they'll pave the way for the necessary paperwork."

"Next Friday?"

Keepsake shook his head.

"This Friday, Dennis. Let's get this show on the road, already."

"Yes, sir!"

Chapter Twenty-four

Before the task force assembled that Friday morning, Keepsake had a talk with McQueen.

"Part of being a good captain is knowing when to delegate authority, Dennis. I let you put this squad together because you're a detective and I'm not."

McQueen waited for the zinger. Keepsake was going to make it clear who was really running the squad. Fine with McQueen, he'd be satisfied to work the investigation and not run it.

"Dennis, I'm not going to pretend to be running this show. You put this whole thing together, and I want you to go ahead and run it."

"Captain, that's a bit more than I was looking for. I didn't even want to be made a sergeant. The responsibility of running a squad, well—"

"Dennis, that's not what I mean," Keepsake said. "I want you to run the investigation, but I'll take the responsibility for the squad."

"And the credit."

Keepsake frowned and said, "Now, Dennis—"

"Take it easy, Cap," McQueen said. "I don't care who gets the credit, as long as we catch this bastard."

"Catching this killer is going to be good for all our careers, Dennis, but if we don't catch him, it's my ass that's going to be whistling in the wind."

"Got it, Cap."

"All right," Keepsake said, "let's get ready for the others."

McQueen had made photocopies of the folder he'd taken with him to the chief of detectives' office, one for each detective and one for the captain. He had decided to share his desk with Detectives Velez and Scalesi, leaving the room's remaining two desks for the other three detectives. He put three folders on each desk.

The room's setup was simple. Keepsake's desk was at the head of the room, putting his back to the wall. McQueen's desk was to the right, against that wall. The other two desks were in the center of the room, facing Keepsake's. To the left of Keepsake's desk stood a blackboard on wheels. The only other thing in the room was an old four-drawer metal file cabinet.

Velez arrived first, followed by Scalesi. She walked right over to McQueen and planted an impulsive kiss on his cheek.

"Hello, Marie."

"You don't know what this means to me, Dennis," she said, her eyes shining.

"Hey," McQueen said, "I needed a good detective, all right? That's all there was to it."

She had cut her dark hair shorter and—like the suit she wore—it was very businesslike. Her olive skin seemed to glow. She was a tall woman, five eight in her bare feet, and she was big and strong. Although not classically beautiful, she was decidedly feminine and attractive.

She'd had to put up with the worst kinds of sexual harassment during her years on the job, and she had never been shy about filing complaints. Because of this she was not a popular figure in the New York Police Department. That's why she had been assigned to the academy as an instructor. It was only Keepsake's carte blanche from the chief of detectives that had gotten her out.

McQueen made the introductions.

Detectives Chapman and Van Shelton walked into the room together, talking animatedly.

"The colors ain't so bad, my man," Chapman said to Van Shelton. The bald black man with the gold earring was obviously referring to the latter's pink shirt and electric-blue jacket. "But listen, the quality has got to improve."

"Are you married, Chapman?"

"Hell, no."

"Well, I am," Van Shelton said, "and this is as good as the quality of my clothes gets. Why do you think I wear these colors?"

"You're color-blind?" McQueen answered. "Do you two know each other?"

"Met on the elevator." Chapman pointed to Van Shelton. "Man's a Met fan."

"All the way," Van Shelton said, slapping Chapman on the back.

Good, McQueen thought, they'd already found some common ground. If this task force was going to operate efficiently, it was important that the detectives on it got along.

While the four detectives were getting to know each other, the fifth, Sam Lacy, walked in.

"Lacy," McQueen said, "this is Captain Keepsake."

Lacy looked Keepsake over, and McQueen hoped he wouldn't say anything about the captain's youth.

"Glad to be here, Cap," Lacy said, surprising McQueen. "Thanks for having me."

"Thank Dennis, Sam."

Lacy looked slightly taken aback by the Captain's use of his first name, but shook it off.

McQueen introduced Lacy to the other four. The man shook hands with the male detectives without comment. When he shook hands with Marie Scalesi, he leered and said, "Well, this might turn out to be more fun than I thought."

She smiled at him good-naturedly. "In your dreams."

"Let's get started," Keepsake said, raising his voice. "You'll each find a file folder with your name on it. Inside is all of the information we've collected on these mutilation murders. Now that we're a task force, we'll be gathering even more detailed info from the proper precincts and departments. That should be here later this week. However, in these folders is enough information for you to familiarize yourself with what we're up against.

"You will all report to Detective Sergeant McQueen. He put all of this together, and he'll be running the investigation. When he talks, it's the same as me talking. Understand?"

They did, although Sam Lacy's assent was a bit less enthusiastic than that of the others.

"All right, then," Keepsake said, "I'll turn you over to Sergeant McQueen."

Keepsake nodded to McQueen and then walked around behind his desk.

"You've heard most of it from the captain," McQueen said. "There isn't much we can do until you've read the material in these file folders. I expect you to do that over the weekend. Monday, I'll give you your assignments, but there's one thing I want to make very clear. Initiative is very important to me. If you see something in these folders that you feel you can run with, let me know. I'd rather have you working on something you feel strongly about than on something I feel strongly about. Is that clear?"

The detectives nodded.

"Good. You can stay here and read the folders, or go elsewhere and do it. Just check back in with me before you leave for the day."

"What time?" Van Shelton asked.

"What time what?"

"What time do we punch out for the day?"

"Officially, we'll be working ten-hour shifts," McQueen replied. "Unofficially, you'll come in when you're told to and leave when you're told to. If anybody doesn't like that, now's the time to speak up."

Nobody did.

"Good. In addition, you'll be issued beepers. If they beep, it means either the captain or I want you. I don't care who you're in bed with, respond to that signal immediately or you'll be replaced."

The beepers were Keepsake's idea, and McQueen thought it was a good one.

"Okay, that's all . . . for now. Monday, we really get down to it."

Van Shelton and Chapman left together to find someplace to go over the material while they discussed the Mets' chances at the World Series.

"Maybe what you need to get yourself," Chapman was saying to Van Shelton on the way out, "is an earring . . ."

Marie Scalesi sat down at one of the desks and immediately started reading.

Sam Lacy told Velez he'd be at his desk in the 63 squad and left.

Velez walked over to McQueen, carrying the folder under his arms.

"You did all right, Dennis. I think you were born to this boss stuff."

"Fuck you, Ray. Go read your file."

"I'll read it, though I been listening to you for so long I've got the case down pat."

"Oh, yeah? Well, then go out and find the killer."

Velez hesitated a moment, and then tapped the folder. "Maybe I'll just refresh my memory a little."

As Velez left the room, McQueen took a deep breath and turned to Keepsake.

"Good job, Dennis," Keepsake said approvingly. "I think you were born to this boss business."

McQueen made a face. He couldn't very well tell a captain to go fuck himself, could he?

Chapter Twenty-five

Before they left for the day, McQueen collared Marie Scalesi and asked her to stay for a few minutes. Earlier, he had spoken to Keepsake about a particular tack he wanted to take.

"Like I said, Dennis, you're in charge," Keepsake said after listening to the explanation. "But if you want an okay from me, you've got it."

McQueen thanked him, then waited until he left to talk to Scalesi.

"What's up, Dennis?"

"Uh, are you busy tonight? I mean, do you have a hot date, or something?"

She appeared puzzled. "I haven't been dating much since last year. I had a, uh, bad end to what I thought was a good relationship."

"I'm sorry, Marie."

She gave him an ironic smile. "I don't have much luck with men, you know?"

"This is all business, believe me. I've come up with an approach for the investigation, and I want to bounce it off you."

"Why me?"

"Frankly? Because you're a woman. Our man was hot shit with women. Can you spend some time talking tonight? I'll spring for dinner."

She smiled then and asked, "Italian?"

"How about Chinese?"

"Sold."

McQueen's history with Marie Scalesi was more involved than he had led Keepsake to believe. McQueen had worked with her on a case requiring the presence of a woman. It was before she'd gotten her gold shield, before his separation. He was unhappy at home—as was his wife. They weren't communicating at all. They hadn't had sex for months.

As Scalesi had pointed out, she did not have much luck with men. At that time she was feeling lonely, as well. They drifted into a relationship that went on for about six months before they realized that it was not only wrong, but destructive. They were not compatible, though they were both so desperate for some kind of relationship that they continued to force the issue. Emotionally, they were at opposite ends of the spectrum. While McQueen had almost

176

endless patience, Scalesi had a temper like a Roman candle. McQueen enjoyed an occasional Mets game, or Knicks game, or Rangers game, and even liked to go to the track. She preferred something a bit more lively than spectator sports, like making the club and bar scene in Manhattan, usually some place with dancing.

Sexually, they were hopeless. There was no question that they were attracted to each other, but they just never seemed to fit. Every session in bed was like a battle for power. They finally admitted that they weren't happy together, just in time to remain friends.

They went on with their lives, even worked together one more time, months after their breakup. That had been awkward. McQueen was determined that this would not happen this time.

They took a department car to a Chinese restaurant in Mill Basin called The Great Wall. He started his pitch while they waited for their main course.

"This thing goes too far back for us to be able to look into every individual case. We could do it, but it would take too much time."

"What's the hurry? The killer's been at it for a long time as it is."

"That's just it. Suppose he just stops?"

"Would that be so bad? If he stopped killing?" She picked up an egg roll and took a bite.

"Then we wouldn't catch him." McQueen

leaned forward, putting his elbows on the table and speaking urgently. "I don't just want the killings to stop, Marie. I want to catch him and put him away."

She chewed on her egg roll, then picked up another, but instead of taking a bite, she used it as a pointer.

"How did you get involved in this, Dennis?"

He explained the situation to her from the beginning of his involvement, the Medco case. She listened intently, asking a few questions. He stopped briefly when the waiter brought their food. He had pepper steak and she had chicken subgum.

When he was finished she said, "I'm impressed, Dennis—and you managed to get yourself a promotion."

"I wasn't looking for that." He immediately recognized his tone as being too defensive.

"I know you too well to think that was behind it."

"I'm sorry. To tell you the truth, I'm not really comfortable with the promotion, Marie, or with being second in command."

"You could have turned it down."

"Not after I got Keepsake involved. That would have been like throwing him to the wolves. As he points out, I put this thing together, I have to see it through to the end."

"So what do you want to do? Why do you need me, Dennis?"

"Like I said before, we can't go back to all those old cases. What I want to do is concentrate on recent ones. Go back maybe . . . five. Now, three of those are women and my guy, Medco, was a ladies' man."

"You think a woman is going to be the answer to all of this?"

"I think it's possible, yeah."

"Well, maybe you're right. What do you want me to do, specifically?"

"Well, first off, I want you to get your hair done."

Monday morning he explained to the rest of the task force what he had explained to Marie Scalesi the night before.

"Five cases. One for each of you. Sam, I don't want you working Bonnie Green."

"What?" Lacy's face turned red. "That's my case. You said you wanted me on this task force because of it."

"I know, and I do want you, but I think somebody with a fresh outlook should go over the old ground." He'd figured Lacy would be miffed, so he tried to mollify the man. "You're the one who's going to go over my case, the Medco killing."

Lacy sat back in his chair and smiled. "I can live with that."

McQueen was hoping he'd say that.

"I'll make my files available to you." He

turned to Marie. "You'll handle Bonnie Green."

"Right."

She had agreed to that over dinner.

"Ray?"

"Yo."

"I want you on Ruth Nash. Get the files from Jack Dent."

"Right."

Next McQueen gave out the two cases that came before Medco.

"Jason, I need you on Thomas Bennett."

"That was Queens, right?"

"Right."

Greenpoint, Brooklyn, where Van Shelton had been assigned, was close enough to Queens for the detective to know his way around.

"I got it."

"Neil. There was a woman named Sara Hart who was killed in the East Village. That's yours."

"That's cool."

McQueen noticed that Chapman had arrived that morning dressed a little more casually, sans tie and sports coat, wearing a leather jacket instead. The task force would not have a strict dress code. However, the young detective sported a gold ball in his nostril. He wondered what Keepsake was going to have to say about that.

"All the information you need about who to

contact is in my file. Where appropriate, go and see the detectives who originally worked on these cases and get their original case files. If there's any problem, call here and we'll take care of it." McQueen looked over at Keepsake to see if the captain wanted to say anything. When the man shook his head, McQueen said, "Let's get to work."

The detectives filed out.

"Dennis?"

McQueen turned at Keepsake's voice.

"Everything okay with Lacy?"

"Sure, Cap. No problem."

"Giving him your case was a clever move."

McQueen waved the intended compliment away.

"It made sense, is all."

"What are you going to do?"

"Well, I can't sit behind this desk all day. That's not my style. I might give Ray a hand with the Ruth Nash case. I was the first detective on the scene, with Dent."

"I remember. That was a nasty one."

"They're all nasty, Cap."

McQueen walked down the hall to the office of his old squad and found Ray Velez talking with Dent, who did not look happy. As McQueen entered, the man looked past Velez at him.

"This stinks, Dennis. Taking this case away from me."

181

"It's an old case, Jack. Let Ray handle it for a while. A fresh outlook might turn up something new."

"Yeah, well, it stinks, too, that you didn't ask me to be on the task force. After all, this case is mine. You were there with me."

"I know, Jack." McQueen chose his words carefully. "We only had room for five men on the detail. I'm sorry."

"You boffin' her, Dennis? Is that how the broad got on the squad?"

"Take it easy, Jack," Velez warned.

McQueen counted to ten, but it didn't do much good. He felt his ears getting hot.

"I'm going to forget you said that, Jack. Now give Ray your case file."

"I'll give it to him, but I ain't forgettin', Dennis. Count on that."

"Suit yourself." McQueen touched Velez's back. "Come back inside after you get it. I want to talk."

"Okay, Dennis."

"Who does he think he is?" Dent muttered after McQueen left. "They make him a sergeant and he gets all full of himself . . . well, fuck him . . ."

"Jack, you're an asshole if you think that way about Dennis. You've known him long enough that you should know better."

Dent pulled a file and slammed the drawer

shut. He turned to face Velez. "He should have picked me for that task force."

"Instead of me? Is that what you mean?"

"Look, Ray, you're a good guy, all right, but you haven't been a gold shield as long as I have."

"Can I have that file, please?"

Dent hesitated a moment, then passed it over.

Velez glared at him, then walked away. He wanted to explain that he hadn't been picked for the task force simply because he was McQueen's partner. Velez knew he was a good detective, and so did Dennis.

He knew everyone saw him as the young, confident up-and-comer. If they could get inside his head, though, they'd see that he was just as insecure as the next guy, maybe even more so.

Detective Marie Scalesi was pleased with the way her life was going now. She found it odd, though, that Dennis McQueen was the reason. Oh, not personally. The dinner with him the night before was enough to tell her that working with him on this was not going to be a problem. And even if it was, this task force was just too good to turn down.

Over the past year she had come to terms with being alone. At forty-three, it was time she grew up. While it would have been nice to have a man in her life, she didn't need to have one.

She continued to put in for a transfer. She would have gone anywhere to get out of the academy, but all she heard was, "As soon as a spot opens."

Then along came Dennis McQueen.

Her personal life was in order, and now she was working on a major task force, trying to stop a vicious serial killer. If they caught the perp, it was going to benefit everyone on the squad.

It finally looked as if she was going to be able to get her personal and professional life in sync.

Chapter Twenty-six

It took a week for the task force to discover the latest murder. It took that long for them to start getting copies of reports from all over the city on cases that had even the most remote connection with sexual mutilation.

They even got the copy of a report on a male body with damage to the penis. The M.E. finally pronounced that the dead man had most likely gotten his organ caught in his zipper a day or two before he was killed. Painful, yes; mutilation, no.

McQueen further angered the members of his old 61 squad by commandeering PAA Bobby Callan to do clerical work for the task force.

When Lieutenant Guiliano heard the news, he marched into the task-force office to confront McQueen. His anger waned, however, when he saw that Captain Keepsake was also present.

"Can I help you, Lieutenant?" McQueen asked.

"Dennis, what are you doing to my squad? First you leave, then you take Velez, then you anger Dent by not taking him, and now you take away my clerical."

"Sorry, Loo. But I need someone to go through all of the sixty-one's and the DD fives we get from other commands. This is important."

"So is having my squad run smoothly."

"Is there a problem, Lieutenant Guiliano?" Keepsake got up from his desk and approached the two men. "Dennis?"

"No problem, Cap." It was McQueen who spoke first. "The lieutenant just wishes we had taken our clerical PAA from another command."

"Well, I'm sorry, Lieutenant, if we're affecting the operation of your squad, but we needed a good clerical man, and Dennis recommended

Callan. You'll have him back as soon as we're done."

McQueen knew what was going through Guiliano's mind. Some of these task forces went on forever. By then, Guiliano would have broken in a new clerical, but lost precious time doing it. A squad's effectiveness, as far as paperwork was concerned, could be retarded by the absence of a competent clerical man. They could find themselves drowning in paper in a week.

"Look, Loo, why don't we do this? If you come up with a problem your new clerical can't handle, we're just across the hall. If he's available, we'll loan Bobby back to you to clear up the mess. How's that?"

Grudgingly, Guiliano said, "Well, I guess that'll have to do." Guiliano, who had marched angrily into the task-force office, was reduced to saying, "Uh, thank you, Captain."

As the lieutenant left, Keepsake said, "I got a call today. The chief would like to know what progress, if any, we've made."

McQueen made a face. What the hell could they be expecting after just a week? "Tell him Detective Scalesi got her hair done. Other than that, all we've done is go over old ground."

"Dennis?" Bobby Callan called from the other side of the room, "I think you've got one here."

"One what?"

"Another mutilation murder in Stony Brook."

"Don't they have their own police?" Keepsake asked.

"We sent flyers out to the police in Long Island, New Jersey, and Connecticut, remember?" McQueen said. "Let me see it, Bobby."

Callan handed over a copy of the preliminary report.

"What's it look like?" Keepsake asked.

McQueen didn't reply until he'd finished scanning the report.

"White male, was killed in his dorm. His neck was broken, and his genitals were removed. 'Hacked out,' their M.E. said."

"What about the way he was killed?" Keepsake asked. "A broken neck?"

"I don't think that matters," McQueen said. "A blade was used to mutilate him. Maybe the neck got broken in a struggle before the knife could be used to kill him."

"Well, someone will have to check it out," Keepsake said.

"I guess I'm elected," said McQueen. "Everyone else is involved with something else right now."

"Okay, get going, then."

It was early on a Monday, before noon. He had plenty of time to get out there, even though it was more than a three-hour drive.

"Good work, Bobby." He handed Callan back the report. "Keep digging."

"Sure, Dennis."

"How about the old files?"

"Still going through them."

One of Callan's duties was to go back even farther than McQueen had. "Okay, keep it up. If by some miracle we can find the very first case, it might tell us something."

McQueen went to his desk and dialed the Stony Brook police. When his connection was made, he asked for Detective Woodrell.

A woman's voice said into his ear, "Woodrell."

"This is Detective Sergeant Dennis McQueen of the New York City Police Department."

"What's your shield number, Sergeant?"

She was careful. That was good; she knew her job. McQueen gave her his shield number and waited a moment while she wrote it down.

"Where are you calling from?"

"The Six-One Precinct in Brooklyn. I'm with a special task force that's headquartered here."

"When I call back, what do I ask for?"

"Just ask for the task force. They'll connect you."

"I'll call right back."

"Thank you."

McQueen hung up and waited. The phone rang a few moments later and he answered it.

"Sergeant McQueen, Task Force."

"Yes, Sergeant, this is Detective Woodrell. What can I do for you?"

McQueen explained what the task force's

assignment was, and the reason he was calling her.

"I remember the case, but why don't you give me the case number so I can pull the file?" She returned in a moment. "Okay, I remembered it, but it happened in February. I needed to refresh myself. Now I have the file. This matches your other cases, huh?"

"It's close."

"I was hoping this was an isolated incident, Sergeant. I'm sorry to hear that someone is making a habit of this sort of thing."

"How's your investigation going?"

"Not real well."

"I've only seen the preliminary report. I'd like to see the rest of your paperwork."

"I could send it along—"

"How would it be if I drove out there today to pick it up?"

"If you don't mind making the drive, I'll be here."

"That'd be great. I'd really appreciate it."

"No problem. If I can help catch this sicko, I'm glad to do it."

"That's fine, then. It's . . . what, eleven now? Why don't we say . . . three o'clock? Just to be on the safe side."

"Three's good. See you then, Sergeant."

Before he could say anything else, the line went dead.

"That's a very businesslike lady," he said to

no one in particular. He looked over at Keepsake as he hung up the phone. "Guess I'll be putting a few extra miles on the car today, Cap."

Chapter Twenty-seven

Detective Rita Woodrell of the Stony Brook Police Department was waiting when McQueen arrived.

She offered her hand. He was not surprised by how firm her handshake was. Marie Scalesi had the same handshake, and Woodrell struck McQueen as being in the same mold, not only determined in her job, but good at it.

"I appreciate your help in this, Detective Woodrell."

"Not at all. Now that I know there are more cases like this it explains why I'm not finding an obvious motive for the killing."

"Can you tell me what you've got?"

"Yes, while we walk."

She was about five three or four, but her strides were longer than those of someone that height. McQueen hurried to catch up with her.

The facility was small, and new, a two-story brick building that had been built just a couple of years before. She led him down a hall to a stairway.

"There's not much, really. He was found in his dorm room by a friend. He knocked on the door in the morning, and then went in. He needed to borrow a book, he said. That was when he found the body. He called the police right away."

"Were you the first detective on the scene?"

"I was. It was gruesome. Blood everywhere."

"Did you notice right away that his . . . his genitals were missing?"

"No, not right away, but by the time the medical examiner got there, we did. He confirmed it. Here's my office."

They entered a room with five or six desks. It had the universal look every squad room shares, drab, bare walls, holding cell, right down to the coffee maker in the corner. She led him to a desk near the window. There were two other men sitting at desks. They watched as she and McQueen crossed the room.

He sat in a hard plastic chair across from her.

She opened a drawer in her desk and pulled out a fat file folder. "The dead boy's name is Brian Jordan," she said as she handed him the folder. "These are copies. You can keep them."

"What's in here?"

"Everything. My initial report, which you've seen, plus follow-up reports concerning interviews with people who knew him on campus. Teachers, other students, friends . . ."

McQueen leafed through the copies.

"What are you free to tell me about your task force, Sergeant McQueen?"

McQueen looked up at her. Her penciled eyebrows were knitted together and he found himself wondering what she looked like when she woke up in the morning.

"Why don't you call me Dennis? It'll be easier."

"All right. I'm Rita."

He told her everything there was to tell about the task force and she listened without interrupting.

"And all this began when you caught that first case? I'm impressed."

"Don't be." He looked down again at the folder in his lap. "It was just police work."

"Detective work, and not the kind you run across anymore, these days."

He looked at her. "You don't appear old enough to be using a phrase like 'these days'."

"I'm not. My father was a detective with the NYPD for years. He died when I was sixteen, and that's when I decided I wanted to be a detective, too."

"How did you end up out here?"

"I put up with the bullshit in the New York

department for about three years, and then came here. I know, it sounds like I ran, and maybe I did, but I've never regretted my decision. I got more of a fair shake in a smaller department. I don't think I'd be a detective right now if I was still in New York."

McQueen didn't doubt it. It had taken Marie Scalesi a long time to break in.

"Would you like to go over to the campus?" she then asked. "Seems a shame to drive all this way and not. I'll take you over there. You can leave your car here and we'll go in mine."

McQueen found himself wondering if she was attracted to him. He found her attractive, but it had been a while since he'd felt that. He hadn't been out with a woman in a long time, maybe he could . . .

"All right," he said finally. "Thank you."

She drove a small blue Toyota Tercel. "It's my own car. Sort of a settlement from my husband."

"Divorced?"

She nodded. "Last year."

"Me, too, five years, now."

"Bad?"

He hesitated. "Bad enough."

"Mine wasn't. We simply decided there was no point in taking it any farther."

"How long were you married?"

"Seven years. You?"

"Almost twenty."

"Kids?"

"A girl, sixteen—no, seventeen. You?"

She shook her head.

"I never had the time or the inclination. Hell, I got married at twenty-seven, was already involved with my career. I didn't want to take time out to be a mother."

"Did he understand that?"

"He said he did. I found out later he didn't." She hesitated, then added, "I found out a lot of things later."

He decided not to pry. He did some mental math and came up with thirty-five as her age. He thought thirty-five was an extremely good age for women. By then all of their girlishness was gone, their personalities complete, they were who they were and who they were going to be for a long time. His own wife had changed drastically when she hit thirty, and then thirty-five, and even when they divorced, he didn't feel that she was happy with herself.

He wondered if Detective Rita Woodrell was happy with who she was.

Maybe he'd get the opportunity to ask.

It was late when McQueen got back to Brooklyn. He decided not to stop in at the task force; if anyone had anything to tell him, the chances were good that they would leave a message on his answering machine. When he entered his apartment and saw that the red light on his machine was not blinking, he gave a silent cheer. He hated getting messages. If he hadn't gotten the damned machine for free, he wouldn't even have one.

He sat down at his desk and placed the Brian Jordan file on top. He and Woodrell had gone to the campus, and she had walked him to the dorm where the body was found. The witness was not on campus, she told him, but had gone back home again. His home number was in the file. He had talked to a few of the students who had rooms near Jordan's, but no one had offered anything new.

When they got back to the station, he screwed up enough nerve to ask her out for dinner. She smiled and said she couldn't, she had someone waiting for her at home. He drove back feeling like a fool. He'd been reading signals that just hadn't been there.

He scanned the file, intending to read it more fully in the morning. The six hours on the road had been tiring.

Ever since he'd given every member of the task force one case each to work on he'd lamented the fact that there was no individual case for him. Well, now he had one. He'd have something to keep him busy, and he'd also have a reason to call Rita Woodrell again.

He fell asleep and dreamed of Marie Scalesi and Rita Woodrell.

Chapter Twenty-eight

McQueen carried a container of coffee into the task-force office and put it on his desk with the Brian Jordan folder. Keepsake was the only other person present, so he told him about the case.

"Well, who's going to work on that one?"

"I figured I'd work it myself, Cap."

"You're a supervisor, Dennis."

"Not really, but I know what you mean. Don't worry, I can work it and still oversee the whole investigation."

"Are we going to get cooperation from the Stony Brook police? I don't want to step on anyone's toes."

"Full cooperation. But as far as stepping on toes, Cap, I'd trample the commissioner's if it would get me this killer."

"Let's just hope that won't be necessary, Dennis."

McQueen went to his desk to have his coffee and read the Jordan file. The other detectives might or might not arrive any minute, depending on how they were working their cases. They might spend the morning doing interviews, and then come into the office in the afternoon. After all, they weren't really on a clock.

He read the file from cover to cover, impressed by Rita Woodrell's thoroughness. She and her partner—a Detective T. Burke—had conducted countless interviews with teachers and other students about Brian Jordan's activities the day before his body was found. They had also talked with his closer friends, who said he had seemed fine, in good spirits. He had last been seen at a nearby bar and grill, a popular student gathering place. Brian Jordan did not have a steady girlfriend, and that night he had left the place alone. He had said he had to study for an exam.

There was no forced entry by either the dorm room's door or window. Woodrell assumed Jordan had let his killer in. However, McQueen conjectured, if Jordan had been grabbed outside, he could have been forced to open the door and then been killed inside.

From the amount of blood at the scene, it was obvious he had been killed right there.

McQueen looked up from the folder and realized he hadn't drunk his coffee. He sipped it now and made a face. It was cold.

He went through the folder again, this time looking to see if Woodrell had asked questions in and around the dorm to see if Jordan had been seen with anyone in the vicinity. He was about to pick up the phone and call her when Bobby Callan walked in.

"Dennis, I'm glad you're here." Callan took off his coat and hung it on a nearby rack, then set down a paper lunch bag. "I have to tell you what I did yesterday after you left." Callan smiled broadly. "You're gonna love this, Dennis. I went downstairs after the eight to four was finished and let myself into the computer room."

"Couldn't you get into trouble for that?"

"I could, but it seemed worth it. I got into NCIC and started checking for sex crimes and murders in Connecticut and New Jersey. I had to cross-reference a few times, and get through some road blocks, but I finally managed to come up with three more murders that might fit the bill."

"You're kidding."

"No, I'm not. I printed out the information. All *you* have to do is get in touch with the departments and get copies of the files."

"Well, where are the printouts?"

Callan smiled, pleased with himself. "They're in the top drawer."

McQueen looked down and opened the drawer. He took the papers out and placed them on top of the desk. McQueen looked at the paper bag that was on the end of the desk.

"Is this your lunch?"

"Yeah, why?"

McQueen picked up the bag and deposited it in his trash basket with his cold coffee. "Lunch is on me today, Callan. Good work."

Two of the cases matched up: one in New Jersey and one in Connecticut. The third was a closed case, where the husband confessed to killing his wife.

In New Jersey, fifteen months earlier, a man was found in a hotel room, badly "slashed." The case had not come up on the computer until Callan had cross-referenced for the word "mutilate" or "mutilation."

The Connecticut case was the same, except that the man had been found in his own apartment eighteen months ago, the way Paul Medco had been found. "Stabbed repeatedly" had been the phrase used, and the case had not appeared until Callan did his cross-referencing.

McQueen looked up from the printout sheets with two things in mind. One was to check all the other medical reports for the condition of the male victims. If none of them had sex before they died, but some of the women had—indicated by the presence of semen—you thought of the killer as a man, simply because it was not generally considered a woman's crime. All McQueen would be doing then was supporting the assumption with some facts.

Second, since NCIC was a national data base, he was going to ask Callan to check beyond the tristate area. First the East Coast, then the Midwest, then the West Coast.

What if this animal was operating nationwide? McQueen hated to think this way, but the more crimes the man had committed, the more chance there would be that he had left some clue behind.

He wrote himself a note so he wouldn't lose his train of thought, then called the police departments in New Jersey and Connecticut to ask that they send copies of the reports on those cases. Once he had established who he was he thought he'd get all the cooperation he needed, as he had from Rita Woodrell. Instead, both departments told him that any such requests had to come through channels.

When he hung up on the second call, he determined to ask Captain Keepsake what could be done to circumvent the proper channels.

Chapter Twenty-nine

In the afternoon, the task-force detectives began putting in appearances one by one. During most of that time, Keepsake was away from his desk.

Ray Velez came in, shaking his head.

"So what have you been up to?" asked McQueen.

"Talking to Ruth Nash's girlfriends. They say she never fooled around. They say that once in a while some men would approach them when they were in a bar, and that usually embarrassed Ruth."

"But she continued going out with them to bars, right?"

"To be one of the girls."

"You think they fool around on their husbands?"

"Oh, yes."

"Then keep at them. Maybe a guy showed a preference for Ruth one night, and they don't want to admit it."

Velez thought a moment and then said,

"That's possible. Thanks, Dennis. I gotta go and talk to the husband today, though I dread it. If Cookie were found like that . . ."

"Ray, don't forget what we're trying to do. You've got to worry about that, not the guy's feelings."

"Yes, Dennis, sure." Velez's voice sounded anything but all right.

Sam Lacy showed up around three.

"How's it going, Sam?"

"This Medco was some pussy hound, huh, McQueen?"

"That he was."

"He even nailed a teenager on the block, and her mother, too. Jeez." Lacy shook his head. McQueen realized that Lacy was impressed with the dead man's prowess. "Man, I'd love to—"

"Save it, Sam. Any developments on the case?"

"Dennis, I'm still going over old ground. This guy had himself quite a collection of pussy, you know? Anybody could have killed him."

"Okay, Sam, just keep at it."

"That's my job, Sarge." Lacy's tone was cold. "I do it pretty well."

McQueen didn't want to argue. He nodded.

Lacy was typing out his DD 5 when Marie Scalesi walked in.

"Hiya, babe!" Lacy greeted her.

Scalesi ignored him. Lacy blew her a kiss as she walked by his desk to McQueen's.

"Marie, you want me to—" McQueen began.

"Forget it, Dennis. I can handle guys like him."

"Okay. Hey, you got a new hairdo, didn't you?"

"I got a trim." Her hair didn't look much shorter, but it did look different. "A whole new do would have cost too much. I don't mind giving some hair for the cause, but not my own money. Then again, I think I'll have to go back again next week."

"I'll see if I can't get you some money for the hair visits, Marie. What else did you get besides a trim?"

"I talked to some of the gals at the beauty parlor, and some of the customers. Sounds like Bonnie Green was a real pistol."

"She was hot, huh?"

"Lots of boyfriends, and she liked to talk. She was heavy into the bar and club scene."

"In Brooklyn or Manhattan?"

"Both. When she wanted to do clubs, she went to Manhattan. Here in Brooklyn she frequented some of the local bars."

"Local?"

"Yes. Marine Park and Mill Basin, mostly."

McQueen rubbed his jaw and stared off into

space. "I'm wondering if our pistol ever ran into our pussy hound."

"What?"

"Medco, my original case." He proceeded to make himself clearer. "A girl as active as she was might have run into him in some local bar. See if you can find out what specific bars she frequented. I'll have Lacy do the same from his end."

"Okay."

"Type up your five, Marie." He got up to give her the desk. "I'll go and take a walk."

She nodded and seated herself.

On his way out of the room McQueen stopped by Lacy's desk.

"What is it . . . Sarge?"

"Just a possible connection, Sam." McQueen outlined what he and Scalesi had just talked about.

"Sounds plausible enough. I'll look into it."

"Good. Oh, one other thing, Sam."

"What's that?"

"Lay off Marie."

"Scalesi?" Lacy smiled lewdly and looked over to where the female detective was typing. "Broad's got the hots for me, Dennis. I can always tell."

"I don't think so, Sam."

Lacy stared up at McQueen.

"You tellin' me to clear a path for you?"

"I'm telling you to let Detective Scalesi do her job, Detective Lacy." He stood straight up.

"Is that an order . . . Sarge?"

"Just do it, Sam."

Part IV

Best-Seller

Chapter Thirty

April 1994

Nick Turner came up from the subway at 57th Street and Seventh Avenue. He looked down at himself. He was wearing a suit and tie, and for a moment he couldn't recall why. Then it hit him. He was on his way to meet his agent and his editor for lunch. Nick straightened his wig and headed for the Russian Tea Room.

In February he had killed Brian Jordan, the boy next door, the one his Gina had seduced—or vice versa. When killed, Jordan had almost become a man. Now he would grow no older.

In March he had killed Alan Simson in Staten Island. It was Turner's only murder in that borough, for which he was grateful. He didn't like Staten Island. He had unpleasant childhood memories of it. Going back was not a pleasant experience, and Alan Simson had paid for that fact.

Now it was April and he hadn't killed anyone. In the world of Nicholas Turner, murder had become the norm. A luncheon meeting with an agent and an editor was unusual.

Turner took several deep breaths. He had his bearings now. He knew who he was, where he was, and what he was doing.

He crossed the street and started toward Sixth Avenue.

Last month he had talked to his agent, Daniel Foster.

"We got the money, kid." The agent was ecstatic. "A quarter of a million for two books, but they want the first book by August one."

"Why?"

"They want it on their winter list for ninety-five. That will put it on the stands with the paperback of your first one—I mean, with 'Ned Tailor's' first one. Why'd you pick that name, anyway?"

"I like it."

There was a long pause, and then Foster said, "You know, Nick, you've changed."

"Have I?"

"Yeah, you have. I don't only mean your writing. Are we, uh, gonna get together before we meet with the editor?"

"What do you mean, meet with him?"

"Oh, I didn't tell you. That's another condition. She insists on meeting you. She says if she's gonna work with you and pay you that much money, she wants to meet you face-to-face. I told her no problem."

"I didn't agree—"

"This might be a deal breaker, Nick. Do you want to push it? What's the harm?"

The harm, he remembered thinking, was that he had not had to operate in a normal environment for some time.

"Nick? Talk to me, man."

"Okay, I'll meet with her—but you've got to be there, too."

"Hey, no problem. I'll set up a lunch."

"And I want to sign the contracts at lunch."

"I'll need time to go over them."

"Get them early, bring them to lunch. I want to sign them there. I don't want to have to come back into the city again."

There was a pause, and then he heard the agent take a deep breath and let it out slowly.

"When do you want to do this?"

"Set it up."

"How do I find you?"

"I'll call you at this time next week."

"Nick, Nick, what's the problem with giving me your phone number—"

Nick hung up.

When he called the following week, Daniel

Foster informed Nick he had set up a lunch for the first week in April.

"Nick, we need to make a good impression. Is that a problem? In the past, you haven't done very well at these sorts of meetings."

He remembered. Meetings with editors had always made him nervous. When he got nervous, he got diarrhea. That meant he couldn't eat and had to leave the table every few minutes. That was when he was the nervous type.

"I've changed."

"What I don't know is how much."

As he walked to the restaurant, Nick clenched his buttocks. He hadn't had breakfast, and he was going to eat lightly at lunch. Maybe he'd just have a beer or two.

This meeting was important. It meant getting enough money to carry on his mission. There was only one problem. He had been at this for three years now, and he was starting to run out of names. He had three, maybe five, left. Once they were dead, what would he do with himself? Write? The killing and the writing had become connected: After each killing, he'd go back to his place and write up a storm.

In the beginning, one killing would carry him through a couple of months of writing. When the writing started to get difficult, he'd go out and kill again, and then it was back to the computer. Lately, however, he was lucky if the killings carried him through a month. In the beginning he killed for a simple reason—justice. Then it got tangled up with the writing. What would he do when he was out of victims?

Then again, there was a whole world out there.

His agent had directed Nick to the Russian Tea Room. One of the tourist attractions of Manhattan, it was also a popular spot for meetings between agents and writers, actors, directors, producers, and the like. Lunch at the Russian Tea Room usually meant seeing at least one famous person.

He went through the revolving door and found himself in a small reception area next to a coat-check room. Straight ahead was a small bar, and beyond that the dining room. Off to his right was a stairway that led upstairs to a cabaret.

From just inside the door he saw Daniel Foster. The agent had changed. He had always been a little man with thinning hair who tended to be overweight. Now he was a small, fat man who was sitting at a table for four, already halfway through half a loaf of bread with butter. A partially finished tall glass of beer stood in front of him.

"Sir?"

Turner turned his head and looked at the maître d'.

"Are you here for lunch?"

Turner pointed. "I'm meeting the bald man with the bread in his mouth."

"Oh . . . him. This way, sir."

He followed the man past the red leather booths that lined the walls to a table almost in the center of the room.

The fat agent looked up at the maître d', then at Nick, then back to the maître d'. "Yeah?"

"Your guest has arrived, sir." The maître d' turned to Nick and said, "Enjoy your lunch, sir."

"Thank you."

Turner sat opposite Foster, who stared at him, a puzzled frown on his face.

"What's the matter, don't you recognize me?"

The agent's eyes widened and he dropped the half a roll he was holding. It fell into his lap, smearing his pants with butter. He grabbed a napkin off the table, dipped it in his glass of water, and swabbed at his pants.

"Nick? Is that you?"

"Who were you expecting?"

"What did you do to yourself?"

"I changed, for the better."

"God." The man sat forward and peered intently into Turner's face. "You know, I can see the Nick Turner I used to know in there, but it's eerie."

A waiter came over and asked Turner if he wanted a drink.

"A beer, imported, German."

"Yes, sir."

The waiter, a gray-haired man dressed like a cossack, left. Turner looked back at Foster, who was still studying him.

"I knew you changed. I saw it in your work and could hear it in your voice, but this—"

"You don't have to get used to it, just accept it. We won't be having other meetings like this."

"Nick—"

"After this, after these two books, we'll do everything through the mail. After these books make the best-seller list, I'll be calling the shots."

Foster sat back and touched his mouth nervously. He remembered a nervous man who was happy with what he could get for one of his books. This big man with the bad hairpiece and the weird eyes was something else entirely. He was scary, but he might also be the agent's ride to the big time.

The waiter brought Turner's beer. The agent picked up his own and held it out. "Okay, let's drink to calling the shots."

Chapter Thirty-one

When Victoria Dreyer arrived, Foster introduced Nick as "Ned Tailor." In Nick's mind there was no use in calling them anything other than "the Editor" and "the Agent." It was only in those guises that they had any effect on his life. Their names meant nothing to him, just as his real name meant nothing to them.

"Such a pleasure to meet you, Ned," Victoria said once she had a glass of white wine in front of her. "You're a very talented writer. We have high hopes for your books."

"That's nice to hear." He felt a faint urge to move his bowels, but it was manageable at the moment. He hadn't eaten, and he would just order a salad. He shifted slightly in his seat and continued to look at the editor, hoping that she would not notice his discomfort.

In the old days he would have gone to the men's room twice already.

Victoria looked at Nick and shivered again. A chill had gone through her when she first saw him. She felt it again now when he looked at her. She had never reacted this way to a man before. It was fairly obvious that Ned Tailor was wearing a hairpiece, but he was still an attractive man, a very big man, well-built and looking very uncomfortable in his suit and tie.

She was thirty-five years old, very attractive, and had risen rapidly in her profession. For the past seven years she had been single-minded in her pursuit of success in the publishing world, and during that time she had had very little opportunity to develop any personal relationships. However, she felt some unnamed thrill when this man looked at her with his penetrating eyes.

Then there was his apparent lack of interest in the entire author/editor lunch process.

She was used to lunching with authors and agents who would bend over backward to compliment her and gain favor. This man seemed bored, uninterested by the whole thing. It was the agent who carried the conversation, talking about his writer's book and plans for future books.

Toward the end of lunch, Victoria looked directly at the quiet man. "Ned, are you interested in being a best-selling author?"

"I'm interested in making money." She found his reply frank and refreshing.

"Does that mean you will do what it takes to make your books best-sellers?"

"No, it means I'll write the books, and you'll

pay me the money. What happens to it after that is up to you."

She sat back, staring at him with her eyes wide.

Foster misinterpreted her look and jumped into the fray. "What Ned means is that he's really more interested in the actual writing of the book than the marketing that goes into—"

"I know what Ned means," the editor said, cutting him off. She still stared at Nick.

"Is that a problem?"

"No. You're devoted to your writing. That's good. The sales and reviews on your first book will help, especially the paperback sales, which have been good."

"Good. Then what do we need to discuss?"

"Well . . . your ideas for what these two books will be, delivery dates . . . perhaps you and I could have dinner and talk further—"

"I want to sign the contracts now." Turner looked at his agent. "Did you bring them?" The big man looked at the editor.

He signed all three copies of the contracts and then passed them to the editor.

"When will I get the first check?" Turner asked.

She smiled. "As soon as I get back to the office, I'll put through the request for payment. It shouldn't take more than a couple of weeks . . . maybe three."

Turner needed the money; he could wait a

couple of weeks, but probably no longer than that. The urge to kill was coming more frequently. He was feeling it already.

"Then we're finished," said Nick.

"Don't you want coffee?" She pouted, disappointed.

"I don't drink coffee."

"A drink, then? To celebrate?"

She felt his eyes bore into her, but his face remained expressionless. She became aware of the fact that she was holding her breath.

"I'll have another Beck's," he finally said.

She smiled and said, "Wonderful."

Victoria left the restaurant first, leaving Turner and Foster there. At least she paid the bill, the agent thought.

"She likes you," the agent said.

"She does?" Nick's stomach was bloated with gas.

"I mean, she really likes you. Didn't you see the way she looked at you? That's one turned-on lady. Believe me, I've known her some time, and she doesn't turn on easy. She must go for the, uh, muscles."

"Keep after her for that check. I need that money badly."

"I understand." The agent nodded his head. "Bills."

Turner stood up and said, "Yes, bills."

Daniel Foster watched Turner walk toward

the door. Before going out, though, the big man stopped in the men's room. He couldn't believe Nick Turner's transformation. He knew that the man had reacted drastically to the death of his wife. Was this a product of that? He had never known a man to change his appearance so totally. And not only his appearance, but his personality and—more important—his writing. Turner had always been able to churn out readable material, but now the man was damn near writing literature. Of course, it was literature with a hard, brutal edge, but it rivaled the stuff that passed for best-sellers these days.

It didn't matter how or why the man had changed, only that he had—and the change was going to carry them into a much higher income bracket.

After he stopped in the men's room to release the painful gas that had built up in his system, Nick Turner walked purposefully back to the subway. He was in a hurry to get out of the city. He was feeling cramped

Something else was bothering him, too. The urge to kill had been different these past few months. He didn't like the way it felt. Oh, he liked the killing itself. It was the feelings and emotions that led up to them that he didn't like.

And then there were the journals. Reading them used to fuel his desire for justice. The people he was killing owed their lives to him because of what they had done. Over the past few months, though, he hadn't seemed to need the journals to do that. He was quite capable of killing without the help of the journals. He didn't like that. He was smart enough to know that something like that might get out of control. He was no common killer.

He had to get back home as quickly as possible. He wanted to read Gina's journals tonight. He wanted to get back on track.

The people around him on the street and on the train were ceasing to look like people. They were all starting to look just like victims.

Chapter Thirty-two

Two weeks later Turner called his agent from a pay phone.

"I don't have your check yet, Nick."

"Why not?"

"I don't know. I've been calling and leaving messages, but I haven't heard back from Victoria."

"Keep trying. I'll call you again at the end of the week. I need this money."

"I know you do, kid. Listen, I'll send her a letter by messenger saying that if we don't have the money next week, the deal is off."

"No!" Turner squeezed the phone so hard that he didn't know which would crack first, his bones or the plastic.

"Don't worry, Nick, it's just a ploy. And anyway, I can easily sell you to another publisher if I have to."

"That would take even longer."

"Look, I told you she had the hots for you, didn't I? Maybe it would be better if you called her yourself."

Turner thought about that for a moment. "I'll call you at the end of the week," he said finally. "We'll talk about it then."

"Okay, kid. Leave it to me, then. Have I ever let you down?"

Turner hung up.

Victoria Dreyer had never done anything like this. Oh, she had held up payments on contracts before, but never for this reason.

Since her lunch with Ned Tailor and his agent she had thought about the man quite a bit. She had never met anyone like him. He was brutal, of that she was sure. It showed in his writing, and his appearance had made it a certainty. His size, his obvious strength, his cold eyes. She shivered again every time she thought about the way he had looked at her.

"Victoria?"

Her assistant, Kevin Murphy, stood in the doorway. He was the latest in a long line of assistants, none of whom lasted six months, most of them young, male, and gay. Kevin had been promoted from within the company. He had been on the job a couple of months, but he was already finding out that the stories about her were true. She was extremely difficult to work for.

"Yes, Kevin?"

"Um, I've got another message from Ned Tailor's agent—" He came into the room and handed her the pink message slip. "It's the same as the others, urgent that you call him about the Tailor contract."

"Thank you, Kevin."

"Um, I was wondering if there was a particular reason why you were, uh, avoiding him?"

She set the message slip down on her desk and coldly looked up at her assistant. She didn't know it, but she looked at Kevin Murphy in almost the same way Ned Tailor had looked at her at lunch.

"I wasn't aware that I had to clear my actions with you, Kevin."

After he left the room she looked down at the slip of paper he'd just given her. She touched it with her right forefinger, moved it around some, wondering when she would be getting a call from the author himself.

That was what she was waiting for.

* * *

Daniel Foster handed the envelope to the messenger and said, "Make sure that gets right into her hand, all right?"

"You got it, Mr. Foster."

"Good."

He gave the boy a dollar and let him out the door, then went and sat behind his desk.

The Daniel Foster Agency was housed in a small two-room office in the West Village, near Washington Square Park. Foster had liked the location when he'd first taken it eleven years ago. He could see the arch from his window, and the park, which was always filled with activity. When the weather started to get nice like this, the walkers and joggers and skate boarders and skaters came out. Many of them were young women, and he often sat by the window to do his work so that he could watch them.

The sights and sounds of the Village had changed very little over the years, but it was all beginning to wear thin. He wanted to move uptown and saw Nick Turner—no matter what name he was writing under—as his means of doing just that. Now this bitch Victoria Dreyer was holding up progress.

Foster was not one of the top agents in the business, but he considered himself good. He was a shrewd negotiator, and he watched out

for his clients. At fifty, physically unimposing, he knew he did not fit the mold of a high-powered businessman, but he'd often thought that would change if he signed a high-powered client. He'd been looking for eleven years, ever since he quit his job as an editor. Now one of the authors on his client list was threatening to break out, and it was probably the last one he'd have expected it from.

Nick Turner had always been a nice, quiet man, competent at the type of work he did. Foster never held out much hope that Turner would break out with a major work, and when the man disappeared after his wife's death, he had given up on him. In fact, he'd even moved the man's file into his inactive drawer. When he'd gotten the manuscript in the mail—*Too Dead to Live*—he'd expected the same kind of low-level schlock or true crime or how-to the man had been producing for the past ten years. He'd been, in fact, one of Foster's first clients. When he read the book, however, he was shocked. It was good, damned good, so much so that he'd gotten excited about it. That hadn't happened in years.

Three publishers had made comparable offers, but he had decided to go with Victoria Dreyer at Pembroke Press because the company was a major player. While Victoria was difficult to work with, she was still the fair-haired editor in that company, rising by leaps and bounds over the past five years to her present position as associate publisher.

All he'd expected from Victoria was her normal level of professionalism, but that had gone down the tubes when she'd met Nick Turner.

Foster had seen it in her eyes. With his new look, Nick was, to say the least, interesting-looking. Foster thought he was scary, but that appealed to some women.

He was sure Victoria was holding the check up so that Nick would have to call her. Foster would give her two days to respond to the message he'd just sent, and then try to phone her again. After that, he was going to play hardball. He owed it to his client. He could sell Nick elsewhere, and it wouldn't hold things up all that much. In fact, maybe he would be able to give the kid an advance to tide him over.

Yeah, it was definitely time for Daniel Foster to start playing hardball.

Chapter Thirty-three

Turner called the agent again on Friday, and the man told him everything was under control.

"I've got a handle on it, kid," the man said confidently. "The matter will be resolved by the middle of next week."

Turner took him at his word. He needed that money by next week if he was going to continue his mission.

The names left on the list had been left until last for a reason. They had disappeared from the Brooklyn neighborhood where they had become involved with Gina, and it would take money to track them down.

The urge was upon him.

Victoria Dreyer grew impatient waiting for Ned Tailor to call. When Daniel Foster called on Monday, she reached for the phone.

"Victoria, honey, I've been having a helluva time getting through to you."

"I'm sorry, Daniel. It's just been really hectic."

"I know how it is, been up to my ears myself.

Listen, my man Ni—uh, Ned's been a little nervous lately. We haven't gotten that on-signing check, you know."

"I'm so sorry about that. There's been some sort of foul-up with our computers. It's holding our checks up. I'm sure it's been approved, it's just sitting somewhere. You know how it is."

"Yeah, I do, Victoria, but my writer needs to get paid. He signed the contract in good faith."

"It hasn't even been a month, Daniel."

"Well, you did promise three weeks, Victoria." And she was wrong; it had been closer to five weeks.

"I was overly optimistic." She sat forward in her seat and gripped the phone tightly in her left hand. With her right she played with her hair, winding a lock round and round her finger.

"Listen, Daniel, why don't you have Ned call me? Maybe I can buy him dinner, you know, to make up for the wait?"

"Ah, I doubt he'd call you, Vic. Besides, he lets me handle all his business. That's what agents are for."

"I just thought I could explain it to him—"

"Victoria, we need this check. I'm afraid the deal hangs in the balance."

Victoria felt her face flush. Who did this little shitheel think he was, William Morris?

"Listen to me, Daniel, don't threaten me—"

"I'm not threatening, Vic—"

"And don't call me Vic!" Her father had called her that, and she hated it.

"Sorry, uh, Victoria—"

She could feel Foster backing up from her anger. "I think you better have Ned call me, Daniel. I'm not sure I want to talk to you right now."

"Victoria, come on—"

"Tell him to call me or the deal's off!" She slammed the phone down and glared at it. The flush that had invaded her face began to fade and she smiled. If that didn't get Ned Tailor to call her, nothing would.

Two days later, Turner called his agent and asked about the check.

"She's jerking us around, kid. I told you she had the hots for you, right?"

"That's silly."

"Silly or not, she's a woman, you know? I don't think she's had a decent fuck since the eighties."

Turner couldn't believe what he was hearing. Why did women always control his life? First his mother . . . Christ, he hadn't thought about his mother in years! Then Gina with her journals. And then Stacy in Kansas, and now this with Victoria Dreyer.

He frowned. "The slut."

"You said it. You know, maybe I'm wrong. Maybe she has been fucked since the beginning of the decade. She uses her position against male writers."

"What did she say?"

On the other end of the line Foster was chilled by the angry tone of Turner's voice.

"She doesn't want to deal with me anymore. She said that if we still wanted this deal, you had to call her."

"What do you think?"

"Like I said, I can sell this somewhere else."

"No. We have a contract. She can't do this."

"She's doing it, kid."

Turner felt as if a leather band were constricting his chest. "She should die." The words were out of his mouth before he realized it.

"A little harsh, Nick. But then again, if she did, we'd get a new editor and the money would go through. That's too much to hope for, though. We're going to have to deal with her, Nick. Call her, see what she wants."

"We know what she wants, don't we?"

"Sure. Maybe you should give it to her. After all, she's not bad-looking. That's up to you, though."

"Give me her number."

The agent read off the number. Turner immediately hung up and called Victoria Dreyer.

The call took up all of twelve minutes. He agreed to go to her Manhattan apartment and discuss the "problem." He hung up, walked back to his apartment, and stared at his inactive computer for a few minutes. Soon he would be working again.

He went to the closet where he kept his gym bag, the one packed for his excursions. He took out the knife and stared at it, marveling that he was still using the same weapon after all this time. He ran his thumb along the blade. It was still sharp, with that little nick he liked to roll his thumb over. At one point, he'd considered throwing it away and using a commando knife, or something like that, but then he decided against it. This was the knife he had used for his first killing. He hoped to use it for his last.

Whenever that was to be . . .

Chapter Thirty-four

Victoria Dreyer primped for the mirror, stepped back, and took another look. A simple V-necked dress to show some subtle if not exciting cleavage. It was short, too, to reveal her legs and thighs. She had good legs, and wore heels that would also show them off. She turned to one side, then the other, sucking in her tummy and sticking out her chest. Too good for mortal man, she thought. She'd spent years trying to play down her sex appeal so that it wouldn't interfere with business, but she still knew how to play it up when the time came.

She picked up a bottle of perfume. After a lot of thought, she had finally decided on White Diamonds. If it was good enough for Elizabeth Taylor, it was good enough for her. It was a gentle, teasing scent that snuck up on a man. The bigger the man, the harder he fell. White Diamonds would probably bring Ned Tailor to his knees.

She shuddered. Just the thought of it gave her a rush.

She squirted the perfume in strategic areas, then put the bottle down and regarded herself once more.

"Bad girl," she pouted at her reflection. Then she smiled and went to see to the hors d'oeuvres.

Nick Turner hated Manhattan, especially taking the train to Grand Central, and then the shuttle and subway uptown. He'd considered renting a car, but then there would be someone who could identify him. This way he was just another body on the train. Carrying his gym bag, he just looked like another jock on his way to a workout.

Victoria Dreyer lived on the gentrified Upper West Side. She had an apartment in a building on West End Avenue between 74th and 75th streets. It was eight o'clock by the time he got there. She had wanted him to come earlier, but these days it got dark late. He wanted the dark—if not for when he arrived, surely for when he left.

At this time of the evening the only people on the street were neighborhood people out walking their dogs or on their after-dinner stroll. In front of Victoria Dreyer's apartment house, though, at the moment Nick mounted the steps, there was no one.

He entered the lobby, found her name on the bank of buttons. She was in 10B. There were four apartments on each floor. He pressed 10A and there was no reply. He pressed 10C and somebody asked who it was. He asked for someone and apologized when told there was no one there with that name. He pressed 10D and there was no answer.

He rang 10B then. She didn't bother with the intercom. She simply buzzed him through the door. Cocky bitch.

He got into the small elevator, pressed the button for the tenth floor, then stepped back and held the gym bag to his chest with both arms around it. He was wearing a stocking cap on his bald head, and a green khaki jacket with a brown collar. Underneath he wore a sweat-shirt; jeans and simple canvas shoes finished his outfit.

At the tenth floor, he looked around. The way the apartments were situated, 10C, where he had gotten the reply, was not right next to 10B. That was a good. He went to 10B and rang the bell. He wondered if the elevator could be heard from inside the apartment.

The door opened. Victoria Dreyer wore an expectant look. "Well, hello."

Turner didn't hear her. The smell of her perfume wafted toward him. White Diamonds, the same perfume Gina had worn.

"Ned?"

Her voice brought him back from the memory of his dead wife.

"Hello," he managed.

"Come in, please."

He entered, moving past her, the scent of the perfume growing more insistent. She closed the door and faced him. They stood in a hallway. She waved at him to precede her.

"May I take your coat?"

"Sure."

"And your . . . bag?" She gave the bag a puzzled look.

He put the bag down at his feet, removed his jacket and handed it to her, then picked up the bag again. She noticed that he was dressed rather too casually, but then decided it didn't matter. If she got what she wanted, neither of them would be dressed much longer.

God, she couldn't believe she had actually planned this. It was going to happen.

"I'll hold onto the bag."

She frowned again, then brightened.

"Did you bring me something, you naughty man? A surprise, maybe?"

He wondered if she realized how ridiculous she sounded. And she probably thought her ridiculous dress was seductive.

"Well, I can wait. I'm not one of those women who can't, you know. May I take your cap?"

He hesitated, then removed the cap, revealing his bald head. He wasn't sure how she'd react.

"I knew you were bald." Her tone was triumphant. She cocked her head to one side. "I like you better this way."

She went to a closet in the hallway, hung up his jacket, and then returned.

"I have some beer. Beck's. I remembered."

Beck's. It wasn't a favorite, just what had been available.

Victoria went to the kitchen. She was surprised at what a thrill she felt when he removed his hat. He shaved his head, and she found it sexy.

She used an opener to take the twist cap off the beer, then poured herself a glass of white wine. She carried both to the living room, where Nick Turner was still standing, still holding his gym bag.

She raised her glass. "To new friends . . . and relationships."

She sipped her wine; he didn't drink.

"Is there something wrong?"

"This is silly." He put the bottle of beer down on her coffee table.

"What is?"

"This dance we're doing. I know what you want, Victoria."

She smiled. "You do?"

He put the gym bag down at last, taking a step toward her, grabbing her wrist hard enough that the glass of wine in her other hand spilled.

"Ned—"

He took the glass of wine from her before she dropped it and put it on the table next to the beer.

"Ned, I don't—"

"Yes, you do. Tell me what you want."

"Ned—"

"Are you wearing a bra?"

Before she could answer, he thrust his other hand into her dress and cupped her right breast. She caught her breath, suddenly realizing she was aroused and wet.

He was right. This was what she wanted.

Then just as suddenly, he was gentle. He slid his hand inside her bra, touching her hard nipple.

"Tell me what you want."

"I . . . want you to . . . to make love to me."
She was breathing hard, speaking in gasps.

"No."

"Wha—" He tightened his hold on her breast and she gasped.

"Say it in plain English. Tell me what you want, bitch."

The marriage of pain and pleasure surprised her. Her eyes widened, her legs grew weak.

"I don't understand—"

"Yes, you do. Say it."

Then she understood. It excited her even more. "I want you to fuck me."

"That's it. Say it again!" He squeezed harder.

"I want you to fuck me," Victoria Dreyer said. "Fuck me, oh, fuck me!"

Chapter Thirty-five

The next half hour was a blur.

Turner tore her clothes off and carried her to the bedroom. She tore at his shirt, pulling it from him. By the time they reached her bed, she had her mouth on his neck and his shoulders. He roughly threw her onto the bed. She watched as he got out of his pants and underwear, and then he was on her.

"Wait—"

But Turner didn't, not in the mood for foreplay. He thrust. She was so wet that he slid right in. She gasped as his thickness filled her. She wrapped her legs around his waist and held on tightly.

He slid his hands over her, squeezing and pinching her small breasts, then slid them beneath her, cupping her firm buttocks. With each thrust, he pulled her to him. She cried out each time. No man had ever filled her so utterly, or manhandled her so easily. She was small and light in his hands. She heard him growling in her ear and that turned her on even more. She started to rake her nails across his back and he reared back.

"No!" he shouted, and for a moment she thought he was going to strike her.

"What—" She stared up at him wide-eyed and frightened, but still very aroused.

"Don't mark me."

His voice was cold, his face calm despite the beads of sweat. He showed her his forefinger, sticking it right in her face.

"Don't ever mark me."

"A-all right, Ned." Her voice was meek.

He kept his finger there and she opened her

mouth and sucked it. It turned him on. He remained there for a moment and she was able to examine his upper torso. He sweated so profusely that he gleamed, like a Greek god. He was still inside her, still rock hard.

"Come on."

She ran her hands down his back until she was rubbing her palms over his buttocks. As smooth and hard as marble.

"Come on, Ned. Fuck me. Fuck me good."

He stared down at her. She still smelled like Gina, but now she sounded like that whore, Stacy.

He drew away.

"Oh, no . . ." she moaned as he left her. She saw his penis then, rigid, engorged with blood, big and beautiful. "Come back . . ." She writhed on the bed, still feeling pleasure even though he'd left her. She ran her hands over herself.

"I have something for you," he said. He left the room, but only for a moment. He returned with his gym bag.

"Show me," she said, anxious, playful, a finger perched on the edge of her bottom lip. "Show me my present, Ned. Show me!"

He would show her. When he was ready.

He growled and descended on her again. He dropped the gym bag next to the bed, grabbed her by the hips and literally flipped her over on to her belly.

"Ned, wha—"

She had a fine ass. "I want to fuck you from behind!" He lifted her up onto her knees, positioned himself between her legs and then slid his penis up between her thighs and into her, hard.

"Oh, God . . ." she cried out. He slammed into her, holding her hips tightly. Sweat dripped from his chin onto the small of her back as he leaned over, mixing with her own.

"Lying bitch . . ."

She wasn't hearing what he was saying, just responding to the sound of his voice. "Yes, yes . . ."

"Cheating bitch . . ."

"Yes . . ."

He withdrew from her, wet and shiny and throbbing. He parted the cheeks of her ass then and probed her anus with the head of his cock.

"Ned, no—I never—"

She lifted her head up, trying to look at him over her shoulder.

"Shut up!" He pushed her head down. "You're a bitch and a slut. We'll do this my way or not at all!"

After a moment he released her head, but it remained where it was. "Yes, all right . . ." She surrendered herself.

With a quick thrust, he was inside her. She cried out, again surprised at how she could feel pleasure and pain at once. She had never had a man inside her in this way before. Her body was alive with new sensations.

"Oooh, God, yes," she said, "please, Ned, don't . . . stop . . ."

He grabbed a handful of her hair and pulled, bringing her head up painfully. With his other hand he reached down and slid something from his gym bag. Her "present."

"What about my check, Victoria?"

"Wha—" She wasn't sure she had heard him right. "What did you—"

"My check, you bitch! For my contract."

"Ned—you're hurting me—"

He thrust his hips forward. The pain was mixed with pleasure again.

"Oh, God, Ned, please . . . I want you to—"

"What about my check, bitch?"

"It's coming, Ned, it's coming . . ." She laughed suddenly, an ironic laugh and said, "It was mailed today."

"You mean this trip wasn't necessary?"

"Oh, God . . . it would have been mailed anyway . . . I couldn't delay any longer . . ."

"But you're getting what you wanted from me, aren't you?"

"Y-yes—b-but my neck is starting to—"

"I'll take care of your neck, Victoria," Nick Turner said. He started moving in her again, in and out as hard and as fast as he could. The sheets were soaked with their sweat. The room was filled with their scent, their heat. She felt as if he was tearing her up and he was still holding her head up painfully.

"N-Ned—"

He couldn't hear her. He hadn't been with a woman in a long time. He could feel his orgasm building, boiling up from his ankles, through his thighs, and then suddenly he was erupting inside her, coming like he'd never stop.

He brought up the hand with the knife, pulled one last time on her hair, drawing her neck muscles taut. When he brought the knife across her throat, the blood shot out over the wall and the headboard, then kept spurting. The pillow and sheet beneath her turned red with it. Her head came back further then, and the wound in her neck yawned. He had a vision of himself standing beside the bed, triumphantly holding her severed head in his hand by the hair, like a Viking with the head of a vanquished enemy. He released his hold on her hair before he almost did tear her head completely from her shoulders.

He pulled free of her and a last few gouts of semen splashed onto her back. He turned her over. Her eyes were open wide. In death she stared at him. As he brought the knife down on her again and again, he knew that in death she was Gina, Stacy, his mother. She was dying because she deserved it, so that he could write again.

His check was in the mail.

Chapter Thirty-six

May 1994

In the next day's newspaper, Daniel Foster read about the murder of an unidentified Manhattan woman in her apartment. The story said she had worked as an editor. They were not releasing her name until her family could be notified.

He lowered the paper, shaking his head. "It couldn't be."

He called Victoria Dreyer at work, but her assistant said she hadn't come in. "She called in sick."

"Will she be in tomorrow?"

"I don't have any way of knowing that."

Foster hung up. Well, at least Victoria couldn't be the woman who was murdered. A dead person didn't call in sick. What was he thinking, anyway—that Nick Turner went to see her and killed her?

He waited that whole day for Turner to call. It didn't happen. The eleven o'clock news said the victim's name was still being withheld.

However, an informed source had told them that she worked for Pembroke Press.

"Jesus . . ." Foster shakily covered his mouth with his hands. He didn't sleep well that night at all.

He had fallen asleep late and consequently woke up late. He didn't get into his office until nearly eleven. He bought a newspaper on the way, but waited until he got to his office to read it. As he entered his office, he saw the mail on his floor and spotted the Pembroke logo. It was the signing money for Nick Turner's contract.

At last! Victoria had come through after all. That meant she had to be alive, right?

He sat at his desk with the check and opened the newspaper. The story was on page 1, continued on page 3. The first line on page 3 identified the dead woman as thirty-five-year-old Victoria Dreyer.

Foster dropped the newspaper.

He stared at the phone, willing it to ring. And it did, startling him so badly he cried out, then felt foolish. "Hello!"

"Did we get the check?" Nick Turner's voice.

"Nick, Jesus, have you seen the paper?"

"Did the check come?"

"Yes, damn it, the check came. It's here. Christ, Victoria's dead. What happened?"

There was a long pause during which Foster could hear Turner breathing.

"What do you mean, what happened? Why are you asking me that?"

"You were supposed to call her, see her. What happened with you and Victoria?"

"I called her Monday morning, like you told me to."

It was now Wednesday.

"She told me that the check was going in the mail that morning. Did it come?"

"You didn't see her?"

"I didn't have to. She said the check was being mailed Monday morning."

Foster frowned. Had Victoria changed her tune over the weekend? She'd been giving him the runaround for weeks. Turner calls once and she puts the check in the mail?

"Nick, what did you say to her?"

"I told her I needed the money."

"So you didn't see her?"

"I told you I didn't see her. What's wrong with you today?"

"I'm just shook up. Jesus, I knew the woman, and now she's dead."

"At least we weren't in the middle of an edit."

"Thank God for small favors." Foster immediately felt like a shit for saying that.

"Send me the check."

"Same P.O. box?"

"That's right."

"The other checks I sent were made out to Cash, but they weren't for anywhere near this

245

amount. If this gets lost in the mail, you're fucked."

He listened to Turner's breathing.

"Good point. Make it out to Ned Tailor."

"That ain't your real name—"

"I can open a bank account in any name I want. Just do it."

"What about the new book?"

"I've started it. I'm really on a roll these days."

"What's it called?"

"Don't worry about it."

"Gee, thanks, kid, that's real—" But he was talking to a dead line. "Jesus." He stared at the phone, then hung up.

He looked at the check. One hundred and twenty-five thousand dollars. He'd deposit it in his account and then write a check to Nick for a hundred and twelve thousand, five hundred.

This was just the beginning. Victoria Dreyer's murder was unfortunate, but it had nothing to do with Foster and his author. They'd get a new editor and go on with business as usual. A few more checks like this and he wouldn't even think about Victoria Dreyer anymore.

He wished he could stop thinking about her now.

Nick Turner hung up the phone and faced his computer.

Before leaving Victoria Dreyer's apartment he had to take a shower to wash her blood off him, off his knife. He then put the knife back in the gym bag, removed a fresh shirt from the bag, and got dressed. He had been in her apartment just an hour and a half.

With the slow night schedule of the trains, it took hours to get home. Still, it was the most satisfying ride he had taken in quite some time. He felt calmed, his mind racing with ideas for his new book.

When he returned to his apartment, he changed into fresh clothes, sat down at the computer, and immediately started to write. Since then—over a period of thirty hours—he had stopped only to eat a couple of snacks, go to the bathroom, and shower one more time.

Now he refocussed on the screen. He had a working title already: "The Check Is in the Mail."

It seemed fitting.

Part V

Composite

Chapter Thirty-seven

May 1994

By May first, Dennis McQueen had the first
reports from the task-force detectives. They had
gone over all the old ground and had unearthed
as much new material as they could. It was now
up to him to try and construct a composite picture of a killer.

Three copies of the reports were prepared.
One for the detectives' own files, one for Mc-
Queen, and one for Captain Keepsake.

In the task-force office McQueen and Keepsake
sat at their desks with piles of reports in front of
them.

"I'm going to take them home and read them,
Dennis, but as I've told you before, I'm not a
detective."

"Looking at it from your point of view, you might see something that I didn't. We'll only know after we compare notes."

Keepsake loaded the files into a black leather attaché case, a gift from his wife last Christmas. "And when do we do that?"

McQueen grinned wryly.

"When we have notes to compare."

Keepsake nodded. "See you in the morning, Dennis."

"Right, sir."

"Oh, wait," Keepsake said, "I almost forgot. I got this for you."

He took a sheaf of papers out of his briefcase and handed them across to McQueen.

"What's this?"

"It's a report on the psychology behind the serial sex killer. I think you'll find it interesting. It was prepared by a friend of mine who teaches at John Jay." John Jay was a prestigious university that specialized in criminal justice and criminal law. "Take a look through it, Dennis. You might find it interesting."

McQueen looked down at the papers. He had read other such reports, all having a basic premise that he rejected: All serial killers started out as abused children.

Keepsake left and McQueen unfolded the *New York Post* lying on his desk. On the front page was a story about a Manhattan woman who had been raped and murdered in her apartment Monday night. It had happened too late for the Tuesday editions to have all the facts, but here in the Wednesday paper it was all there.

Victoria Dreyer's throat had been savagely cut, she had been stabbed, slashed, and mutilated. Two of her neighbors had been out until late, and another had not heard any noise. The phone rang while he was reading the account.

"Detect—I mean, Sergeant McQueen." Rank took some getting used to.

"Sergeant, this is Kyle Weatherby of the *New York Post*."

McQueen knew the name. Weatherby had a column in the paper, a slot that had opened up for him when Mike McAlary left the *Post* for the *Daily News*.

"What can I do for you, Mr. Weatherby?"

"I was wondering if you would confirm a rumor. I've heard that a task force has been set up to investigate a series of sexual-mutilation murders. Is that true?"

"I can't confirm or deny that, Mr. Weatherby."

"Can't or won't, Sergeant?"

"Take your pick. Would you mind telling me where you got this information?"

"From an informed source."

"You heard this from a cop?"

"I'm afraid I can't confirm or deny that,

Sergeant," the reporter said, hanging up before McQueen could.

"Damn it!" McQueen slammed down the phone. Somebody had opened his mouth. McQueen wasn't going to waste time trying to find out who it was. He did, however, plan to talk to all of the task-force detectives in the morning and advise them as to what would happen if any other information made it into the hands of a newspaper reporter.

He turned his attention back to the *Post*. He located Kyle Weatherby's column. It dealt with the murder of Victoria Dreyer.

He decided to go somewhere else and read the article, the files, and the report he'd gotten from Keepsake. He'd read it over dinner.

Chapter Thirty-eight

McQueen picked up some takeout on his way home from work. Once in his apartment, he took a shower, made a pot of coffee, and went back to his reading.

He looked down at his yellow pad. He had written a name at the top of each of six pages: James Hart, Thomas Bennett, Bonnie Green,

Paul Medco, Ruth Nash, Brian Jordan.

These were the last six victims of their killer that they knew about, the six cases on which they were concentrating their efforts. Thomas Bennett had been killed first. He opened Detective Jason Van Shelton's report. Bennett was found at the bottom of a set of subway stairs at a closed entrance. His murder had obviously taken place right there.

September 1992

Turner had been following Thomas Bennett for a week. The man lived in Middle Village, Queens. He had moved while Turner was in Kansas. Luckily, he still worked at the same place in Manhattan.

Bennett was a door-to-door salesman and, according to Gina's journals:

> When he came to the door to sell me pots and pans, I had no idea we'd be fucking on the living-room floor fifteen minutes later. I didn't buy anything—he didn't mind. He left me his business card, told me he lived in the area, in case I wanted another free sample.

Turner remembered the entry with remarkable clarity. She had even written down the name of the man's company.

Bennett was married, but his wife must not have been a very good cook. Every evening when he emerged from the subway in Queens, he stopped at a burger place before going home.

Bennett had worked late; Turner, having decided that this would be the night, was willing to wait. He stood patiently outside Bennett's Manhattan office building. When the man came out, it was after nine P.M. By the time they came up from the subway in Queens, it was ten-fifteen. Turner feared Bennett might not stop for his burger, then heaved a sigh of relief when the man crossed Queens Boulevard.

It was a mild night. Turner remained outside until Bennett had ordered. He then entered, stopping at the counter and ordering a coffee from the bored-looking clerk. She spoke with another clerk, saying she was glad they were closing in forty-five minutes.

Turner walked to the table where Bennett sat. He put his gym bag down on the floor and sat across from him. Bennett looked around. He and Turner were the only people in the place. He stared in surprise.

"I'm sitting here."

Turner took the plastic cover off his coffee cup while the man continued to stare.

"There are other tables, pal," Bennett said. "Why don't you sit at one of them?"

"I like this one, Tommy."

"How do you know my name?" Bennett frowned, then started to pick up his burger, fries, and soda. If Turner wouldn't move, he would.

"Sit still."

"What did you say?"

"I said stay where you are. You're not moving."

Bennett was in his mid-thirties, and looked to be in good shape. If he stood up to Turner, there might be an attention-getting scene. Turner headed it off. He reached across the table, took hold of Bennett's wrist and squeezed. Bennett's eyes widened in pain.

"H-hey—"

"Just sit quietly," Turner said. "If you try to move, I'll hurt you. Understand?"

Bennett nodded jerkily as sweat popped out on his brow from the pain. Turner released his wrist, and Bennett immediately cradled it, flexing his hand to see if anything was broken.

"It's not broken," said Turner. "Go on, finish your burger. We'll be here another forty minutes."

"What do you want from me?"

"I want you to eat your burger, drink your soda, and shut up."

"Mister, look, if you want money—"

"I don't want your money."

Bennett studied Turner, trying to figure him out.

257

"Are you gay, is that it? If you don't hurt me, we can go into the men's—"

"I don't want a blow job, and if I did, I sure wouldn't want it from you. Look, Tommy, do yourself a favor and eat. Don't make me hurt you."

For the next forty minutes Bennett nursed his burger and fries. Turner finished his coffee and then started on the other man's drink. The second clerk came out with a mop and washed the floor. He gave Turner and Bennett an odd look now and again. When Turner caught him looking, he glared, and the boy went back behind the counter.

"Hey! We're closing," the girl behind the register yelled to them.

"Time to go outside," said Turner. He stood up with his gym bag in one hand, then grabbed Bennett under the arm with the other, jamming his thumb into the man's armpit. Bennett had little choice but to stand. "We're going for a walk . . ."

They left and crossed Queen's Boulevard. Halfway across there was an island with a subway entrance, closed off with bars at the bottom of the stairs. Anyone coming or going would have to use the stairway across the street.

Turner said, "Go downstairs."

Bennett looked down and said, "I got to get home. Why are you doing this?"

"Go down the stairs, and I'll tell you." Turner opened the gym bag and pulled the knife halfway out, just to show it. "Downstairs."

Bennett went down the steps, stopping before the bottom.

"All the way."

He went down the rest of the way.

Now Turner could watch the burger place across the street, and keep an eye on Bennett without fear that the man might run.

By eleven-thirty the workers had left. It was dark, the street around them practically deserted.

"Can I come up now?"

"No."

"Y-you said you'd tell me why you're doing this."

"And I will." Turner took one last look around to make sure no one was nearby, then started down the stairs. "You sell door-to-door, right?"

"T-that's right."

"Must catch some young housewives home during the day, maybe bored, watching the shopping channel while hubby's at work?"

"What are you—"

"Some of them pretty?"

"Sure."

Turner reached the bottom of the stairs now, and Bennett cowered against the gate.

"You can tell me. You fucked some of them, didn't you?"

The man's eyes flicked about nervously, and then he decided that if he told this crazy bastard what he wanted to hear, maybe he'd let him go.

"Okay, yeah, yeah, I fucked one or two. You know, when they asked for it?"

"Remember Gina Turner?"

"W-what? Hey, man, I don't remember names. I see a lot of people, you know?"

"A pity." Turner put his hand in the gym bag and wrapped it around the handle of the knife. He let the bag fall to the ground, freeing the knife.

"Oh, hey, man, no—"

"I would have preferred you remembered."

Bennett bolted then, trying to get past Turner, but Turner turned the knife up and drove it into the man's belly. Before Bennett could scream, the big man slapped his other hand over his mouth.

"Should have kept your dick in your pants, pal," Turner whispered into the dying man's ear. "Now I'm going to take it out for good."

He lowered Bennett to the ground and went to work. Later Turner came up from the subway steps and looked around. He replaced the knife in his gym bag, and donned the trench coat he had brought to cover the blood on his clothes. Thomas Bennett's penis was put in a Ziploc bag and deposited in his tote.

Chapter Thirty-nine

The report mentioned a hamburger chain across from the subway station. Its staff had been interviewed. They stated that someone who looked like Thomas Bennett might have been in the place that night. Customers didn't usually stand out, they said, not like the guy they had one night who ordered a coffee and stayed until closing.

"That dude was weird, man," said an employee. "This big sucker had him a wicked black mustache, carried a gym bag. Had a way of lookin' right through ya, ya know?"

But there wasn't anything outstanding like that about Thomas Bennett. He was an ordinary-looking guy who people saw and forgot in the blink of an eye.

McQueen took a break to get another cup of coffee, then carried it back to the desk and turned to a clean yellow page. He opened Detective Neil Chapman's report of his investigation into the murder of James Hart and began to read and make notes.

* * *

December 1992

James Hart was not the first man Nick Turner had killed whom he'd known. Hart didn't live in Brooklyn. He lived and worked in Manhattan. Gina had met him when she had a part-time job in his office. Turner met him at a company outing, and again at a Christmas party. The outing was at Coney Island. Turner remembered losing track of Gina for about an hour, and found out later from her journals what she had been doing:

I knew James Hart liked me, Journal, because he had asked me to lunch from time to time. He's single and handsome, but I resisted until the outing at Coney Island.

I got separated from Nick after the roller coaster and was about to look for him when Jim grabbed my arm. He wanted me to go on the Ferris wheel with him. There was something in the way he looked at me, the way he asked—I just couldn't say no. When the ride started, he touched my breast. He took my hand and put it on his crotch. I pulled down his zipper. He kissed me. Oh yes, Journal, we did it on the Ferris wheel.

That was one ride James Hart was going to pay for, Turner thought. He sat in a West

Village bar Hart frequented, wearing a waist-length blond wig. For good measure, Turner had donned a phony beard and mustache. His gym bag was at his feet.

The White House Inn was on Varick Street. Hart lived on Horatio Street, near Eighth Avenue. The man was good with women, and he often left the bar with one. His routine didn't vary. After work he went home, changed, then went to the bars, usually ending up here. Turner decided that the first night Hart left the place alone, he'd keep him company.

It was child's play to come up behind the man as he was unlocking the lobby door to his building.

"What the hell—"

"Open it up, Jimmy boy."

"Who are you?"

"I'm somebody who wants to make sure you're not lonely tonight."

Hart closed his eyes, then opened them in disgust. "Are you a faggot?"

"No, Jimmy. But if I was, you wouldn't be my type." Jesus, Turner thought, what a town. Everybody thought he was gay.

"Look, pal, I work out—"

"I know, three times a week at the Y. You're in good shape, Jimmy, but don't try me. You'll get hurt. Let's go upstairs. I want to talk."

"Why should I—"

Turner had anticipated this problem. He had

a heavy pipe in his bag, and he took it out now and pressed it to Hart's back. It was just the right size at one end to be mistaken for a gun, and wide enough at the other to fit Turner's hand comfortably. He'd used the pipe before.

"Jesus, is that a gun?" Hart was frightened now. "Take it easy, man."

"Upstairs."

Hart unlocked the door, went into the hall, and stopped.

"Come on, Jimmy. You're in 2D. Let's go up."

"How do you know where I live?"

"I know a lot about you, Jimmy. I know you like to ride the Ferris wheel at Coney Island. Let's go."

They went up the flight and into Hart's apartment. Turner dropped the pipe back into his gym bag.

"Sit down at the kitchen table, Jimmy, hands on top where I can see them."

Hart obeyed. He stared at Turner.

"You don't remember me, do you?" Turner got a kick out of this.

"Should I?"

"We've met, Jimmy. In fact, you knew my wife real well. You worked with her."

"I did? I'm sorry, but I don't place—"

"Gina Turner, that ring a bell?"

Hart frowned. "Gina Turner?" He shook his head.

Just like Thomas Bennett. Poor Gina put out for these guys, and they didn't even remember her.

"You should remember the women you fuck, Jimmy, even once."

"Hell, man," Hart shook his head helplessly. "I fuck 'em all once."

"Bragging, Jimmy?"

"Look, what do you want from me? I don't remember no Gina Turner, and I sure as hell don't remember you."

"Too bad. I would prefer that you remember, but if it has to be this way . . ." He reached for the bag.

Hart shouted "Fuck you!" and came out of his chair.

Turner acted instinctively. His hand closed over the handle of his bag and he swung it. The bag with the heavy pipe struck Hart over the eye with a thud. He staggered back, bleeding.

Turner pulled out his knife. He followed the staggering man back and brought the knife up and down. He missed his belly, got him in the sternum. That was just as good.

It got the job done. Or started, anyway.

McQueen read the M.E.'s report on Hart. In addition to the stab wound in the sternum and the mutilation, the deceased had a head wound. It was difficult to determine what he had been

265

struck with, but it had left an impression, an indentation, in its wake.

McQueen went through the entire file and couldn't find anything that described exactly what the impression had been. He'd look into it in the morning.

The Brian Jordan report he'd gotten from Rita Woodrell was next. If he didn't get some shut-eye, his brains would be shit tomorrow. And someone else might be dead; he had to keep reading.

Woodrell's report was excellent, though nothing stood out in it—like the head wound on James Hart, or the location of the Bennett murder. Maybe tomorrow she could tell him something that would change that.

He took another hour to make notes before he had had enough. Somewhere along the way he had decided to turn all of this shit over to Bobby Callan to enter into the computer. If there were common denominators to be found, that was the way to find them.

He stacked the files. As he started to get up from his desk, his eyes fell on the serial-killer profile Captain Keepsake had given him.

"Shit." He was going to have to read that before he went to bed.

He stood up and stretched, prepared another pot of coffee. He would read Keepsake's report, if for no other reason than to argue against its contents in the morning.

Chapter Forty

The report had been written by a Dr. Floyd Thomas, who had a Ph.D. in psychology. McQueen wondered how much experience he had in dealing with these killers before they were caught, like cops did, and not after. He knew he would dream about the words and phrases used to describe these "poor, miserable, unfortunate creatures." How many of these killers' bloody victims had this doctor seen up close?

A passage explained the difference between serial killers and mass murderers. The serial killer claimed his victims over a period of time, while the mass murderer killed his all at once—like the seven nurses killed by Richard Speck, or the twenty-five people slaughtered at a McDonald's by James Huberty.

Some of the most famous serial killers were David Berkowitz—Son of Sam—and Richard Ramirez—the Nightstalker—or more recently, Ted Bundy and Jeffrey Dahmer.

As far as McQueen was concerned, they

should all have simply been lumped under the heading "Killer."

The report claimed that the serial killer was a unique criminal who can seem normal when he's not actually killing. He drags his killing spree out over a period of months or years, stalks his victims before he actually kills them. The serial killer, the report went on, is addicted to killing, and between crimes he simply blends back into the normal fabric of society. The most frightening statistic was that the FBI estimated that at any given time there were five hundred of these animals at large and unidentified in the United States. Also, the United States, which accounted for only 5 percent of the world's population, also accounted for seventy-five percent of the world's serial murderers.

According to the report, a serial killer operated according to a ritual, which criminologists had broken down into seven phases: the Euphoria phase, the Trolling phase, the Wooing phase, Capture, the Murder, the Totem phase, and the Depression phase.

The serial killer became euphoric when he was planning his murder, before "trolling" for his victim. When he found the victim, he would "woo", or lure them, then capture them and kill them. The Totem phase was the sickest, the one McQueen found the most interesting. The high a serial killer got from his crime faded very quickly, so the killer often took a part of the victim with him, as if trying to keep that feeling alive. This fit with what they knew about their killer, who had been carrying away the genitals of his victims. Finally, the killer fell into a state of depression, and then the cycle started all over again.

As far as McQueen knew, his killer fit at least the sixth phase. How many of the others did he fit?

Further into the report McQueen found something that he just flat out couldn't accept, which was that being a serial killer is a "disease." There were also discussions of "episodic explosions of violence," and something called "episodic aggressive behavior."

"Sorry, Doc." He wouldn't be reading this much longer, he thought, if the doctor was going to continue in this vein. McQueen had a huge problem in dealing with killers as victims.

The doctor had prepared a list of over twenty behavior patterns that a person suffering from this "disease" might exhibit. That meant that all he and his task force had to do was find a suspect who displayed "ritualistic behavior, masks of insanity, suicidal tendencies, head injuries," and on and on.

Hell, they didn't even have a suspect to watch, even if he did believe in this stuff.

Before giving up he tried to find something on the sexual aspect of the crime.

The doctor began to lose him again when he

called crimes "sex crimes" even when the victim had not been sexually assaulted. He seemed to feel that if the killer was driven to kill by a sexual incident in his past—such as being sexually abused as a six-year-old—it meant that his crimes were sex crimes.

According to the reports McQueen had read about his killer, some of the victims were sexually assaulted, some were not.

Most criminals were caught when they slipped up, made a mistake. That was why he had the task force going back over old crimes. Maybe they'd be able to find a critical mistake the killer had made. Son of Sam had been caught because he got a parking ticket near where he'd committed his last murder.

In the long run, McQueen didn't care what kind of killer he was after, or what had happened in his past to turn him into a killer. It was his job to catch the maniac and put him away.

Chapter Forty-one

For someone who had stayed up very late reading reports, McQueen felt remarkably good the next morning—until he went across to the 7-Eleven to buy a copy of the *New York Post* and a cup of coffee before going to work.

The paper's headline read: "Task Force Formed to Investigate Sex/Mutilation Murders."

"Terrible, isn't it?" the clerk asked.

McQueen closed the paper and stared at the man.

"You don't know the half of it."

Two phone lines had been strung into the room for the task force. When McQueen arrived, both were ringing. He ignored them.

He set his stacks of files and notes down on his desk, then sat and spread the newspaper out again. The *Post* had a reliable source who stated the New York City Police Department had formed a task force to investigate a rash of sex/mutilation murders that stretched back two years, possibly farther. The story was written by

271

Kyle Weatherby. Weatherby said that official police sources had denied comment.

McQueen wondered what other sources, if any, the man had tried beside himself. Both phones started ringing again. McQueen picked one up.

"McQueen."

"Who's this?"

"Sergeant Dennis McQueen."

"Are you with the task force? This is Andy Wilson from the *Daily News*, Sergeant. I was calling to find out about—"

"Call the Public Information Department." He hung up. As he did, the phone on Keepsake's desk started to ring. McQueen had a button on his phone for the other one, so he pressed it and answered.

"Sergeant McQueen."

"What the hell is going on over there, McQueen?"

It was Inspector Pyatt from the chief of detectives' office.

"How do you mean, sir?"

"Don't be obtuse, Sergeant. Somebody leaked the story about the task force to the press."

"I saw the paper, sir."

"Who talked?"

"I don't know, sir."

"Damn it, do you realize this could jeopardize the task force?"

"Yes, sir."

"Stop being so blasted subservient, Sergeant!"

"I'm just being respectful, sir."

"Hold on. The chief wants to talk to you."

"Yes, sir."

The line went dead, and when it came back on Chief Robert Sands was booming in his ear.

"What the fuck is going on there, McQueen? Where's Keepsake?"

"He's away from his desk, sir."

"Obviously. Is he hiding in the fucking men's room?"

"No, sir, he's—"

"The commissioner called me at home!" Sands was shouting now. "Do you know why?"

"Uh, yes, sir—"

"Because the goddamned mayor called him at home wanting to know why there's a serial killer loose in his city and he doesn't know about it!"

"Yes, sir, I can see how the mayor would be upset."

The line went quiet then. McQueen thought he could hear Sands sucking on one of his cigars. When the man came back on the line, his tone was softer.

"Sergeant, what do you think I should tell the commissioner to tell the mayor about this?"

"Sir, that's not for me to say—"

"Oh, but it is, Sergeant, because I'm fucking telling you it is."

"Uh, right, sir. If I were you, I'd tell the commissioner that the task force was formed to determine whether or not a serial killer is active in the city. I'd tell him that as soon as I—that is, you, sir—receive a report indicating that this is indeed the case, you would notify the commissioner immediately. He, in turn, would then notify the mayor."

"When can I expect this report, Sergeant?"

"Well, sir, I'll have to check with Captain Keepsake, but I'd imagine you could have it sometime late this afternoon."

There was a moment of silence followed by Sand's voice saying, "I'll hold you to that, McQueen. After all, it was on your word that I authorized the task force, wasn't it?"

"Well, yes, sir, but the captain—"

"You and I both know that Keepsake is an administrator, Dennis." McQueen was surprised by the chief's use of his first name. "You're running the investigation, are you not?"

"Well, sir—"

"That's right, you are. I want three things from you, Dennis. I want that report on my desk by noon. Two, I want you to catch this sonofabitch before he costs all of us our jobs. Can you do that for me, Dennis?"

McQueen hesitated, then thought, Oh, why the hell not?

"Consider him as good as caught, sir."

"Three, I want the skell who talked to the newspapers. Report to me directly, Sergeant. I'll be waiting for the good news."

"Yes, sir."

He waited for Sands to say something else, but the chief had hung up. McQueen imagined he could smell the cigar smoke, like a malevolent cloud, hanging in the air above the chief's head.

Catch the sonofabitch.

Yes, sir, I'll get right on it.

Chapter Forty-two

"Dennis, your handwriting is for shit."

McQueen looked up from his desk at Bobby Callan.

"What is it?"

Callan leaned over and placed McQueen's notes on the desk.

"What's this say . . ."

It was almost twelve-thirty in the afternoon, just half an hour after a report signed by Captain William Keepsake went by special messenger to the chief of detectives' office. It stated that it was the belief of the task force that a serial killer was at large in the city of New York, and had been for two years or more. The report further stated that there was a possibility that the same killer had struck in other states, as well. The task force was awaiting confirmation of this fact.

Bobby Callan had been entering McQueen's notes into the computer, pausing every so often to have them deciphered.

The task-force detectives had wandered in during the course of the day, wondering what was going on. They had all seen the story in the *Post*. Each detective had been instructed by McQueen to not leave the building.

"The captain wants to talk to all of you at one time."

When Velez was informed of this fact, he asked McQueen, "Is this about the newspaper, Dennis?"

"Oh, it sure is."

"You think it was one of us?"

"I don't know what to think, Ray. It could have been a morgue attendant. You never know."

Ray hesitated, then said, "Uh, Dennis . . ."

McQueen looked up at his partner. "Relax, Ray, I know it wasn't you."

"Well, uh, that's just it . . ."

"What are you telling me, Ray?"

Velez winced and lowered his voice "Can we talk out in the hall?"

"Jesus, Ray—" McQueen followed his partner outside.

"You talked to the newspapers, Ray?"

"No, not to the newspapers."

McQueen waited. When nothing else was forthcoming, he got annoyed.

"Ray, Jesus, don't make me drag it out of you. If you got something to say, say it."

"Well . . . I told Cookie what's been going on. You know Cookie's brother is a photographer, right?"

"Yeah. So?"

"He's sort of been trying to catch on with one of the newspapers."

"Aw, Ray . . ."

"Cookie told him what I told her."

"Aw, Ray . . ."

"I think maybe her brother, Carlos, leaked the story to the *Post*."

"Aw, shit, Ray!"

"I'm sorry, Dennis."

McQueen looked around to see if anyone could hear them.

"Keep quiet about this, Ray."

"Dennis, how much trouble could I be in?"

McQueen studied his partner for a moment. "Ray, you don't know for sure that Carlos is the one. Don't get yourself jammed up, okay? Just leave it with me for a while."

"Okay, Dennis. Thanks."

"*De nada*, partner. Now get back in there."

"Sure, Dennis."

McQueen went back to his desk, sat down, and almost covered his face with his hands but caught Keepsake looking over at him. He took a deep breath and looked down at the files piled infront of him. Business as usual—the last thing he wanted to do was give Ray Velez up.

Chapter Forty-three

"The what?" Sam Lacy asked.

"The Totem," McQueen repeated.

"Why the hell are we gonna call him that?" Lacy asked.

"We got to call him something," Neil Chapman said. "Why not that?"

Lacy looked over at Chapman and sneered once again at the gold ball in the black detective's nose. That and the earring in his ear convinced Lacy that Chapman was gay.

McQueen saw the look on Lacy's face and

jumped in before he could say something he'd be sorry for. If Chapman got it into his head to kick the white detective's ass, Lacy wouldn't stand a chance.

"I did some research on the psychology behind serial killers," he announced, reclaiming everyone's attention. He explained the seven phases, and when he got to the Totem phase, some of the detectives began to nod.

"It makes sense to me, Dennis," Marie Scalesi said.

"Me, too," Jason Van Shelton said. McQueen looked at him and winced. The predominant color of his outfit today was lavender. McQueen knew from hearing snatches of conversation that Chapman was still trying to get the man to pierce his ear.

"Anybody object?"

Lacy sat back with his arms crossed over his chest.

"Okay," McQueen said. "Among ourselves, our maniac is the Totem."

"I've got something to say to everyone, Dennis. I'm sure you've all seen the story in the newspaper," Keepsake said, loudly. "They've seen it at Police Plaza, too, and the chief wants somebody's head. When I find the person who leaked this story, I'm personally going to chop it off."

"Begging your pardon, Captain," Chapman

said, "but why would one of us have leaked it? This is a plum assignment for us. We wouldn't risk losing it."

"Let me put it to you this way. If the newspaper gets hold of this nickname, this 'Totem' . . . well, we'll know where to look then, won't we?"

The detectives exchanged glances, then looked back at Keepsake. Velez bit his lip, as if to keep himself quiet.

Silencio, McQueen thought.

"Am I understood? That's all, then." Keepsake went back to his desk.

"Okay," McQueen said, "everybody get to work."

As the detectives were leaving, Marie Scalesi came over to McQueen.

"So, the lamb turns into a lion, huh?" she asked, looking over at Keepsake.

"Can't say I blame him. The commissioner and the chief are out for blood."

"Who do you think did it?"

He stared at her for a minute, then changed the subject. "Do you have any plans for dinner?"

"No, why?"

"Because I need somebody to talk to."

"About what?

He hesitated a moment, then said, "Things."

"Well, okay," she said. "That's good enough for me."

Chapter Forty-four

Entering the Precinct upon his return from lunch, McQueen was greeted with unpleasant news.

"Captain Austin's looking for you." It was the desk officer, a lieutenant whom McQueen knew only slightly.

McQueen scowled. He'd managed to avoid him, lately.

"Okay, thanks." He headed for the stairs.

"He's in his office!" the desk officer called out.

McQueen waved with his back turned and fled up the stairwell. If Austin wanted to talk badly enough, he'd eventually come upstairs.

When he entered the task-force office, Bobby Callan met him with another message.

"That detective from Stony Brook called." He handed McQueen a message slip. "She said she had some information you'd find very interesting."

McQueen looked at the slip. She had called just about the time he'd asked Marie Scalesi out to dinner. Why had he done that? Maybe he was tired of eating alone, but there were other dinner companions he could have asked.

"And Captain Austin was looking for you, too," Callan added. "I told him I didn't know when you'd be back."

"Thanks, kid."

McQueen walked to his desk, noticing that Keepsake was not at his. Marie Scalesi was just hanging up the phone.

"Gotta go, Dennis."

"See you tonight?"

"I'll pick you up, okay?" She looked down at the desk and put her hand on the psychological report on serial killers. "Can I take this to look at?"

"Sure," he said. "I'll get it back from you tonight."

She left and McQueen sat down and dialed Detective Woodrell.

"I've got something for you," Woodrell said, getting right to the point. "An eyewitness."

His heart rate went up. He sat straighter. "Who?"

"A student who had to go home early because of a family emergency. That's why he wasn't around to come forward earlier. It was only on the follow-up interviews that I found him."

"And what did he see, exactly?" asked McQueen.

"He saw Brian Jordan go into the dorm with a big man."

"That's it? A big man?"

"This kid was packing his car, in a hurry to leave. He didn't pay too much attention."

"Nothing else?"

"He also said this big man was carrying a bag of some sort."

"A bag . . . a gym bag?"

"Well, he said it was a small bag, not like a suitcase. I guess it could have been a gym bag. Why?"

"I can't seem to . . . I either read something about a gym bag or heard it from someone . . . I have to go back over the reports. Anything else?"

"That's it."

"Can I have this witness's name and number?"

She read them out. He jotted the information down on the back of the pink message slip.

"I hope this helps, Sergeant," she said, "I know it's not much . . ."

"It's more than we had before," he said, wondering how they had gotten back to "Detective" and "Sergeant." "Thanks for the information, Detective."

"I'll still be working on it from here," she said. "If I come up with anything else, I'll let you know."

He thanked her again, and they hung up. He tried to call the witness then, but there was no answer. He walked over to where Callan was working.

"You got all that stuff in the computer, Bobby?"

"Just finished."

"Add this." He took out Rita Woodrell's follow-up report of her interviews. "Let me know as soon as you're done, and we'll start cross-referencing."

Callan took the report, shaking his head.

"What is it?" McQueen asked.

"I can't believe an old dinosaur like you is becoming computer friendly."

"I'll marry the fucking thing if it helps me catch this guy."

Keepsake walked in, and McQueen filled him in on the phone call from Woodrell.

"Oh, by the way," Keepsake said when McQueen was done, "did you know Austin is looking for you?"

"Yes, sir," McQueen said, "I did."

The first thing McQueen had Callan cross-reference was any mention of a big man with a bag, or a gym bag.

"There you go," Callan said. "It's mentioned in the report from Stony Brook and in the report on the Bennett killing. Something about a big man with a gym bag in the burger joint."

"That's where I remembered it from." McQueen's tone was triumphant.

"Dennis, I ran some words at random to see what came up. Want to see?"

"Sure."

"Okay." Callan's fingers flew over the keys. "I tried the word 'bar'. It turned up in almost every report. It seems most of our victims like to frequent bars. Medco and Bonnie Green, definitely."

"So they could have met in a bar." He remembered theorizing about that with Scalesi.

"Ruth Nash didn't barhop, but she did go to a bar with her girlfriends once in a while. And in an interview with one of the girlfriends, there's a mention of a bodybuilder type."

"I remember that . . ."

Callan looked up. "Your big man, Dennis."

"Nothing about a gym bag?"

"The interviews with James Hart's friends say he was a barhopper and a ladies' man."

"Like Medco."

"Right."

"Did he ever barhop in Brooklyn? Did Medco go to Manhattan?"

"I don't have anything on that."

"We'll look into it. What else?"

"Okay. Bonnie Green was a hairdresser, so I ran that. Look." Callan pointed to the screen. "Ruth Nash had her hair done at the same salon where Bonnie Green worked."

"We'll have to find out if Green actually did her hair. Also, if they work on men's hair there."

It would be Scalesi's job to find that out from the Bonnie Green end. Meanwhile, the others would have to find out where their victims had their hair cut.

"No other cross-reference on that?"

"No."

"You got more?"

"I got more." Callan typed in "Brooklyn," and all the names but one came up. James Hart was the exception. The others either lived in Brooklyn at the times of their deaths, or had lived in Brooklyn at one time.

Next, Callan typed in "Marine Park." Up popped Nash, Medco, Bennett, and Brian Jordan.

"What about Bonnie Green?"

"She lived and worked in Mill Basin."

"Close enough. That's the best common denominator we've had so far. We'll have to look a little deeper into Hart's past and see if we can find a Brooklyn reference. This is great, Callan. All of these people might have known each other, having met either in Brooklyn, or at a bar. And the killer has got to be this big man. Anything else on him?"

Callan shook his head. "The counter clerk in the burger joint said something about a black mustache, but the Stony Brook reference has no description other than big."

McQueen was growing excited. "We need to check the bar scene for a big man who may or may not be carrying a gym bag, and who may or may not have a black mustache. A mustache can be grown and shaved, or it could be a phony for the purposes of disguise."

"You want me to keep playing with this, Dennis? Maybe I can come up with something else."

"Definitely, Bobby." McQueen put his hands on the civilian aide's shoulders. "You're going to get written up for this, Bob. I promise."

"Stick it in my folder." Callan made light of it, but he'd had a few commendations over his eight years on the job, and he appreciated them. "Hey, Dennis, you gonna see what Captain Austin wants?"

"Not if I can help it," McQueen said. "Keep at it, Bobby."

McQueen went to his desk and, while everything was fresh in his mind, he made notes as to what he wanted each of the detectives to do.

Chapter Forty-five

Late that afternoon, McQueen regarded the assembled task force. "The captain and I have gone over your reports. As a result, we've come up with some assignments for you."

"New assignments?" Sam Lacy asked, frowning.

Rather than give each detective an assignment verbally, McQueen had written everything down. "You've all done good work, but the facts you've turned up have raised other questions. The sheets I'm handing out will instruct you on what your next step should be."

Lacy accepted his sheet from McQueen, but not without comment. "I usually run my own case."

McQueen didn't answer, and Lacy switched his gaze to the captain.

"I usually—" he started again. Keepsake didn't let him finish.

"Sergeant McQueen and I have evaluated the work you've done. You'll appreciate the fact that you have all been working on one case, while we have been looking at the bigger picture." Keepsake stared at Lacy, who finally looked away.

"Yes, sir."

McQueen returned to his position in front of everyone while they went over their assignments.

"We have to find out where they got their hair cut?" Van Shelton's tone was puzzled.

"Some guys care about their hair, man," Chapman said.

Van Shelton looked at Chapman's bald head. "How would you know, Kojak?"

Chapman smiled and stroked his pate, then turned his attention to McQueen. "What about this big man? This could take a while."

"Don't let it," McQueen said. "We've established links between some of the victims. We're hoping to establish a link between as many of them as we can. On one point we've connected five of the six. Neil, it's going to be up to you to tie your guy into it."

"I'll do my best."

"The captain is authorizing overtime. Put in as much time as you think you need, and submit your overtime hours in writing. In two days, people, I want a comprehensive update. Get to work."

The detectives milled about, comparing their assignment sheets, talking among themselves. Lacy left the room without speaking to any of the others.

One by one they filed out, until Velez was the only one left. He walked over to McQueen's desk. "What's going on, Dennis?"

"What do you mean?"

"Don't we get to find out how we're doing? How close we're getting to Totem?"

McQueen looked up at his partner. "Ray, I want each of you working on your own case with no distractions. In two days' time, when you come back with all I need, I'll lay it out for the rest of you."

"Well . . . how about coming over to the house for dinner tonight?"

McQueen hoped it was a sincere invitation, and not an attempt to pump him.

"Can't. I've got a previous engagement."

"Who's the lucky girl?"

"It's just a dinner, Ray."

"With who—"

McQueen gave Velez an exasperated look, pointed at the door and said, "Go."

Then Keepsake waved him over. "The newspapers are still calling. Apparently, the information leaked only to the *Post*. What's his name . . ."

"Weatherby."

"I'd like to know who he got it from. The chief called again and reamed my ass. He told me to stay out of your way while you find out who the leak is."

"Let's keep this in perspective, Captain. I'm trying to find a serial killer. I don't have time to stop and check for the leak."

"He was adamant."

"Cap, are you ordering me to devote most of my time to finding the leak?"

"No, Dennis, I'm not," Keepsake said. "As the chief so kindly pointed out, you're running this investigation."

"Hey, look, Cap—"

"Talk to Weatherby. That's all I ask."

McQueen wondered how the young captain was holding up under the pressure. He seemed all right, but there was no way of knowing what was going on inside the man.

Unexpectedly, Lacy was waiting for McQueen downstairs in the lobby. Maybe it shouldn't have been so unexpected.

"I don't like being told how to run an investigation," Lacy said, blocking McQueen's way.

"Get used to it. You're on my task force, Sam. You want to stay on it, get used to doing what you're told. If you can't, then you're off. Now, let me by."

Lacy hesitated a moment, then stiffened his jaw and stepped aside.

McQueen had tried tact with the man, to no avail. Maybe he'd finally hit on the way to handle him.

He was about to go out the door when he heard a voice call out behind him. Actually, it did more than just call out—it screeched.

"McQueen!"

"Oh, hello, Captain."

Austin's face looked paler, his cheeks even more hollowed-out and cadaverous than before. "I've been leaving messages for you, Sergeant."

"I know, sir, but I've been real busy—"

"Yes, I know," Austin said, coming toward him. "Running the task force, right?"

"Begging your pardon, sir, but Captain Keepsake is in command of the task force."

"That pup?" Austin said, snorting. "He couldn't run a nursery school. I want you in my office, Sergeant."

"I don't have time, Austin."

"Captain Austin, to you!" Austin's loud voice carried. They had an audience now, every cop in the lobby, and even the lieutenant on the front desk. "I don't care what your new rank is, McQueen. You still answer to me."

McQueen almost snapped back, but decided to move in closer and lower his voice. "No, sir, I do not answer to you." He put a sarcastic emphasis on the word "sir." "I answer to my CO, Captain Keepsake, and beyond that to Chief Robert Sands."

"Goddamn it—"

"Don't fuck with me on this, Austin! How

would you like me to tell the chief you've been interfering with the running of the task force, just to bust my balls?"

"I've—" Austin started, but he bit it off and tried again. "I just wanted to talk—"

"I don't have time to talk, Austin," McQueen said, "I have a serial killer to catch. You want to talk to me about something? Call upstairs and take it up with my CO. Now, if you'll excuse me, *sir*, I have some work to do."

He left Austin in the lobby with his mouth hanging open. Oddly, the satisfaction he felt at having been able to tell the man off was not as great as he would have expected. In fact, it had probably been a foolish thing to do. Once the task force was done, he'd be returned to the 61 squad, and would once again be under the command of Austin. He was not the type to forget.

Chapter Forty-six

McQueen was waiting downstairs when Marie Scalesi pulled up in her Mazda Miata. It was her one indulgence, one she could barely afford. He got in, immediately noticing that she wore a burgundy suit that matched the purse on the seat next to her. Her gun and shield would be inside.

"What's the matter, don't want me to see where you live?" She nodded toward his building.

"This is a nice car, but it's not built for grown-ups." He tried to stretch out his legs.

"Reach down between your legs. You can slide the seat back."

He reached around under the seat, found a lever, and slid the seat back so that he could sit fairly comfortably.

"Where are we going?" she asked.

"Drive straight. There's a place in Sheepshead Bay I want to show you."

She pulled away from the curb and drove straight on Nostrand Avenue.

"Don't want to answer my question?"

"About what?"

"About your apartment."

"It's just an apartment."

"Oh."

They drove in silence for a few moments and then he said, "Maybe later."

She hesitated, then said, "Oh . . ." in a different tone of voice.

They went to Maria's, a restaurant he thought had the best Italian food in Brooklyn.

Over dinner he told her how he and Bobby

Callan had used the computer to find similarities in the cases they were working on.

"That stuff about the big man with the bag showed up in one more case. We're looking into the others to see if we can find him there."

"We're getting closer to our Totem, then."

"Carrying his weapon in that gym bag."

Marie dipped some bread in a bowl of sauce. "You know, in this day and age a killer like this is leaving himself wide open to AIDS infection. I mean, with his exposure to all the blood."

"He should get so lucky that he'd get AIDS and die."

He said it with such feeling that she looked across the table at him with a small frown.

"Dennis, I wanted to ask this before. Why are you taking this so personally?"

He opened his mouth to answer, stopped, and started a few times before admitting, "I'm not sure I know, Marie."

"I think you want to catch him yourself."

He frowned. "I don't usually get emotionally involved in my cases, but this is different. It's been going on for too long. I want to stop him, that's all."

"And you want to meet him."

He hesitated again. "I want to see what kind of man does this."

After dinner they stopped at a small cappuccino shop on Emmons Avenue for dessert. Then she drove him back to his place. They sat awkwardly in the car once she cut the motor.

"It's late," she said.

"Uh-huh."

"I should be getting home."

"I know."

They turned their heads and looked at each other.

"Would you like to come up? To see the apartment, I mean."

"Sure."

They walked into the dark apartment, and he peeled the burgundy suit from her body with the lights off. He saw her body first with his hands and then, after they had adjusted to the darkness, with his eyes.

Her breasts were full and heavy, the skin remarkably smooth. He ran his hands around to her back and down to her buttocks, which were almost chunky. She had put weight on since the last time they were together. He liked it, and said so.

"I'm too heavy . . ." she murmured.

"Not as far as I'm concerned."

He kissed her, a searching, hungry kiss. It had been a long time for him, and her eagerness matched his. She reached between them and took him in her hands. He caught his breath and closed his eyes. When he opened them he could see her face, even in the dark. He'd never seen a woman look so sensuous.

"Where's the bed?"

He took her hand and led her to the bedroom.

"If we don't turn the lights on, you can't see the apartment," he said.

"We'll turn them on later," she said.

They lay side by side, staring at the ceiling, alone with their thoughts.

"What was that you said?" she asked.

"When?"

"While we were making love."

She put her head on his chest. With her right hand she played with his chest hair.

He frowned. Had he said something wrong? Maybe his wife's name? No, it had been too long for that.

"It sounded like 'Gaah'."

"I didn't say 'Gaah'."

"Then what did you say?"

"Well . . . maybe I said 'God'."

"No, it was more drawn out."

"Oh, that's because I said G-o-h-h-h-d." He drew it out, made it long and guttural. For effect he arched his back.

"Oooh," she said, sliding her hand down over his belly. "When did you start doing that?"

"Now, I guess."

"It's so sexy."

She took him in her hand again, and he moaned.

"And so's that moan."

He wasn't aware that he had moaned. He always thought he was pretty quiet during sex.

While she stroked him, he ran his hand up and down her back. He was responding to her touch, growing hard again.

"Well, look at you." Her tone was admiring. "You've still got it, McQueen." She slid her hand down to the base of his penis and touched the tender spot just below his scrotum.

"God . . ."

Chapter Forty-seven

When the phone rang in the morning, they both instinctively reached for it. She was closer, so she answered. "Whozit?"

McQueen lay on his back and waited.

"Oh, just a minute." she said nervously. She rolled over and looked at him, both of them suddenly wide awake. She whispered, "It's your daughter."

He brought the phone to his ear as she buried her head in the pillow, embarrassed.

"Daddy, that was a woman." His daughter's tone was shocked.

"Uh, yeah, it was, Margaret."

"Daddy, you have a girlfriend?" The tone changed, sounding delighted.

"Well . . ."

After struggling through the conversation with his daughter, he got dressed, then ran downstairs and back with bagels and coffee. Marie had already showered and was wrapped up in his terry-cloth robe.

From his kitchen nook she could see the living room, with his desk piled high with papers.

"Is that Totem Central?" She looked at him over her container of coffee. There was a smear of butter at the corner of her mouth. He was about to wipe it away when she got it with her tongue.

"That's it."

"May I?"

"Sure."

She walked over to the desk, carrying the coffee. She didn't really move much, just a light touch as she read a few words. Also on the desk was yesterday's paper, with the screaming headline about the murdered editor.

She turned to face him, one arm crossed in front of her and the other holding the coffee. The robe hid her feet. She had put her hair up in a towel. He had never had a woman in his apartment, and he liked it. The whole place smelled of her.

"I read this story, the one about the woman editor who was killed? Think it's our boy?"

He frowned. "Sure sounds like it."

"How does it differ?"

"I don't have all the facts, but she was raped. Not all the female victims we're investigating were—although it's hard to tell since most of their genital area was removed."

The phone interrupted.

"Dennis, it's Callan. The weapon is the same."

"What?" McQueen was momentarily confused.

"According to some of the reports entered in the computer, the weapon that was used left distinctive marks on the edges of the wound. Apparently, the blade has an imperfection, a 'nick' a couple of M.E.'s called it. It left a jagged edge to the wound in some cases."

"Jesus, that's great, Bobby. Good work. Is Keepsake in yet?"

A moment, and then, "Yes, Dennis."

"Cap, can we get the reports on the woman killed on the Upper West Side?"

"You think that was our man?"

"I don't know. The sexual aspect of it raises questions. I'd like to see those reports, and ask the M.E. about the wound. Did Bobby tell you about the knife?"

"Yes, he did."

"Okay, that's how we can pin it down. If she was killed with the same weapon *and* raped, then maybe our man has finally made a mistake."

"I'll get on it, Dennis."

"Also, ask Dr. Bannerjee to look at all of the reports, or make calls to the other M.E.'s about the wound. Let's see if they all have that nick Bobby was talking about."

"I'll take care of it."

"Thanks, Cap. I'll keep in touch."

He turned to face Marie. He started when he saw that she was naked. She'd removed the towel from her head. Her wet hair contrasted sharply with the white skin of her shoulders. Her beauty was in comforting contrast to the grim matters he had just been discussing.

"Marie—"

"I know, we have to go to work, but you haven't showered yet."

It was no use arguing, he could see that, so he kissed her.

Chapter Forty-eight

Before leaving his apartment that morning, McQueen had phoned Kyle Weatherby at the offices of the *New York Post* and arranged to see him.

"Oh, so now you want to talk to me." Weatherby's voice was smug.

"That's right. What's it going to cost me? Drinks?"

"Hell, *and* lunch. Meet me at Mac's. It's a bar and grill a couple of blocks from the office."

Mac's was a typical, old-fashioned New York workingman's watering hole. A big bar curved at both ends was on one side of the room, and on the other a cafeteria set-up. You could get any kind of sandwich imaginable, and innumerable hot plates.

Since Weatherby's photo appeared at the head of his column, he was easy to pick out, sitting at the bar with a bottle of beer in front of him. At least the man didn't drink expensive. In person, he looked younger than in his photo, even though his hair was prematurely white. McQueen didn't think he was forty yet.

"Weatherby?"

The man turned on his stool and gave the policeman the up and down. "Sergeant McQueen, pull up a stool. It's a busy time, and there are no tables. I hope you don't mind eating at the bar."

"That's fine."

"What will you be drinking?" the bartender asked.

McQueen sat on the stool and inspected the line of beer bottles behind the bar. "I'll have a St. Paulie Girl."

"The roast-beef sandwiches are great here," Weatherby told him.

"Okay."

"Two," Weatherby told the bartender. "Plus an order of rings, and fries. My friend here is paying."

Weatherby was clearly pretty regular to warrant the bartender going and getting his food for him.

"I wrote this place up once and business doubled. They treat me good."

"It must be nice."

Weatherby got down to business. "Okay, Sergeant, why the turnaround?"

"I want to know where you got your information, Mr. Weatherby."

"Hey, you're buying me lunch. Call me Kyle."

"Okay, Kyle. The fact that this information got out is dangerous. This task force was

303

formed to evaluate whether or not there was a serial killer operating in the city."

"Is there?"

McQueen paused. "Yes."

"Is this for publication?"

McQueen hesitated. "Yes, why not? You already printed it."

"But it's still unconfirmed, remember? You told me to call Public Information."

"I had no choice, and I have no choice now."

"So, for the record, there is a serial killer working New York, right?"

"The tristate area."

Weatherby took out a pad and started scribbling. He looked at McQueen again when done.

"If you write this, Kyle, you've also got to write that there's a serial-killer task force working on the case."

"That's fair."

"That much is on the record. Not much else is, all right?"

"If you tell me something off the record, Sergeant, it's off. If you try to stonewall me and I find out something on my own, I'm gonna print it. Do you see? If you talk to me, we'll both be happy." Weatherby paused. "But don't expect me to tell you my source. I can't."

"Look, I need to know if it was somebody on my squad. You can understand that, can't you? I've got to be able to talk freely in my own house."

"If you're not going to talk to me, then I need an ear in your house, as you put it. You can understand that."

"Then the leak is on my squad?"

"I said I can't tell you."

"You can't tell me who it is. How about telling me who it isn't?"

Weatherby picked up his beer, thought for a moment, then put down his glass, saying nothing for a time. "Let's make a deal."

"What kind of deal?"

"When you wrap this thing up, I want an exclusive. I want all the facts eight hours before anyone else gets even a whiff."

McQueen made a show of thinking the offer over. The bartender brought their food. The sandwiches were thick, on kaiser rolls, with little plastic cups of au jus on the side. The onion rings, fried in beer batter, were huge. The fries were the kind he didn't like, shoestring.

"Eight hours?"

"That'll give me the jump on everyone."

McQueen grabbed a ring and took a bite. "All right."

"It's a deal?" Weatherby sounded surprised.

"It is. I'll call you personally. You don't talk to anyone else on my squad. Okay?"

"Sure."

"Now who's the leak?"

"Take it easy. It's not a cop." Weatherby took a bite of his sandwich and shook his head.

McQueen was annoyed. "I'm not getting enough from you to justify our deal. You and I know that there's a big true-crime book in this. Without me, you get nothing and somebody else cashes in. Think it over." He turned away from the man and bit into his sandwich.

"Two more?" the bartender asked, looking at their empties.

McQueen nodded, and they were brought fresh beers.

"Fine. Who's your source?"

"He's got a relative who's married to a cop. The cop came home and told his wife, and the wife told this guy. My source wants to break in as a photographer. He gave me the information in exchange for an introduction." McQueen's heart sank. How could he turn in his own partner?

Chapter Forty-nine

McQueen called the task-force detectives together to go over the evidence, using a chalkboard to illustrate the connections among the victims.

First, he went over the similarities he had initially found. After the detectives were apprised of these, he continued on with the information they had gathered over the past two days.

"The most important thing we've found, though, is this big man with the gym bag. Chapman interviewed many people who frequented the same bars James Hart did. Two of them remembered a big man with long blond hair and a blond beard."

"Lots of big men around," Lacy said.

"This one always had a gym bag at his feet. The word we get is he stopped coming around the same time Hart did. Also, one of Ruth Nash's girlfriends remembers that they were all approached one night by a big man who was built like a bodybuilder."

"And the gym bag?" Marie Scalesi asked.

"They didn't see one. It doesn't mean it wasn't there. One of the girls who worked with Bonnie Green said she spoke of a new man she was interested in. She referred to him as a 'big hunk' and said his name was Ned."

"That's slim," Scalesi said. "And what can we do with just a first name?"

"It's something," McQueen argued. "He apparently wears disguises, but there's not too much that can disguise the fact that he's over six feet and built like a bodybuilder—and most of the time he's carrying a gym bag. That's where we think he carries the knife."

"And a change of clothes," Lacy chimed in.

"He'd have to have some clean clothes with him. He couldn't have killed all of these people without getting blood on him."

"Good point, Sam."

"Okay, I asked you all to look for unusual incidents with anyone involved in your case. We came up with two divorces—in the families of both Green and Bennett—a sex-change operation—that was James Hart's cousin—and a case of Paul Medco's brother beating his wife. She won't press charges, keeps going back to him and keeps getting beat up."

"He's violent, then," Lacy said.

"Yeah, but what's his motive to kill his own brother, let alone all these others?" Velez said. It was his case. "Plus, he's only five eight, and on the fat side. I looked into it. He's a scumbag wife beater, but he's not a serial killer."

"There's nothing else unusual except for this: About four years ago, Brian Jordan's neighbor's wife died. She was young, and she went suddenly."

"So?" Lacy said. "It was a natural death."

"Was it?" Scalesi asked.

"No doubt," McQueen said, "but afterward the husband started acting strange. He eventually sold the house and disappeared."

"Disappeared?" Scalesi said. "Did they have kids?"

"A daughter was left in the care of his in-laws."

"Have they heard from him?"

"We don't know. I'm talking to the grandparents later today."

"What did the husband look like?" Chapman asked. He was running the tip of his index finger back and forth over the ball in his nose. When his question brought everyone's eyes to him, he stopped.

"Ray?" McQueen said.

Velez had handled the interview of Brian Jordan's parents. "According to Jordan's parents, he was a big man, over six feet. But not like a bodybuilder. They said he was kind of sloppy."

"That could be changed with a weight-lifting program," Chapman said.

"What did he do for a living?" Scalesi asked.

McQueen smiled. This fact had excited him more than anything else they had gathered over the past two days.

"They said he was some kind of a writer," Velez replied.

McQueen slammed a piece of chalk into the board so hard that it broke, half of it shooting across the room. Using the other half, he made circles on the board.

"Which brings us to Victoria Dreyer." This was the name on the board he had drawn the circles around.

"Who the hell's that?" Lacy asked.

309

Scalesi answered. "The woman who was killed in Manhattan."

"What's she got to do with this? She was raped."

"True, but we also determined that the murder weapon was the same as in our other cases. Also the disappearing neighbor wrote books," McQueen said triumphantly. "Dreyer was a book editor."

There was a short silence in the room. Then Sam Lacy finally spoke. "You think that while he's been killing people, he's been writing books?"

McQueen looked at his staff. "That's what we have to find out. The Dreyer case is now ours."

McQueen assigned Scalesi and Van Shelton to go to the Upper West Side and canvas Victoria Dreyer's neighborhood.

"What are we looking for?" Scalesi asked.

"How about a witness?" suggested Keepsake.

McQueen told Lacy and Chapman to go to the offices of Pembroke Press. "See if she was talking about anyone lately, a writer who might fit our description of the big man with the gym bag. Ray, you come with me. We're going to go and talk to the sloppy neighbor's in-laws."

"What's this guy's name, anyway?" Chapman asked before going out the door.

"The slob's name is Nicholas Turner," Velez said.

Chapter Fifty

Evelyn and Anthony DeBartolo lived in a three-story house on Marine Parkway, in Marine Park, the same section of Brooklyn their daughter had lived in with her husband.

Marine Parkway was twice the width of any other street in the area, and the homes went for three times as much. It was not unusual for one to be purchased for three hundred thousand dollars, gutted and done over and resold for twice that much. However, the DeBartolos had lived in the same home for years, building it up to its present impressive stature themselves.

Both DeBartolos were home. McQueen and Velez were escorted by Mrs. DeBartolo to the den to meet her husband. Along the way they passed a room where a little girl sat in front of a TV playing Nintendo games.

"Lisa is nine, now," Evelyn said. She was a well-kept woman in her sixties, trying and failing to pass for forty. Her eye makeup was too heavy, she had painted her eyebrows too high. Her skirt, of

Oriental design, was too short and too tight. The odor of her hair spray and dye permeated the air.

"She hasn't seen her father in over three years, and we haven't heard from him in over a year. She did receive some gifts now and then, but not for a year or so."

"I hope the sonofabitch is dead," Anthony DeBartolo said.

"Tony!" his wife scolded.

"Fuck 'em," DeBartolo said. He had a bald head surrounded by hair that looked like steel wool. His lavender V neck showed more steel wool sticking out. He wore jeans, and open-toed sandals. He had lived a hard life and earned enough money to dress the way he wanted to in his own home. The only nod to vanity he might have shown was a very carefully trimmed mustache and Vandyke beard.

McQueen and Velez sat on a sofa.

"Would either of you gentlemen like some tea?" Evelyn asked.

"Nick Turner was never good enough for my daughter," DeBartolo said. "Do you know what he did for a living?"

"What?" McQueen knew, but asked anyway.

"He wrote books." DeBartolo shook his head. "What kind of a profession is that for a man? Books! Women write books. She reads them." He nodded his head toward his wife. "What are some of the names, Mother?"

"Danielle Steele," she recited, an obedient wife. "Jackie Collins. Sue Grafton. Patricia Cornwell."

"Yeah, see? Women. How could he support my daughter on books? You know how? She worked, that's how. She worked herself to death so he could write his books. The sonofabitch should die. I ain't gonna apologize to anybody for wishing that!"

"Mr. and Mrs. DeBartolo, we have some questions about your son-in-law," Velez said.

"What's he done?" DeBartolo asked.

"Nothing we know of right now."

"Has something happened to him?" DeBartolo's voice indicated his hopes were raised.

"We don't know that, either," said McQueen. "Let's get to it. After your daughter died, how did your son-in-law take it?"

"He took it very hard—" Evelyn started, but her husband interrupted her.

"Sure he did. Without her to support him, he'd have to go out and get a real job."

"For a couple of months he was just very quiet," Evelyn said. "I would call him and he would just mumble on the phone. I'd go over to take some dinner—you know, so that Lisa could eat properly—and he wouldn't talk or eat."

"Then what happened?"

"He came to us and told us he was leaving,"

DeBartolo said, breaking in. "He was selling the house and wanted us to take Lisa. He was giving us his daughter and, believe me, I was glad to take her. I can't think of anything that would have hurt that kid more than to stay with him."

"Why?"

"He was strange, that's why," DeBartolo said.

"The truth, Officer," Evelyn DeBartolo said. "Nick hated me, I think. I reminded him of his mother."

"His mother?" Psychobabble, McQueen thought.

"Yes, I don't think Nick had a very good relationship with his mother. Gina told me."

McQueen purposely changed the subject. "What about physically. How was he built?"

"I have a wedding picture," Evelyn said. "He hasn't changed much since then—at least, he hadn't the last time we saw him."

"Would you have any other pictures, also?"

"Probably. I'll go take a look." She left the room.

McQueen turned to DeBartolo. "After Nick sold the house, where did he go?"

"Sergeant, we don't exactly know where Nick went. He sent some gifts, but there were never any return addresses on them. There was one postcard he sent Lisa. The poor girl kept it, has it hung up in her room. We don't talk about her father in this house anymore, but she keeps that postcard." He bellowed out to his wife. "Mother, get that postcard, too!"

Evelyn DeBartolo returned carrying a photo album and a postcard.

"May I see the postcard?" McQueen asked.

"Certainly."

She handed it to him. It had a fountain on it, and at the bottom said very simply, KANSAS CITY. On the back were two sentences: "Daddy loves you. Be a good girl." There was no return address. He handed the card to Velez. "Now the photos?"

Evelyn opened the book. "It was a beautiful wedding."

"For Chrissake, show the man the pictures he wants to see."

She flinched at her husband's tone and turned several pages before she came to an eight by ten wedding photo. Nick Turner towered over his wife. In the photo he had a baby face, and a shapeless body.

"Do you have a more recent picture?" McQueen asked Evelyn.

She turned to the book's final page. On it were two photos, both five by sevens, one of Gina and one of Nick. Gina had been a lovely woman, with short hair and a heart-shaped face. In his photo, Nick still looked rather shapeless, although older and less baby-faced.

"When was this taken?"

"A couple of months before Gina died. I think it was October 1990."

"Mrs. DeBartolo, may I borrow the wedding photo and this one of Nick?"

She looked at her husband.

"Give them to him, Mother. These are the police, you know."

"Yes, of course."

She took both photos from the book and handed them to McQueen.

"We'll get them back to you as soon as possible."

"If they help you catch the bastard and put him away, you can keep them!" DeBartolo said.

"Thank you both for your help." McQueen and Velez stood up.

"I'll see you to the door," Evelyn said. Once there, she put her hand on McQueen's arm. "The postcard? Lisa will miss it."

McQueen looked to Velez. He shrugged. "I guess we don't need it."

"All right," McQueen said. Velez handed it back.

"Thank you, but there's something you should know." She spoke in a hushed whisper. "I went over to the house one day a couple of months after Gina died. Sometimes, I took him food. I had a key, so I let myself in. I heard something upstairs, like someone crying. When I went up I saw Nick sitting on the floor in the bedroom. He was crying, and he had some books spread out on the bed and the floor. He didn't see me, and I left."

"What kind of books, Mrs. DeBartolo?"

"They were my daughter's journals."

"Did you know what was in them?"

She looked away then, embarrassed. Instead of answering, she took a white business card from her pocket and handed it to him.

The card said: DR. JAMES FORSLUND. The address was on Livingston Street, downtown Brooklyn.

"He was my daughter's psychiatrist. Maybe you should talk to him."

"Mrs. DeBartolo, can you tell me—"

She shook her head vehemently and said, "Talk to him. Please! My husband doesn't know anything about this. He thinks only crazy people go to psychiatrists." She closed the door.

"Jesus, that poor kid, Lisa," Velez said when they got in the car. "Her mother dies, her father goes off the deep end, and now she's stuck being brought up by that pair."

McQueen started the car. "They really love her. That's more than most kids get." The older man stared rigidly straight ahead.

"Margaret knows you love her, Dennis."

"Ray," McQueen said. "Shut up."

Chapter Fifty-one

Dr. James Forslund had an appointment cancel and was able to give McQueen and Velez some time, even though they had not called ahead.

"Yes, of course I remember Mrs. Turner."

"What was wrong with her, Doctor?"

Dr. Forslund smiled benignly. He was in his fifties, with a mane of gray hair that appeared lacquered in place. He wore a brown three-piece suit. His office was spare, with only his glass-topped desk and two black metal chairs. His window offered a view of the East River. There was no sofa. He sat back in his leather chair, calmly regarding McQueen.

"My patients don't necessarily have anything wrong with them, Detective."

"He's a sergeant." Ray pointed to McQueen. "I'm a detective."

"I understand, Doctor," McQueen said, ignoring Velez. "Let me rephrase the question. What was Mrs. Turner's condition?"

The doctor did not immediately reply.

"Doctor, your patient has been dead for four

years. You're not about to invoke doctor-patient confidentiality, are you?"

"I know the law, Sergeant. I know there is no confidentiality when the patient is dead. However, please understand, I'm not used to talking about my patients, dead or alive."

"I understand, Doctor."

"Also, I am very curious as to what this is all about. Why are you investigating my patient's death after all these years?"

"We're not, Doctor. This is part of an investigation into another matter."

"It's about Mr. Turner?"

"Doctor, we'd appreciate it if you would just answer our questions," said Velez. "What was Gina Turner's condition—uh, in layman's terms, please?"

"She was depressed. Her marriage wasn't satisfying to her."

"Was her husband abusive?"

"No. He was wrapped up in his work and was often apathetic toward her."

"Did Nick Turner ever come in to see you with his wife, Doctor?" McQueen asked.

"Once. I asked her to bring him several times after that, but he refused to come again."

"And just how depressed did all of this make her? Suicidal?"

"All depressed people do not contemplate suicide, Sergeant McQueen."

"Did she?"

Forslund hesitated. "She did not consider it when she first came to me, but she did later. Sometime in 1989."

"And when did she first come to you?"

"1986."

"How is it you remember the dates so well, Doctor?"

"She became a . . . pet project of mine." The doctor shifted uncomfortably in his seat. McQueen gave him all the time he could.

"In what way, Doctor?"

"When she started talking about suicide, I tried a new course of treatment."

"Medication? Something experimental?"

"Prozac?" Velez asked.

"No."

"Doctor, what was this experimental treatment?" asked McQueen.

"I suggested to Mrs. Turner that she keep a daily journal."

McQueen exchanged a glance with his partner. "Doctor, if Nick Turner read these journals after his wife's death, do you think they would have upset him?"

"Sergeant, I think it's safe to say that Mr. Turner would have been very upset."

McQueen asked the doctor, "Do you know what was in those journals?"

"Yes, Sergeant," Doctor Forslund replied, "I do."

* * *

On the street, Velez asked. "Is Turner our man?"

"It gives him motive."

"But the guy's a writer. Would he be capable of that kind of violence?"

"What would you do, Ray, if you read something like that written by Cookie after she died?" McQueen asked as they reached their unmarked vehicle.

"I'd wonder why she didn't tell me she was that kinky when she was alive. We could have had a ball!"

"You're a sick fuck. Get in the car."

Part VI

McQueen and Turner

Chapter Fifty-two

June 1994

Daniel Foster had spoken to Nick Turner twice since Victoria Dreyer's death, right after she was found, and then earlier this week when Turner called about his replacement editor.

"His name is Tom Douglas, Nick. He isn't going to be permanent, but he'll probably work on this next book."

"Is he any good?"

"He's been around a while."

"I want somebody really good."

"Well, we had Victoria. In spite of how difficult she was, she was a good editor." He paused and then added, "But she's dead . . ."

He waited to see if Turner would respond in any way, but there was only silence from the

Robert J. Randisi

other end of the phone. It made Foster surer than ever that Turner had killed her.

He worried if knowing it made him some sort of accessory. What would he do if the police came and questioned him?

He was getting paranoid. It was getting so anytime he saw a couple of men standing out in front of his office he thought they were cops coming to arrest him. He looked out his window toward Washington Square Park. There were two men out there right now.

Oh, Jesus, he thought, these two really do look like cops. What were they doing standing right in front of his door like that?

Suddenly, the older one said something to the younger one. They turned and approached his door.

He would be calm. He took a deep breath when he heard the door buzzer.

The man who answered the door was short, bald, and fat, nothing like McQueen's image of a slick literary agent.

"My name is Sergeant McQueen and this is Detective Velez." They showed their ID. "May we come in and talk to you?"

"About what?" The man was skittish. His eyes were big, round, and watery.

"We'd rather talk inside, if you don't mind."

Foster hesitated, then nodded and stepped back from the door. "Come in."

326

They followed him into a disheveled office. The agent circled his desk and nervously sat down. They each sat in a chair across from him.

One reason McQueen appreciated Velez as a partner was that the younger man followed his lead. For some reason, it was McQueen's instinct to sit silently for a while and see what occurred.

"Well? W-what was it you wanted to see me about?"

Foster grew more nervous and agitated the longer McQueen and Velez maintained their silence.

"Is this about Victoria Dreyer?"

McQueen looked over at Velez. The younger man raised his eyebrows and looked back at Foster.

Finally, the agent couldn't take it anymore.

"I never expected him to kill her," he blabbered. "You've got to believe me. I didn't have any part of that. I didn't think he'd kill her!"

"We do believe you, Mr. Foster," McQueen said. "Now tell us who you're talking about."

When Nick Turner hung up the phone after speaking with his agent, he remained in the booth a few minutes, thinking. Daniel Foster sounded nervous, and he obviously thought Turner had killed Victoria Dreyer. There was no way the man could prove it, he had been too intimidated to come right out and ask. Turner left the phone booth and walked back up the road to his apartment.

When he'd found this neighborhood in New Milford, Connecticut, he'd thought it ideal. Aside from the small apartment complex he lived in, and the nearby convenience store with the phone booth outside, there were few buildings in the area. Most residents of his building worked regular nine-to-five jobs, so he was virtually alone during the day. When he did see any neighbors, he ignored them. His appearance discouraged friendly overtures.

Nick Turner didn't want or need friends. Friends were people who could hurt you. No one would hurt him anymore.

Including his agent.

Chapter Fifty-three

Now that Daniel Foster had opened his mouth, he realized it had not been a smart thing to do. "Well," he said then, "I don't actually know for sure whether he did it."

"But you suspect he did?" McQueen asked.

"What does it matter what I think? I-I'm no policeman."

"But you do know the man in question, and we don't."

"Know what man?"

McQueen and Velez exchanged a long glance.

"Backpedaling," Velez said.

"What?" Foster asked.

"My partner suspects you're trying to change your story, Mr. Foster," said McQueen.

"I don't have a s-story."

"Why do you think Nick Turner killed Victoria Dreyer?" McQueen now spoke fast, angrily.

"Nick—uh, I didn't mention his name."

"Nick Turner is the client of yours we came to talk about, Mr. Foster. He wasn't the one you meant when you said he killed her?"

"Yes, Mr. Foster," Velez added. "Why don't you tell us what you do mean?"

Foster sat in confused silence, his shoulders slumped. There was no way out for him but to talk. He finally had a writer he thought he could turn into a best-seller, and the guy turns out to be a killer. "Nick Turner," Foster said. "I—I th-think he might have killed Victoria."

"Lots of people have been killed, Mr. Foster," said McQueen. "Miss Dreyer is just one of them."

Foster's jaw dropped. "He's killed more?" Foster felt a coldness in his stomach, like a stone. "H-how many?"

"Over a dozen," McQueen said.

Robert J. Randisi

"Well over a dozen," said Velez.

"Where is he, Mr. Foster?" asked McQueen.

Foster was lost in thought and didn't hear the question. He was suddenly contemplating the thought of a best-selling true-crime nonfiction novel written by the killer himself.

"Where's Turner?" Velez demanded.

"I don't know."

"Come on, Foster, he's your client. Aren't you negotiating a big contract with the publishing house Victoria Dreyer worked for?"

"It's all signed, sealed, and paid for—well, half is paid for."

"Turner signed the contract?"

"Yes. He signed at a lunch with Victoria— only she didn't know him as Nick Turner. She knew him as Ned Tailor."

McQueen felt a slight rush, and knew Velez was feeling it too. Another piece of the puzzle fell into place. This had to be the right guy. Now all they had to do was track him down. "Turner already got paid?"

"I already sent his check to his post-office box in Connecticut."

"I'd like that post-office box, Mr. Foster," said McQueen.

The agent grabbed a scrap of paper and copied Turner's P.O. box from his Rolodex.

"When was the last time you spoke to Turner?"

"This morning on the phone. I hung up not half an hour before you knocked on my door."

"Do you know when he will be calling you again?"

"I'm not sure."

McQueen pressed his hands together as though praying and touched the index fingers to his lips thoughtfully. "When he calls again, Mr. Foster, we will be here and we will tell you what to say."

Outside, McQueen and Velez stopped to look across the street at Washington Square Park again. "Jesus, Dennis, this has been good work, all of it, right from the beginning. Maybe they'll make you a lieutenant after this."

"Bite your tongue, Ray. Come on, let's get a crew over here and get set up for that next phone call."

"Are we just going to sit and wait?"

"You are," McQueen said. "I'm going to Connecticut to find the sonofabitch."

Chapter Fifty-four

On his bus ride home, McQueen found himself thinking about Marie Scalesi. He had seen her socially several times since that first night, and they had frequently talked on the phone when they weren't at work.

It was nice, but it had come at the wrong time. He needed to concentrate his efforts on catching Nick Turner before he could think about a relationship—or even going on with the rest of his life. Over the past week, there hadn't been a chance to talk at work, and he'd refrained from calling her in the evenings.

He needed to catch this guy. After months of gathering information, forming the task force, putting it all together, the end was nearing.

When he got home, the red light on his machine was flashing once. The single message was from Marie Scalesi. She would be home all night and available to talk. He returned the call.

"Jesus, Dennis, I don't know what to say," she said after he explained to her what had happened, and that he wanted her to go to Connecticut with him.

"Don't say anything, Marie. Can we use your car? I'll make sure you get reimbursed for the gas—"

"I'll pick you up in the morning."

"I can take the train into town."

"No, it's all right. We can hop right on the Belt Parkway by you and go that way."

There was an awkward silence, and he thought she might be waiting for him to ask her to come over right then and spend the night. But he had a lot of thinking to do tonight.

"Dennis?"

Here it comes, he thought. "Yes?"

"Do you think there's a chance we'll catch this guy tomorrow?"

"With luck, we will. It would be a helluva long shot."

Nick Turner couldn't sleep. At midnight he stood in front of his patio door, staring out. He thought about how nervous his agent had sounded. It made Nick uneasy that Foster had his P.O. box address. Now that he had the first half of the contract money in the bank, he wouldn't need the box until his manuscript-delivery payment. Then the publisher would cut his second check.

Tomorrow he'd cancel the box. The jumpy

agent just might be tempted to turn Nick in, based on his suspicions.

Maybe it was even time to get a new agent. Maybe it was time to cancel the old one.

Chapter Fifty-five

When they reached New Milford, they asked directions from a pedestrian for the police department. Driving through the town McQueen was struck by how quiet, peaceful, and pretty it was. They passed a big, white Methodist Church with a small cemetery next to it, a new-looking brick building that housed an elementary school. They followed railroad tracks for a while until they reached a quaint train station. They passed a larger cemetery than the one near the church.

"Oh, I love old cemeteries like that," Scalesi said. "Look, see that big stone. The one with the angel on it?"

"It's beautiful."

"That's what I want when I die, an angel to watch over my grave."

"Talk to your family about it."

She snorted. "The only family I've got are my mother and sister. They'd be too cheap for that."

"Well, if I'm around, I'll remember."

She took a long look at him, long enough to make him afraid she'd drive off the road. "You're sweet, Dennis. I'd forgotten how sweet."

"Yeah, yeah," he said uncomfortably. "Keep your eyes on the road."

At the police station they were directed to Captain Hastings's office. McQueen explained the situation.

"We'd like to cooperate all we can, naturally." Hastings was a tall, handsome, black man in his forties with broad shoulders and a well-cared-for mustache. His uniform was spotless, and freshly pressed. McQueen knew without looking at the captain's ring finger that the man was married. "Tell me what you need."

"I just need one of your men to go to the post office with us, Captain, so that we'll get their cooperation."

"You'd need a court order to get inside the box," Hastings pointed out.

"We don't need to get into the actual box, Captain. All we're looking for is the name and address of the renter."

"I'll go over there with you myself," the captain said, getting up from behind his desk. "If you get an address, you're going to want some backup, right?"

* * *

"You're paid up until the end of the year, sir," the postal clerk told Nick Turner. "There is no refund."

"I know that. I just don't want the box anymore."

"Of course, sir." The look on the clerk's face said that he didn't understand. After all, there were waiting lists for these boxes.

"Take my name off it."

"Yes, sir," the clerk said, "we'll do that today."

"See that you do."

As Turner went around the corner to his parked car, a New Milford police car pulled up in front of the building, followed closely by a Mazda Miata. McQueen, Scalesi, and Hastings gathered on the sidewalk.

"Maybe I should do the talking," Hastings suggested, "so that there's no mix-up."

Inside, Hastings asked for the postal manager, a man named Howard Doyle.

Hastings told Doyle what it was they wanted.

"Captain," the manager said, "this is a federal post office. I can't let you into a box without a court order."

"Let's see what can do for us, then, Mr. Doyle," said Hastings. He looked at McQueen, who handed the manager a piece of paper with Turner's P.O. box number on it. "Who's renting it?"

Doyle went off to look up the information. He

returned looking very put out. "No one is renting that box.

"But someone was renting that box last month," said Scalesi. "Aren't they usually rented for the year?"

"It must have been canceled recently, or the renter's year may have ended at the beginning of this month."

"In any case," she said, "couldn't you tell us who had that box last?"

"I suppose I could look that up for you."

"We'd appreciate it."

Minutes later, Doyle returned carrying a three-by-five index card. He seemed uncertain as to who to speak to, then just spoke to the three of them. "The box was rented by a man named Ned Tyler."

"Is that your man?" Hastings asked.

"It's a name he's used," McQueen said. He couldn't be sure about "Tyler," of course, but the man had used "Ned" three times now. Another slipup. "Do you have an address, Mr. Doyle?"

"Oh . . . my . . . well, yes, I—of course . . ." The man stammered for a few more moments, then finally read them the address.

"Thank you," McQueen said.

"One other thing, Mr. Doyle," Scalesi said. "When was that box canceled?"

Doyle looked at the card and his eyes widened. "Why . . . it was today. Just one moment."

"When?"

"It's not on here . . . I'll ask . . ." He went and spoke to some of the other clerks, eventually returning with a man named Morse.

"He was here not twenty minutes ago," Morse said. "I couldn't understand why he'd canceled. He was paid up until—"

"What did he look like?" McQueen asked, cutting him off.

"Oh, he was a big man, very broad, built like a weight lifter."

McQueen felt Scalesi's hand on his arm as he thanked Morse and Doyle.

Outside, Scalesi said, "Jesus, Dennis, we just missed him!"

McQueen looked around, as if Turner might be on a nearby street corner watching them.

"I can't believe your luck," Hastings said. "The same day you come looking, he cancels the box."

"The question is, why?" McQueen asked. "Why cancel the box now?"

"Captain, can you take us to that address now?" Scalesi asked.

"What was it?"

McQueen read the address Doyle had provided.

"I could take you there, but it won't do you any good," Hastings said. "There's nothing on that street but empty lots."

Chapter Fifty-six

Nick turner was going to kill his agent.

It was unavoidable. The man knew too much and was too nervous. Turner could never feel secure as long as Daniel Foster still lived. As for his second check, he could always arrange to get that directly from the publisher. What did he need an agent for? He already had a two-book deal, and he was confident he could get another deal afterward.

He went to his computer. In the hard drive was half of book one. It was going well, thanks to his editor. She'd provided unique editorial guidance. Over the past few days, however, he had begun to feel the itch again. The money was in the bank, just waiting to be used to track down the last five names on his list. But he had the book to finish.

Nick Turner was being pulled apart by two urges: one to write and one to kill. Or were they the same? He needed to keep writing, but in order to do that, he needed to kill so that the urge to kill would not interfere with the urge to write. Did the writing come from the killing, or the killing from the writing?

He put his hand on the cover of the closed laptop computer. Whatever, he needed to kill the agent. The man deserved to die, anyway.

Daniel Foster sat at his desk and chewed on the nail of his left thumb. Sitting across from him, Ray Velez watched, positive that any minute the man was going to start leaking blood from that thumb. The detective wore a pair of headphones around his neck. Foster noticed Velez looking at him and pulled the thumb from his mouth.

"You want some coffee? I keep a pot of coffee going all day. I need the stuff to keep going, you know? You want some? I'm gonna have some."

"Sure." Velez started to get up. "I'll have some."

"No, no, stay there." Foster bounded up out of his seat, propelled by nervous energy. "Sugar? Milk?"

"Just black."

"Just black, the way I take it. Comin' up."

Foster went through a doorway to Velez's right and he heard the man clanking cups.

"Must be a hell of a job, being a cop," Foster said, handing Velez a full cup.

"It's a job." He sipped the coffee.

"How is it?"

It was weak. "It's fine."

"Good, good." Foster sat back in his chair, still holding his cup in one hand. "Bet you've seen a lot of stuff, huh?"

"I've seen enough."

"Some pretty bad stuff?"

"Some."

"Ever think about writing a book? There's a huge market for true crime these days. What about that? You have any hot cases you could write about?"

"Not that I can think of."

"What about this one? This case, you know, it's gonna cost me a lot. I don't know where he got it, but suddenly Nick Turner's got talent, you know? I could have gone all the way with him."

"All the way?"

"Yeah, you know, *The New York Times* bestseller list! All the way."

Velez was amused. "But you're still helping us."

"Well, he killed people. I don't condone that, you know? Besides, he scares the shit out of me."

"Can't blame you for that."

"So what do you say? Want to write this up? I could sell it, you know. Big bucks. Big time. Talk shows. *Letterman. Leno.* Oh, well, maybe one or the other, you know? But what about daytime? *Sally? Oprah? Phil?*"

Velez shook his head. "Well, if anyone is

going to write about this case it should be my partner, Dennis."

"Dennis?"

"Sergeant McQueen's really the only one who knows enough to write about it."

"He's a pretty good detective, huh?"

"He's real good, the best."

"Well, maybe I should talk to Sergeant McQueen about a career move, huh?"

The phone on the agent's desk rang, and the man jumped. Velez sat forward, adjusted the headphones, and switched on the microcassette recorder.

After the fifth ring, he said to Foster, "I think you better answer it."

Chapter Fifty-seven

Foster finally picked up the phone. "H-hello." The agent sounded scared out of his wits.

"Relax, Mr. Foster. It's me, Sergeant McQueen."

"Oh, Sergeant—"

"You can't let the phone ring that many times, Mr. Foster. Our man might hang up."

"I know, I'm just a little spooked, I guess. Did you find him?"

"Is Detective Velez there?"

"Ray? Sure, he's right here."

Velez came on the line.

"How's it going, Ray?"

"Fine, Dennis. Daniel and I were just having a cup of coffee."

"Oh. It's 'Daniel' and 'Ray' now, huh?"

"He's not such a bad guy, Dennis. He wants to make you a star." Velez sounded amused.

"I'm sure there's an explanation to that, but I'll ask about it another time." McQueen went on to explain about Turner having closed the post-office box just before they'd gotten there.

"What timing. What'd he have in mind?"

"I don't know, but I think I've figured out a way to flush him out. It's really very simple."

They were at a pay phone at a rest stop, and Scalesi was listening to McQueen's end of the conversation. Her expression said that it was about time she found out what he had in mind.

"When he calls, your friend Daniel is going to have to tell him that he's going to the police."

"Tell him what?"

"You heard me."

"Dennis, that means—" Velez broke off and McQueen heard his voice away from the phone ask Foster if he could have another cup of coffee. When he came back on the phone, he had his hand cupped over the receiver and spoke in a low tone.

"You're hanging him out to dry, Dennis."

"We'll use him as a decoy, Ray."

"Bait is more like it. He's not on the job, you know."

"Do you have a better idea?"

"What if he just tells Turner that they have to meet with the new editor?"

"There's no guarantee Turner will show up. Remember, he's got half his money. We need something that Turner can't resist."

There was silence on the other end, then Velez said, "How do you want to work it?"

"Do you want to wait for me to get back so I can talk to Foster?"

"No, I'll do it. What if Turner calls while you're still driving back?"

"Okay, then. Here's how we'll play it . . ."

"There's no other way?" Daniel Foster asked over another cup of coffee.

"If you can think of one, Dan, let me know, I'll pass it along."

Foster sat in brooding silence for a while, then shook his head.

"No, I can't see another way. That'll get the kid here, all right."

"He may be planning to kill you, already. Maybe that's why he canceled his post-office box. He's cutting all ties to you."

Foster opened his mouth a couple of times before he was able to form words. "Hell, I'll do it. Maybe I'll come out of this with an idea for a book I can write myself."

"You can write?"

Foster made a face and said, "Not worth a damn."

He opened a desk drawer and brought out a bottle of Early Times.

"You want a touch of something stronger in that coffee, Ray?"

"Why not, Dan?"

Nick Turner decided to get it over with as soon as possible. He just needed a jolt to keep going on the book for another week or so, and then it would be done. Hopefully, the agent would serve that purpose. Once the book was finished and delivered, and Turner had arranged to receive the remainder of his money, he could finish off Gina's list.

He dialed the agent's number, knowing the man would be surprised to hear from him again this soon.

Velez was holding his cup out to Foster when the phone rang again. Foster answered on the second ring, just managing to keep his elbows out of the bourbon puddle on his desk.

Chapter Fifty-eight

When they got back to the city, McQueen told Scalesi to drop him at Daniel Foster's office.

"Want me to stick around, Dennis?"

"No, I'll spell Ray so he can go home to his wife."

"How will you get home?"

"You people with cars think that's the only way to get around, don't you?"

"You mean there are other ways?" She paused. "Will you call me?"

"Marie—"

"We have to talk, Dennis," she said quickly, "and I want you to know it's okay with me if we do it after we catch this guy, this Totem, or Turner, or whatever we're going to call him now. I understand."

"All right, Marie," McQueen said, "I think it's a good idea, too. We'll talk once we've got this guy."

Ray Velez answered the door at Foster's office. "He called, Dennis. Just about ten minutes after we spoke to you."

"He's moving fast. First he closes the P.O. box, now this. Was Foster expecting the call?"

"No. He said there was no reason for Turner to call him now. Dennis, do you think he's closing up shop, getting ready to move on?"

"We can't lose him now! Not after all this!" McQueen paused to regain control of his voice. "How is Foster doing?"

"How would you be if you were being used for bait? He's scared."

"But he's going along with it?"

"He's gone along with it, Dennis. He told Turner he was going to the police if he didn't agree to meet with him." Velez stepped away from the door. "Let him tell you."

They went into the office. Daniel Foster sat behind his desk. "Ah, Sergeant McQueen. I want to talk with you about a new career, sir. Together, we'll make you a star."

"Is he drunk?" McQueen looked at Velez.

"He had a little bourbon in his coffee."

McQueen stared at Foster in dismay, then looked back at Velez. "All right, Ray. I'll take over now. You can go on home."

"You going to stay with him all night, Dennis?"

"Yeah, all night. Just because he and Turner already talked doesn't mean Turner won't show up here early, or even call to change plans. Where does Foster live?"

"He's got an apartment right upstairs."

Velez took a couple of steps toward the desk. "Dan, I'll see you tomorrow. Okay?"

"Sure, Ray." He peered at Velez owlishly. "Thanks for the company, ol' buddy."

"A *little* bourbon?" McQueen asked Velez.

Velez shrugged and said, "I guess he can't hold it."

"Check in with Keepsake tomorrow, Ray. He'll tell you what your assignment is."

"I thought I'd come back and relieve you in the morning."

"Call Keepsake, all right?"

"Sure, Dennis, sure."

Velez left. McQueen took Foster's coffee cup away from him. "That's enough of that, Mr. Foster. How about some regular coffee?"

"I had enough coffee," Foster said with a frown.

"I mean coffee without bourbon."

Foster's eyebrows went up. "I got a better idea. How about some bourbon without the coffee?"

"I need you sober so we can talk. Where's the coffee?"

"In there." Foster pointed to a doorway.

McQueen found himself in a small kitchen. On the counter next to the stove was a coffee maker with half a pot. He poured a cup for Foster and, as an afterthought, poured one for himself, too. He took them back into the office.

"Mr. Foster, tell me about the call from Turner."

The agent sipped from the coffee cup, nervously holding it in both hands. "He called and said he wanted to see me. I didn't even have to try to talk him into it."

"Why did he want to see you?"

"To talk about his books. Isn't this what you wanted? For him to come into the city to see me?"

"Yes, it is, but it would have been nice if it could have been on our terms."

"Well, I went ahead and told him about going to the police, anyway. I arranged for us to meet here."

"Has he been here before?"

"The old Nick Turner has, but not this version."

"Why did he agree?" The question was directed more toward himself than at Foster.

"I guess he really wants to talk to me . . . or kill me. Your partner and I talked about the possibility that Turner might be preparing to kill me, the way he killed Victoria."

"Well, I'm sorry to say it makes sense. He seems to be trying to close some doors."

"Well, I trust you and the police department won't let him shut this one."

"No, we won't. When is he supposed to be here?"

"Sunday, the day after tomorrow."

"Did he sound nervous?"

Foster laughed shortly. "Not at all."

"How about you? Did you sound nervous?"

Foster gave McQueen a sheepish look. "I'm afraid I did, Sergeant."

McQueen was sure a man like Turner would have noticed that. "Can I use your phone?"

"Sure, go ahead."

As he was dialing the task-force office in Brooklyn he asked Foster, "Do you have any appointments today?"

"No."

"Tomorrow?" The phone was ringing.

"Yes, New York Books starts tomorrow."

"What's that?"

"It's a new publishing convention where companies are getting together to brag about their new product. There's another one, ABA, but some folks wanted this alternative. This is its first year."

"Where is it?"

"At the Jacob Javits Center. I'll have to be there over the weekend."

"I'm going to arrange to have two detectives here at all times, Daniel. They'll be out of sight, one inside and one outside. When Turner shows up, you're going to have to try to play it real cool. Do you think you can do that?"

"Could it save my life?"

McQueen laughed and said, "I'm sure it could."

"Then I'll force myself," Foster said.

Chapter Fifty-nine

McQueen stayed the night after arranging with Keepsake for two detectives to be with Foster the next day. An unmarked anticrime car with two plainclothesmen from the 6th Precinct remained outside. Since Foster had to go to this book thing, one detective would accompany him while the other remained in the office in case Turner showed up as an early surprise.

The men in the unmarked car were given a general description of Turner according to what the task force knew. Six feet to six one, built like a bodybuilder, possibly carrying a black gym bag. Hair color could be anything, or he could be bald. They were told to use whatever force necessary to subdue him.

In the morning, McQueen was relieved by Ray Velez and Marie Scalesi.

"What are you doing here?" he asked Velez

when he opened the door at 9:30 A.M. McQueen
was stiff from having slept on an uncomfortable
couch.

"I talked the captain into giving me the first
shift. We'll be relieved at four by Chapman and
Lacy."

"Is there coffee?" Scalesi asked. She held up a
bag and added, "We brought donuts."

Inside, they found Foster sitting behind his
desk reading some papers that had arrived by
messenger just ten minutes earlier.

Foster grinned when he saw Velez. The grin
turned into a smile when he saw Scalesi. Velez
introduced Scalesi.

"Very pleased to meet you, Detective."
Suddenly, the little man became charming, surprising both McQueen and Velez. "Can I get you
some coffee to go with those donuts?"

As Foster disappeared into the kitchen,
Scalesi said to Velez, "He's sorta cute."

"Did I say he wasn't?"

"You didn't say he was."

Foster returned with coffee for Scalesi. He sat
in his chair and she sat across from him. They
each took a donut, she a glazed, he a powdered
cruller, and began to eat.

"They'll get along," McQueen said to Velez.
"I've got to go."

Velez walked him to the door.

"He's going to leave for that convention

around ten o'clock. Why don't you go with him, Ray. Scalesi can stay here and impersonate some kind of temp Foster brought in."

"A-OK, sir." Velez sniffed. "Hey, what's that smell?"

"Brut," McQueen answered. "It was all Foster had. I had to put something on after I took a shower. I still feel skelly, though. Same clothes as yesterday."

"So go home."

"First I want to go over to the Javits Center and take a look at this convention. Foster says he has to be at this thing all weekend, and we may have to cover him there. After that, I'll go home and change clothes, and be back."

"Why? Chapman and Lacy will be here at four."

"What else can I do? This is it, Ray. All that's left is to catch the sonofabitch, and I want to be there when we do."

"I hope he's the right guy."

McQueen gave him a hard stare. "Don't even think like that."

The Jacob Javits Center was a cop's nightmare. The huge convention center had two full floors of row upon row of exhibitors' booths. McQueen had no idea that there were so many publishers. Covering Daniel Foster here would be nearly impossible. There were people everywhere, aimlessly milling about. He walked around the place and got lost several times. The setup was a maze.

The booths' displays were elaborate. One display had towers like a castle. Another had a giant zebra suspended above the booth. A third had an ornate red "P"—the booth belonging to the late Victoria Dreyer's employer—Pembroke Books.

At a snack area, he stopped for coffee and a Danish. He sat at a table and watched the people walk past. The noise level was painful.

He got up and began his search for the exit. The one and only way to cover Foster would be to stick with him every step. Up to now, Turner had killed up close, using his hands or a blade. He had not used a gun, but that didn't mean he didn't have one. It was virtually impossible to protect someone if another someone wanted to kill him badly enough. President Reagan was surrounded by Secret Service men when he was shot.

McQueen finally found the exit. Before leaving, he turned to survey what looked like a huge rats-in-a-maze setup. He needed a shave and a change of clothes and, just for good measure, another shower.

Oh, yeah, and a different cologne.

Chapter Sixty

McQueen was showered and changed by twelve-thirty in the afternoon, ready to head back into the city. Instead of stopping at the precinct for a car, or taking a car service, he went back in by subway. At that time of day the trains would be pretty empty and he wouldn't have to deal with traffic. The subway was often the quickest way to travel, and he wanted to get back to Daniel Foster's office as soon as possible.

With any luck at all he'd be there before two.

"Jesus, I had no idea there were this many people involved in publishing." Ray Velez was surprised by the size of the convention.

"This is just the tip of the iceberg, pal; ABA is even larger."

They had arrived at about ten-thirty, and for almost two hours he had watched Daniel Foster walk around, backslapping and glad-handing people.

Foster explained that his job was to stop and

schmooze at any publisher's display where he thought he had a chance of placing one of his authors.

"Is there a Spanish word for 'schmoozing'?" Foster asked, but he continued to jabber on without giving Velez a chance to reply.

Velez had the same reaction McQueen had had. If Turner showed up here, keeping Foster alive would take some doing.

Foster looked at his watch. "I have to meet an editor in five minutes for lunch. Uh, Ray . . ."

"Yes, Dan?"

"You'll cramp my style at lunch, you know."

"I have to stay with you, Dan."

"I know that, and believe me I don't want you too far away from me, but do you think you could, uh, sit at another table?"

"It's almost lunchtime," Officer Frank Womack said. "I hate stakeouts." The young policeman looked out the window of the unmarked police car at all the merry goings-on of Washington Square Park.

His partner, Officer Lee Burke, grunted. He liked stakeouts. You sat in one place for a long time, didn't have to chase anybody, and nobody would shoot at you for long periods of time. Burke had been on the job over twenty years, while Womack had been in barely five. Burke was forty-three and wore pants six sizes larger than the day he had graduated from the police academy. His once dark hair was turning gray and he had a knee that stiffened up on him if he was standing too long. If he tried to run, forget it. It couldn't stand the strain of carrying his weight. The department had been after him lately to lose some.

Womack was thirty and worked out three times a week. He was a study in perpetual motion. The only thing Burke didn't like about being on a stakeout with him was the incessant shaking of his feet. Womack could not keep them still. Sometimes it felt as if he were rocking the whole car.

"I hate sitting in one place for so long," the younger cop said.

"A few more years on the job, Frank, and you'll appreciate quiet times like these."

"At least if our killer shows up, it won't be so quiet."

"Relax, enjoy the view. This park has been here a long time. I remember when it was filled with beatniks, then hippies—"

"Are you that old, Lee?"

"Fuck you, and watch the girl joggers," Burke replied. His stomach growled. "And now I'm hungry. Hey, why don't you walk over to the Waverly and get us a couple of burgers and fries. Oh, yeah, and coffee, too."

"Wait a minute."

Womack picked up the radio handset. "Anticrime One to Task Force Two."

There was a moment of silence, and then Detective Marie Scalesi's voice came over. "This is Task Force Two. What's up, boys?"

"You hungry?"

"Starved."

"Burger okay?"

"That would be great."

"Comin' up," Womack said, and replaced the handset.

"Why don't you let her get her own food?" Burke demanded.

"She's stuck inside, Lee."

"Hey, she's got the gold shield, let her figure out how to get fed."

"Ah, come on, Lee, loosen up. Besides, she's a good-looking woman, don't you think?"

"About ten years too old for you."

"Hey, I don't mind older women." Womack opened his door and got out, closed it behind him, then leaned in the window. "If our killer shows up, don't shoot him until I get back, okay?"

"He ain't due until tomorrow."

"Then what are we doin' sittin' here?"

Gettin' out of the line of fire for a while, Burke thought as Womack walked away. He followed his partner's progress in the rearview mirror until he turned the corner, then turned his attention to a ponytailed blond jogger going by.

Inside Daniel Foster's office, Marie Scalesi

picked up her book and continued reading. It was nice of the guys outside to think about her when they were getting food. Too often there was a rivalry between the squad and the uniformed force. The anticrime guys, even though they were in plainclothes, still carried silver shields rather than gold, so they aligned themselves with the uniformed cops. These guys seemed okay, though. A hamburger would go down nicely right about now. She hoped they also brought her some greasy French fries. A big woman, Marie Scalesi never bothered about maintaining a slim waist. Even without it, she had always sported a figure men noticed.

In prowling through Foster's shelves she had found several paperback novels written by Nick Turner. She turned her attention back to the book in her lap. It was a novel about the robbery of Shea Stadium during a Met game. She enjoyed it. She hoped Turner wouldn't show up soon and prevent her from finishing it.

Nick Turner watched the policeman get out of the car and walk away. He followed the man just long enough to determine that he was going to fetch lunch. Good. When the cops were in their vehicle stuffing their faces, they'd be easier to take.

Turner had to laugh. The agent's nervousness over the phone made it obvious that he was working with the police, even now. Turner had guessed they'd be waiting. That's why he'd made his appointment for Sunday. He'd catch them all off guard.

Turner had immediately spotted the unmarked police car when arriving that morning at eleven. The car was in position, across the street from the agent's building. He had to chuckle to himself. He had written a book once about anticrime cops, had even interviewed a few of them. He knew what to expect.

He had been watching them from a doorway for an hour and a half when the younger one went for lunch. Turner wore a heavy down coat that was the largest size he could find. He was roasting, sweat pouring down his face and soaking into his shirt. Still, he needed the disguise. Anyway, he might have looked odd had he been any place but New York, but in this city people wouldn't look twice at you even if you had two heads.

He was back in the doorway when the man returned with a brown paper bag of food. He watched as the cop left the bag with his partner, then crossed the street to the agent's office and left a smaller bag with a woman there. No doubt the woman was a cop, as well. By the time the cop returned to the car, Turner was sure that there were two outside and one inside. The bag of food the cop had handed to the woman cop was too small to be lunch for more than one person. The agent probably wasn't inside.

This woman would have to tell him where his agent was.

He stepped from the doorway, hands in the pockets of his coat, elbows out, and walked toward the unmarked police car like that. There was a pocket inside the coat, and the knife was temporarily in there, handle down. You didn't even have to pad a down coat to make it look like you were fifty pounds heavier than you were. It was all in how you moved.

Left behind in the doorway was his black gym bag.

Chapter Sixty-one

"What do we have here?" Burke watched in his side-view mirror as a man approached the car.

"What?" Womack asked.

"Behind us."

Burger in hand, Womack turned to take a look. He saw a big, heavy-set guy wearing a blank baseball cap.

"Wow, look at the size of that guy. He must

weigh a ton. And look at that coat. He must be boiling. Think this is our guy?"

"We're looking for a bodybuilder, Frank. This guy look like Arnold Whatsenegger to you?" He took another mouthful of burger.

The fat man was about ten feet away.

"What's this guy want, anyway?" With a Styrofoam cup of coffee in his right hand, Burke rolled down his window with the left. The man in the down jacket bent down to the window.

"Hey, fellas, can you help me? I'm lost."

"Whataya tryin' to find?" Burke asked.

The man started to lean into the window, bringing his right hand up.

"Hey, wait—" Before Burke could say anything else, the man's right hand was behind Burke's head. In a quick movement, the man head-butted the older cop, who dropped his coffee in his partner's lap. Turner leaned in, and with his butcher knife neatly sliced Womack's throat before the younger cop could react.

Burke, stunned by the blow to his forehead, which had opened a deep cut, suddenly felt an even worse pain in his neck as the knife cut his throat open as well.

Turner stood up and hid the knife in his coat. He looked around. On the bustling street no one stopped to look. He had moved so quickly that no one had noticed what was happening. There were people jogging and walking through the park, crossing the street, and paying no attention whatsoever.

In the car, the two cops slumped toward each other. From outside they looked as if they were asleep with their heads together.

Turner crossed the street at a leisurely pace, walked up to the agent's door, and knocked.

McQueen cursed. Of all the days to have a "smoke condition" hold up the subway, this was the worst. He wondered now if it wouldn't have been better to have taken a car. But he consoled himself with the fact that, hell, he'd probably have been stuck in traffic on the Brooklyn Bridge.

There was nothing to do but wait for the train to start moving again.

Ray Velez sat two tables from Daniel Foster and his lunch appointment, a young girl with curly hair who appeared barely out of her teens. Could this be an editor from a major New York publishing house? What are your qualifications for this job, little lady? Well, my mother just gave me permission to cross the street by myself. Ah, you're hired!

Velez turned his attention back to his deli platter, glad that he wasn't in publishing.

When Marie Scalesi heard the knock at the door, she was sure it was the young cop coming back with her French fries. Holding Turner's book in one hand, she opened the door and saw a big man in a down jacket.

Turner stiff-armed her violently, slamming his palm into her chest so hard that it drove the air from her lungs. She staggered back and fell to the floor. He stepped inside, closed the door behind him, and bent over her, putting the knife to her throat.

Scalesi lay on her back, trying to regain her breath, staring into the face of a madman. She couldn't see the knife, but she could feel its tip against her throat—and she smelled blood.

"I just killed two cops," Turner said. "A third wouldn't be so hard, understand?"

She nodded.

"Say it."

"I understand."

Her mind raced. Tell him what he wanted to hear. Her gun was in her purse on Foster's desk.

"Lie still." He slid his free hand up her leg and beneath her skirt to her thigh, then did the same thing with the other leg. For a moment she thought about rape, but he was merely checking her for a weapon.

"Gun's in your purse, huh?"

She started to nod but he shook her roughly, using his free hand and said, "Say it!"

"Yes! Yes, my gun is in my purse."

"Women shouldn't be cops. You'd never see a man without his gun on him."

He spotted the book she'd dropped right next to her on the floor, and recognized its cover as one of his. He was flattered.

"What's your rank?"

"D-Detective."

"Okay, Detective, we're going to get up now. If you try to get away from me, I won't just slit your throat like I did your two friends, first I'll gouge your eyes out. Get it?"

"I understand."

He pulled her to her feet. Scalesi's legs felt weak beneath her. She was frightened, and ashamed of it, but she still thought like a cop, looking for a way out. If she could get to her purse . . .

Once she was on her feet, he closed his free hand over her left elbow and held her in a painful grip. This was Turner, she knew. He looked heavy and flabby in his down jacket, but there was no denying the strength in his hand. Now that she was on her feet, she could see his knife. It was covered with fresh blood.

"I have a question for you." He held the knife in front of her face. "I want you to answer me the first time I ask, or I'm going to hurt you."

She couldn't take her eyes from the blood on the knife. She felt as if her bladder were full.

"Here's the question: Where is he?"

McQueen felt like a goddamned fool.

What in hell made any of them think that

Turner would call the agent, make an appointment, and then keep it?

Trapped on the slow-moving train, he realized Turner had no intention of going to Foster's office on Sunday. Turner had his own agenda. He'd closed his P.O. box. Now he would close out the agent as well.

He would do it today.

Chapter Sixty-two

McQueen came up from the subway at 4th Street and ran for Washington Square. On Daniel Foster's block, everything looked normal. He spotted the unmarked vehicle, no problem. As he got closer, he noticed that the two cops' heads were close together in the front seat. Were they sleeping?

He ran to the car. He bent to look in the driver's window and something cold landed in his stomach.

"Oh, God . . ."

Both men were dead, their throats neatly cut, their chests covered in blood. More had pooled around them on the seat.

He would have opened the car door and

reached for the radio to call for help but remembered that Velez and Scalesi were inside. No, check that, one of them would still be inside.

He ran to the door of the agent's office and pounded on it. He tried it: locked. He stepped back and kicked. The door sprang open. Pulling his gun, he stepped inside, holding the weapon out in front of him.

The office was a shambles. There was nothing on the desktop, which had once been full of stacks of papers and paraphernalia. Everything had been thrown on the floor.

"Marie?" McQueen was starting around the desk to go to the kitchen when he saw her sprawled on the floor behind the desk, lying on her stomach. There was a paperback book on her back.

"Marie . . ." He bent over her, turning her onto her back. She was dead. She had to be. Her throat had been cut, her eyes had been gouged out. Her skirt was up around her waist, but there was no evidence of the killer's habitual mutilation. Perhaps Turner hadn't had the time.

"Shit, Marie . . . I'm sorry . . ."

He dropped back on his haunches and crouched down by her, tears stinging his eyes. The blood was wet, with no hint of coagulation. This had happened *very* recently. Jesus, if the crazy bastard had taken the subway, was he going into the station while McQueen was coming out?

He looked for the phone, found it on the floor. The wire had been pulled from the wall. He found Marie's radio under the desk. He used it to call for an ambulance, a lab crew, detectives, a boss, the works. He knew who had done this, but he had to go by the book.

He put the radio down next to Marie and noticed the book that had been on her back. When he'd flipped her over, it had fallen to the floor. He picked it up and noticed the author's name: Nicholas Turner. The man was completely crazy if he signed his work this way.

He picked up her radio again and tried to get Velez. "Task Force sergeant to Task Force Three." No answer. "Goddamn it, Ray—" He stopped short and changed his tack. "Task Force sergeant to Central, 'kay."

"Central." A female dispatcher came on the line.

"Central, I just called for a crew at Sixteen Washington Square. I've got three dead cops—"

"Why didn't you call for a ten-thirteen, Sergeant?" A 10-13 was the call that went out when an officer needed assistance.

"Because they're already dead, damn it!"

There was some static and silence, and then the dispatcher's voice came back.

"What can I do for you, Sergeant, 'kay?"

"Central, I want you to keep trying to raise

Task Force Three. That's Detective Ray Velez. He's protecting a witness at the Jacob Javits Center. I believe the killer of the officers is on his way there."

"Do you want to call a ten-thirteen at the Javits—"

"Jesus, no! Every cop in midtown will respond and scare the killer off. Just get as many anticrime cars as you can to meet me there. No lights, no sirens. Understood, 'kay?"

"Understood, 'kay."

"I want them to meet me in front and not to do a thing until I get there."

"Understood, Sergeant. Do you want to put a description out on the air, 'kay?"

"All I've got is a big man with muscles like a bodybuilder, 'kay."

"Is he armed, 'kay?"

"Yes, with a knife—wait a minute."

He looked around for Marie's bag and found it. When he opened it and looked inside his heart sank.

"Central, the sonofabitch has a gun! Get a car here to take me to the Javits Center, fast!"

The doors to the train opened at 34th Street and Turner got off. The cop's gun was inside his pocket. His knife was back in the gym bag, which he'd retrieved from his doorway lookout.

Up the steps and crossing the street, he began trotting west. As he ran into the convention center, two unmarked police cars pulled up. Four anticrime cops got out. Within minutes, there were eight more plainclothes cops, all waiting for McQueen to arrive.

Chapter Sixty-three

McQueen had to take a regular RMP to the Javits Center, but he told them no lights or sirens. Inside the car he again tried raising Velez, but to no avail.

"Keep trying, Central! And try and raise Task Force One, Captain William Keepsake in the Twelfth Division." That meant he was on a different frequency than the one they were using. "Get him over to the Javits Center forthwith."

McQueen figured he was going to need Keepsake to run interference for him so some overeager duty captain didn't try to take over the play.

"Let one captain deal with another, huh, Boss?" the cop driving McQueen asked.

"Yeah, that's right. Can you go faster?"

"As fast as I want," the cop said. "I'm the police, Boss."

"Don't call me that."

* * *

Turner was refused admission to the convention floor because he didn't have a convention badge.

"I lost it," he told a young black security guard.

"I can't let you in without one, sir."

He could have forced his way past the guard, but that would have attracted attention. Instead, he went to the mezzanine level and found a bench near the men's rest room. When he spotted a badge-wearing man walk in, Turner followed.

There was a third man in the bathroom with them, washing his hands at the sink. Turner waited until he left. The man he'd followed stood at the urinal, both hands occupied.

Turner put down his gym bag, took his knife out, and moved right behind the urinating man.

"Hey, wha—"

"Stand still," Turner said directly into his ear. His right hand removed the man's badge. The man was about to protest when he saw that Turner's right hand was covered with blood.

"Oh my," the man said.

Turner looked at his hand and frowned. He hadn't noticed the blood before, but now that the man at the urinal had . . . With his left hand, Turner thrust the blade into the man's back at kidney level. He covered his mouth with his right. The force of the blow pushed the man into the urinal, but Turner dragged him backward and into one of the stalls. As he sat the man on the toilet he looked into his victim's open eyes. At that moment the life went out of them, like a light bulb winking out. He was dead.

Turner removed his down coat and tossed it over the bleeding corpse. Underneath it Turner wore a sports jacket. He took the gun from the pocket of the down jacket and transferred it to the sports jacket, then pinned on the badge. He had seen a lot of people wearing red badges, but this one was green with the word **PRESS** on it.

It was a pleasure to be rid of that down coat. He felt the huge wet circles beneath his arms and was aware of the sharp odor he gave off. But it couldn't be helped. And he had to keep the sports jacket on to hide both his knife and the bloody patches on his shirt. Before leaving the room he put the knife down on the sink and washed his hands. He watched the water turn pink and carry the blood down the drain. He didn't notice that when he picked up the knife with his right hand he once again became smeared with blood. The knife went back in the gym bag. He adjusted his baseball cap and exited.

Walking past the familiar security guard he simply said, "Found it," and kept going.

The security guard nodded, then frowned. There had been some red on the badge. He didn't recall any badges that weren't solid colors.

Velez stood near a publisher's stall, impatiently shifting his weight while Daniel Foster schmoozed with a young man. Foster had told him that this boyish man was the editor-in-chief of a major publishing house.

This particular publisher's booth had turrets and towers like a castle. A young woman in a Robin Hood outfit was handing out free books. Velez took to watching her and her short green skirt move while he waited for Foster to finish. He even kept his eyes on her as others filed past. The after-lunch crowd had increased, and some aisles were choked with people.

Foster joined Velez. They looked at the pretty Robin Hood.

"Don't tell me, let me guess," the policeman said. "She's president of the company."

"C'mon," Foster said. "We've got to go to the Pembroke booth. I want to see if they have Nick's books displayed. He's still my client, after all."

Mc Queen told the RMP driver to pull the car around the corner, out of sight. He saw that the anticrime cars were double-and triple-parked. A group of men stood nearby.

"Who's ranking here?" McQueen called out as he approached.

A man stepped forward. Gray-haired and red-faced, he had obviously been on the job for a long time. "I am, Sergeant George Jackson."

"Jackson, I'm Dennis McQueen, task force."

"The serial-killer task force?"

"That's right. Our man just might be inside. If he's not already, all these cars will probably scare him off."

"I'll have the cars moved."

"Listen up. This guy has already killed three cops. I want him alive, Jackson. Everyone has to understand that, but I don't want to lose any more cops."

Jackson gave him a look. "Takin' him alive ain't gonna be easy."

"Keep the dead cops info to yourself for now, then. Just tell your men we're looking for a killer. He's got a knife and a gun, and he might be carrying a gym bag. I want him alive if I can get him that way."

Turner had not been in a crowd like this in some time. It unnerved him. With the knife in his bag and the detective's gun in his pocket, he knew he could kill a lot of them right now if he wanted. It would have been nice, but it would blow his chance to find his agent. He suppressed the urge and continued through the aisles, wandering aimlessly. Then it occurred to him that no matter what the agent was doing, he'd have to stop by the Pembroke booth eventually. If he hadn't already.

McQueen entered the lobby of the Javits Center with a dozen anticrime cops in tow. He had taken a portable radio from the car and made sure that the anticrime guys all had theirs.

"You, you, and you," he said, pointing at them in pairs. "You go upstairs with Sergeant Jackson and get floor plans. The rest of you, downstairs with me."

As they passed the security guards at the door McQueen and his colleagues flashed their badges. McQueen stopped to talk to a young black guard.

"We're looking for a big, muscular, Caucasian man. He might be bald or wearing a wig. He might have some kind of hat on, might have a gym bag."

"Mister, everybody who walks through here is wearing some kind of crazy hat or carrying an attaché case or something—"

"This guy kills people. Did you see anybody who looked as if he might be hiding a stain on his clothes?" Turner couldn't have done what he did to Scalesi without getting some blood splattered on him.

The security guard looked blank for a second, as if he were struggling to remember something. "There was a guy, like, six feet, with muscles. He was carrying a bag, might have been a gym bag, but I noticed something else."

"What?"

"Well, on his badge there were smears of red." The guy brushed at his chest where an exhibitor's badge might be. "I noticed it because all the badges are solid colors. His was green with red on it."

"Red? Like blood?"

"I guess it could have been blood. He tried to get by me earlier without a badge. Said he forgot his. Fifteen minutes later, he's back with one."

"What did he say?"

"He said he found it."

"Did you—"

They were interrupted when somebody from the mezzanine started yelling. The guard's radio crackled to life.

"What's going on?" McQueen asked.

"Beats me." The guard produced his radio. Before he could use it, McQueen grabbed it.

"This is the police. What's going on?"

From the radio a man's voice said, "There's a dead man in the men's room. If you're the police, you better get down here."

"Stay put, I'm on my way!" He thrust the radio back at the guard. "Damn it." He read the guard's nameplate. "Jamison, you got men at every door?"

"There's supposed to be."

"You get on that radio and give out the description I gave you."

"You want the dude stopped?"

"If he's spotted, I want your men to call me. Don't—I repeat—don't intercept him. He's dangerous. Just sing out."

"Yeah, sure, but we can help—"

"Just do it!" He turned to the other cops. "I'll check the mezzanine. The rest of you start working the floor—and stay on the air." McQueen then rushed down to the men's room to see who Nick Turner had killed this time.

Chapter Sixty-four

The corpse sat on the toilet. The floor around the bowl was covered with blood.

There was blood on one of the urinals, and more on one of the sinks. McQueen checked the body for a convention badge. He didn't have one. Turner had probably killed the poor slob for it.

"Come with me," he told the security guard who had entered with him. Once outside he said, "Stay here. Don't let anyone in until the police get here."

"I thought you were the police."

"There will be more police here, in uniform. Don't let anyone in until they arrive."

There was a crowd around the men's room and McQueen attempted to disperse them as he worked his way through. It was no use. They parted to let him pass, then closed ranks again behind him. He'd let the boys from the local precinct handle it.

He went back upstairs onto the convention floor. It had seemed hopeless at first, but now he believed that all he had to do was find the Pembroke booth, the only common bond he could think of.

Turner found a discarded layout of the booths and used it to guide him to the Pembroke display. There, he immediately spotted Daniel Foster talking to a man who wasn't a publishing type. He looked more like a cop. The agent walked away from the other man and went into the booth.

Turner froze. He had always been alone with his victims in the past. There were a lot of people here. He couldn't very well walk up to the agent and stab him, and the cop's gun would be too loud. He had to get the agent away from the cop, take him somewhere.

The cop glanced about casually. Turner hid behind a display of a giant kangaroo.

He toyed with the idea of just walking right

up to the cop, sticking the gun in his ribs, and marching him to the men's room.

Turner wondered if anyone had found the dead man in the men's room yet. If so, there might be police flooding the place right now.

Nick Turner realized he had been careless, reckless even. That murder had not been carefully planned. It had been a definite seat-of-the-pants operation. He had been too single-minded in his pursuit of the agent, and now he was caught in the midst of thousands of people, some of them probably cops who were looking for him. If they caught him with the knife on him, that would be all the evidence they'd need. They'd never understand that his killings had all been necessary.

The roar of the convention hall grew loud in his ears. Looking around, it seemed that people were looking at him. He felt dizzy, hot. People brushed against him, bumping into him as they passed. He tried to suppress his rage.

McQueen stopped on a stair level to look down at the convention floor. Even if he had known exactly what Turner looked like, what were the chances he'd spot him from up here? He looked down at the floor plan he'd gotten from the security guard, searching for the Pembroke booth.

Velez noticed the man standing at the far end of the aisle. He'd been lingering there a few minutes, and he had something in his hand. Moving to his left, Velez caught a glimpse of a black gym bag.

His heart started beating very quickly. This was him, Totem. This was Nick Turner.

His first instinct was to rush the man, but that might panic Turner. That might get somebody killed. Besides, he didn't know for sure that the man was Turner.

He moved back toward the booth.

"Daniel." Foster was talking and gesturing with his arms. "Daniel," Velez repeated.

Velez stepped up onto the platform and hissed, "Foster!" urgently.

Foster turned around and frowned. "Ray, I'm working here—"

"Excuse us," Velez said. He grabbed Foster's arm and pulled him away.

"Ray, what's going—"

"Look at the man at the end of this aisle."

Foster looked the wrong way.

"No, not that way, that way."

Foster turned and looked, then froze.

"Is that him?" Velez asked.

"It's him, Ray, it's Turner." Foster's face paled.

Velez took out his gun.

Turner had two choices. He could shoot the cop, or he could run. Maybe they hadn't found the body in the bathroom yet. Maybe there were no cops in the building yet except this one.

He ran.

Just as Velez started after Turner, McQueen turned the corner from the other direction. He saw Velez's back and a stunned Foster.

"Foster! Is Turner here?"

The sweating agent turned and stared at McQueen a few seconds before finally answering, "Ray's after him."

McQueen went the other way, hoping to cut Turner off. At the same time he yelled into his radio.

"This is McQueen! He's on the first level. Seal off the doors. Jackson, get your men down here!"

"Task Force, can we help?" Central's voice came over the air.

"We're in foot pursuit, Central. Stay off the air, please."

"Everyone stay off the air in the eleventh division until further notice," the dispatcher announced. "The task force is in pursuit."

In pursuit in a goddamned maze, McQueen thought, shoving people from his path.

Chapter Sixty-five

Running through the aisles, McQueen spotted Turner. Behind him ran Ray Velez.

The crowd scattered before McQueen, running with his gun drawn. "Police! Out of the way!" he shouted. "Police." Into his radio he shouted, "Jackson, are the doors sealed off?"

There was static, and then Jackson's voice replied. "Security's got them covered, McQueen. Where are you?"

Using the map, McQueen gave his location, as well as Turner's. McQueen was running down Aisle B, while Velez pursued Turner down Aisle C. They were crossing Row 14.

"Get a fix! Get a fix and close in!" he shouted.

McQueen sped up, hoping to get ahead of Turner and cut him off, but Turner was bigger, younger, and faster. McQueen's lungs were burning and his chest was already tightening up.

"I'm in Row Twenty," Jackson called.

"He's coming toward you," McQueen said. "Where's everyone else?"

"Aisle A," a voice called, "Row Twelve."

"Aisle D," someone else called, "Row Twenty-four."

The others called in, and McQueen realized they were well scattered. He, Velez, and Jackson had the best chance of catching Turner. "He's headed for the mezzanine stairway!" he radioed.

"I'm outside in the lobby," a voice called. "I can get to the mezzanine."

"Go, go!" McQueen called out, not knowing who he was talking to. "Make sure security has the door covered."

They'd trap him on the stairway.

Turner kept running toward the mezzanine stairway. He heard people shouting, but could not differentiate between bystanders and the police. He kept his eyes ahead and the stairway came into sight. There were two uniformed security men on it, coming down. Behind them came another man wearing street clothes. He was carrying a gun.

Turner chose another exit. He stopped short and turned down Aisle E, running towards Row 13.

Velez heard all the shouting and thought he could detect McQueen's voice. He heard the familiar sounds of static and squelch and knew there were other cops in the convention hall. All he had to do was stay on Turner until he met up with them.

McQueen saw Turner change direction and relayed it over the radio.

"He's not headed for the mezzanine anymore. He's turned in Row Thirteen and he's headed for the west stairway. Who's listening?"

"I got you," a voice said. "I'm near that stairway."

"Good. Stay off it, and keep security off it. Let's try to trap him on the stairway. Understand? Get him on the stairway!"

"Roger!"

There was no one on the west stairway. This was Turner's way out. Discarding the map, he opened the gym bag and took out his faithful knife. Running, he dropped the bag. With his other hand he dug the gun out of his pocket. If anyone got in his way on the stairs, they were going to be sorry.

Hidden at the top of the stairs was Anticrime Police Officer Westclock, along with two Javits security guards, Kinderman and Wahl.

"Don't move until he's climbing the stairs," Westclock instructed.

"Right," Kinderman said, exchanging a glance with Wahl. They had already decided that they wanted to be the ones to catch this killer. Why let the city cops get the credit? Armed with nightsticks rather than guns, they still felt that the two of them could handle one man.

They kept their eyes on the stairs. Once the man started up, he was theirs.

McQueen slowed down. His legs were getting heavy. He stumbled and almost fell. Turner was starting up the stairs. Velez was between him and Turner, almost to the stairs himself.

They had him.

Turner ascended the stairs, clutching his weapons. If he could get into the lobby, then to the street, he could get away.

Halfway up the stairs, he saw two uniformed guards start down toward him. He didn't hear Westclock shouting at Kinderman and Wahl not to move.

The two guards ran toward him, but Turner didn't slow down.

"Okay, pal, it's all over—" Kinderman started to say, but as he reached Turner, the big man drove the butcher knife directly into his belly. Kinderman's eyes widened and he slumped forward, impaled on the blade. Turner's strength was enough that Kinderman's weight did not even unbalance him.

"Hey—" Wahl shouted. Turner raised the gun and fired. Wahl put both arms in front of him to ward off the bullet. It shattered a forearm, continued on, and struck him in the face.

Turner shook Kinderman off his knife and looked up at the exit. A man with a gun stood there, shouting at him.

At the base of the steps, Velez saw Turner dispatch the two security guards. The killer was now facing an armed anticrime cop who was in a two-handed stance, aiming his gun.

"Hold it, Turner!" Velez assumed the same position.

At the sound of Turner's shot, people hit the ground or rushed for cover. It was suddenly quiet.

Hearing Velez behind him, Turner whirled around and stared. It was the cop who had been with his agent.

"You don't understand!" Turner shouted.

McQueen reached Velez's side and went down to one knee heavily. Gasping for breath, he trained his gun on Turner. Seconds later, Jackson reached his side. At the top of the stairs, two other cops joined the first one. Six guns were now trained on Nick Turner.

"Don't fire!" McQueen gasped. He held the radio to his mouth and tried again. "Damn it, don't fire . . ."

"None of you understand!" Turner shouted. "They had to die because of the journals. I'm not finished."

"You are finished, Turner," McQueen said, finding his voice.

Although six cops had their guns trained on Turner, they couldn't fire without fear of hitting each other.

"Spread out," McQueen said in a low voice to Velez and Jackson. "Sergeant, move your men."

"Understood."

Jackson moved a few feet to his left, held his radio to his lips, speaking quietly, urgently.

"It's over, Nick," McQueen said. "You can't get away."

"But you have to let me go," Turner said, his tone pleading. "I'm not finished. There are more."

"Drop your weapons, Nick."

"And there are books . . ." Turner said. His voice was so low that nobody heard him. "Books to finish . . ."

The cops moved now, adjusting their positions so they were not in each other's line of fire.

"Drop the gun, Nick." The gun first, McQueen was thinking, then the knife.

Turner's gun pointed toward the roof. He was thinking he couldn't give up. He had to get to his book, to the journals, to the other names on the list. This wasn't the end, couldn't be.

McQueen watched Turner carefully, hoping the man would not make a move. But he sensed it was hopeless. He could see it in Turner's face, and in his body language.

Suddenly, the big man brought the gun down, pointing it at McQueen and Velez.

"Shit!" McQueen fired. His shot signaled the others. Six other officers fired.

Nick Turner seemed to dance on the steps momentarily as slugs struck his body. Then he was falling, tumbling down the steps toward McQueen and the others.

McQueen watched him roll down the steps, coming to a stop almost at McQueen's feet.

Velez came up next to McQueen.

"Well, there he is, Dennis."

Turner, bloody and battered, lay unmoving on the floor. The gun and knife were back on the stairs.

McQueen turned to Velez, handed him his radio, and said, "Call it in."

Uniformed police joined the plainclothes cops and the Javits security guards for crowd control. The Manhattan M.E. arrived, his men tagging along behind him.

He didn't know McQueen, but he knew the Manhattan-based Jackson. The M.E. looked at Turner's inert form. "Yours, Jackson?" the man asked.

"No, Doc. This belongs to Sergeant Dennis McQueen. He's with the serial-killer task force. McQueen, meet Dr. Hogan."

The doctor's burly black eyebrows went up, disappearing into his mop of unruly curly black hair. "This is the maniac who's been slicing people up?"

"That's him," McQueen said.

As the M.E. bent over to examine Turner, McQueen saw Keepsake coming down the stairs toward him.

"Dennis," Keepsake said, "everyone all right?"

"No, sir," McQueen said. "Turner killed three people here, and three cops at Daniel Foster's office."

"Three?"

McQueen nodded. "Marie Scalesi was one of them."

"Oh, no," Keepsake said.

"Dennis . . ." Velez said, squeezing his partner's arm.

"I thought you'd be next, partner," McQueen said, "if I didn't get here in time."

"Get a stretcher," the M.E. said to his men.

"You going to bag him, Doc?" McQueen asked.

"Afraid not, Sergeant."

"Why not?"

Hogan stood up and faced McQueen.

"He might be pumped full of bullets, but this sonofagun is still alive."

Epilogue

Chief of detectives Robert Sands arrived at
Bellevue Hospital, where McQueen, Velez, and
Keepsake were waiting to see if Turner was
going to pull through. Behind him, Inspector
Pyatt scurried to keep up. His red hair seemed
particularly orange today.

"This is the guy, isn't it, McQueen?" Sands
asked. "I mean, we're sure?"

"Chief—" Keepsake said.

"In a minute, Captain."

"We're fairly sure, sir," McQueen said. "We have
no witnesses who actually saw him kill anyone
other than the two security guards on the stairs—"

"That's too bad about the guards," Sands said,
"but we've got three dead cops . . ."

"No witnesses there, either."

"What are you telling me, Sergeant?"

"I think this is the guy, Chief, but unless he pulls through and confesses—"

"Dennis," Keepsake said.

"Yeah, Cap?"

"Hastings called from Connecticut."

"Who's Hastings? What's Connecticut got to do with this?" Sands demanded.

Keepsake explained. "Hastings is a policeman from Connecticut, Chief, where Turner was living. Anyway, Hastings followed Sergeant McQueen's advice to check the utility companies. They found gas and electric bills in the name Ned Tyler. He went to Tyler's or Turner's apartment and found, among other things, Turner's wife's journals."

"What journals?" Sands asked.

"He was killing people because he read in her journals that she slept with them. They're all marked up with colored markers."

"Jesus . . . his wife is dead?"

"It's all in a progress report to your office, Chief," Keepsake said.

Sands looked at Pyatt.

"Did I get such a report?"

"Well, sir, I was screening things—"

"I was to be informed every step of the way, Pyatt! You've overstepped yourself."

"Well, sir, I thought—"

"We'll settle this later," Sands said, cutting the man off. He turned back to McQueen. "Tell me more."

"Captain Keepsake has all the details, Chief."

"Keepsake?" Sands said. "Give me an oral report."

"Yes, sir. Why don't we go over here and talk, sir." Keepsake took the chief's arm and steered him down the hall. "They also found some jars in the apartment with the dismembered genitalia . . ."

Pyatt, unsure of what to do or where to go, remained halfway down the hall.

"Think he'll pull through?" Velez asked McQueen.

"The doctors are amazed he's even alive. They actually think they might be able to patch him up."

"So he can go to jail and continue his literary career."

"Huh?"

"Something Foster said."

"If the sonofabitch lives, he'll probably be on *A Current Affair* or something," McQueen said. "Who knows? Speaking of the media, I've got some calls to make." Weatherby at the *Post* was about to get something more than "no comment."

The next afternoon McQueen was at his desk when the phone rang. The members of the task force would be working together for a while longer, until all the loose ends were tied up.

"McQueen," he answered.

"It's the desk," a voice said. "We got a guy down here wants to sell you a monument."

"Send him up."

Keepsake sat at his desk, as did Velez and Chapman.

A tall slender man with a pale face and long black hair drawn into a widow's peak entered and looked around. He carried a large leather briefcase. "Sergeant McQueen?"

"Over here."

The man walked over and placed his briefcase on the desk. "I'm from Proctor Monuments. I hope we can find something you'll like."

"Did I talk to you on the phone this morning?"

"Uh, no, sir, I'm the salesman. You spoke to—"

"Whoever it was, I told them what I wanted."

"Yes, sir, I know that. That's a pretty expensive item. I wanted to be sure we had everything right." He leaned over and started turning pages in his book, which was filled with photographs of headstones and monuments. McQueen slapped his hand down on the book.

"I don't care about the cost," he said. "I made a promise and intend to keep it."

McQueen removed his hand. The man straightened up. "Is that what you want?" He opened the catalog and pointed.

The photo took up almost the entire page. It was of a white marble monument with an angel on top.

"Is the angel crying?"

The man looked closely. "I don't know. But if you want the angel to cry, we can do that."

"Yeah," he said. "I want it to cry."

"We could do it in black if you like—"

"No, white marble is fine."

"All right," the man said. "Just let me write up your order."

"Here," McQueen said, moving away from his desk. "Sit here."

While the man filled out the paperwork, McQueen started out to the hall.

"Dennis?" Velez said.

"Yeah?"

"You okay?"

"Sure, Ray, I'm fine."

"What have you heard from the hospital?" Velez asked.

"He's still in bad shape, and he hasn't awakened yet, but the doctor says he's going to make it."

"Will they call us when he wakes up?"

"Oh, yeah," McQueen said, "I made damn sure they knew they had to call me first. There's something I want to tell this bastard when he wakes up."

"What's that?"

"I want to be the one to tell him that his wife's psychiatrist advised her to write her fantasies in her journals. I want to see the sonofabitch's face when he finds out he killed all those people for nothing."

NIGHTMARE CHRONICLES

DOUGLAS CLEGG

It begins in an old tenement with a horrifying crime. It continues after midnight, when a young boy, held captive in a basement, is filled with unearthly visions of fantastic and frightening worlds. How could his kidnappers know that the ransom would be their own souls? For as the hours pass, the boy's nightmares invade his captors like parasites—and soon, they become real. Thirteen nightmares unfold: A young man searches for his dead wife among the crumbling buildings of Manhattan... A journalist seeks the ultimate evil in a plague-ridden outpost of India... Ancient rituals begin anew with the mystery of a teenage girl's disappearance... In a hospital for the criminally insane, there is only one doorway to salvation... But the night is not yet over, and the real nightmare has just begun. Thirteen chilling tales of terror from one of the masters of the horror story.

___4580-X $5.50 US/$6.50 CAN

Dorchester Publishing Co., Inc.
P.O. Box 6640
Wayne, PA 19087-8640

Please add $1.75 for shipping and handling for the first book and $.50 for each book thereafter. NY, NYC, and PA residents, please add appropriate sales tax. No cash, stamps, or C.O.D.s. All orders shipped within 6 weeks via postal service book rate. Canadian orders require $2.00 extra postage and must be paid in U.S. dollars through a U.S. banking facility.

Name_____
Address_____
City_____State_____Zip_____
I have enclosed $_____ in payment for the checked book(s).
Payment <u>must</u> accompany all orders. ❑ Please send a free catalog.
CHECK OUT OUR WEBSITE! www.dorchesterpub.com

DOUGLAS

HALLOWEEN THE

MAN

CLEGG

The New England coastal town of Stonehaven has a history of nightmares—and dark secrets. When Stony Crawford becomes a pawn in a game of horror and darkness, he finds that he alone holds the key to the mystery of Stonehaven, and to the power of the unspeakable creature trapped within a summer mansion.

___4439-0 $5.50 US/$6.50 CAN

Dorchester Publishing Co., Inc.
P.O. Box 6640
Wayne, PA 19087-8640

Please add $1.75 for shipping and handling for the first book and $.50 for each book thereafter. NY, NYC, and PA residents, please add appropriate sales tax. No cash, stamps, or C.O.D.s. All orders shipped within 6 weeks via postal service book rate. Canadian orders require $2.00 extra postage and must be paid in U.S. dollars through a U.S. banking facility.

Name_____

Address_____

City_____ State_____ Zip_____

I have enclosed $_____ in payment for the checked book(s).

Payment **must** accompany all orders. ❏ Please send a free catalog.
CHECK OUT OUR WEBSITE! www.dorchesterpub.com

Regeneration

MAX ALLAN COLLINS
BARBARA COLLINS

Joyce Lackey is a classic baby-boomer. She has it all: a high-paying position, a beautiful condo, a BMW. But there is one thing she doesn't have any more—her youth. And that is what she needs most. Her boss fires her because he wants someone with "young blood, young ideas." Someone young. Joyce is forced to start all over again. But can she compete with all the beautiful young kids who are so hungry for what she has? That's where the X-Gen Agency comes in. They can give Joyce everything she wants, everything she needs—a new job, a new body, a new identity. In short, a new life. But there is a price. A very high price. It seems reasonable enough when Joyce signs the contracts, and besides, she is desperate. By the time she realizes what she has done, it is too late to turn back. This is one contract without an escape clause.

___4615-6 $5.50 US/$6.50 CAN